Ghosts of the Righteous

JOHN WEEDEN

Copyright © 2024 John Weeden

All rights reserved.

ISBN: 979-8-218-49195-6

To Kristen, my beautiful wife, who continues to walk with me over jagged and gentle terrain down life's path

"Be still and know that I am God."

Psalms 46:10

PREFACE

My name is John. I am fifty-eight years old, and I am a ditch digger. I have been most of my life now. And though it is a humbling, laborious profession, I have never associated any negative connotations with my line of work, which some, with no ill-intent, may tend to do.

My job has no real relevance to this story except to shine light on the fact that I am indeed an ordinary man, but as fate would have it, an ordinary man who would come to experience something that was anything but ordinary. This was something that would ultimately change my life and my perception of the world around me.

I have no claims of being a biblical scholar. I'm just an average guy that for some reason was given a brief glimpse behind the veil that has surrounded me since the day I was born. The same veil that separates each of us from the great beyond. Driven by this unexpected, ineffable experience, I felt moved to tell this story. So, despite my mountainous self-doubt, I put pen to paper and I wrote it.

What follows is a fictional story that is based on what I believe to be the unseen mechanics of good and evil that move each of us throughout our lives. The story occurs close to the present day, and much of the subject matter was taken from today's headlines. I wanted people to understand that there is more going on in our day-to-day lives than what we can see with our eyes or touch with our hands. I tried to break down the great walls that exist between country, race, religion, sexual orientation, social caste, and political party to shed light on the actual core of their source, which is as old as time itself. My hope is not to cast judgment on any one segment of people, but to unite us all through our most common denominator—the binding love that exists at the very core of each of us.

Within this story, there are chapters of light, and as in our lives, there are chapters of darkness. Although you may find it difficult at times, I ask that you push through the dark ones. I believe the light offered at the end is well worth the journey.

I wrote this with the intention of offering a wider perspective on our physical lives. It is my hope that after reading this, you will consider that the answer to eliminating the darkness that plagues our world is accessible to each of us and is waiting for us just beyond our veils. In fact, the very meaning of life itself lies there too.

This book was written as your personal road map to the other side of your veil. I hope with great sincerity it helps you get there.

AUTHOR'S STORY

Looking back over the years of my life, I would say that I kind of believed in God…I guess. But that was as far as I took it, or ever wanted to take it. From my perspective, anything beyond that was simply guessing. Why even worry about it anyway if you could never really prove it, right?

Then one day about twelve years ago, I was chatting with a buddy of mine who is a dentist in Westlake, Ohio.

"How's your boy doing?" I asked him.

When his son was a toddler, he had fallen down a flight of steps. The accident had resulted in some neurological trauma, which had unfortunately left him with some learning disabilities. He was about seven at the time of our conversation and was only able to verbalize a few words.

My friend replied, "He's doing amazing! We began taking him to a new medical doctor that actually prays while he works on his patients. During our first visit, he began to verbalize new words he had never spoken before right there in his office. It was unbelievable!"

More so out of shock than any condescension, I began to chuckle smugly. "What? What are you saying, that because this doctor prayed over your son, he was suddenly able to talk?"

My buddy replied, "I know it sounds crazy, but yes, that's exactly what I'm saying."

He told me that the doctor's name was Issam Nemeh. He originally served as the chief anesthesiologist at Richmond Heights Hospital, then served again at Southwest General Hospital, both outside of Cleveland. Steve told me that, at that time, Dr. Nemeh would silently pray over his patients as he was administering their anesthesia. He prayed simply because he was a devout Christian of great faith and strongly believed in the healing power of prayer. Several surgeons at the hospitals began to notice some unexplainable, even miraculous, changes in their patients' physical conditions while they were on the operating table, and then again as they rapidly progressed through their recoveries. The hospital administrators eventually realized that Dr. Nemeh, the anesthesiologist who was in the operating room in each case, was the binding link that connected each of these miraculous healings. It was not long after that the doctor chose to step away from anesthesiology and start his own practice. He began to treat his patients through integrating Meridian regulatory acupuncture with other innovative techniques, but according to Steve the most important one was his use of prayer.

"He takes no credit for any of the healings that manifest," Steve explained. "He is adamant that they come from Jesus, and Jesus alone. According to the doctor, the success of his prayers is dictated by the connectedness of his patients, himself, and God. And even though the healings come from a higher realm, you don't have to be a Christian or even a believer to receive one. Although there are hundreds, if not thousands, of documented miracles, it's not really about the physical healing at all. The purpose of the healing is just to open our eyes to the larger picture, beyond what we typically see in this physical world. The real healing is the spiritual transformation that occurs in the hearts of those who suddenly understand that there is more to this world than what we can see and touch."

He then added, "If you want to see for yourself, Dr. Nemeh also does healing services for all dominations in a variety of churches all around Cleveland."

I didn't know how to respond. I was sincerely happy for him that his son was doing so well, but healing services and praying over people just seemed, I don't know, unbelievable.

I told Steve, "My only experience with healing services was when I'd catch a glimpse of a ranting television evangelist while channel-surfing late at night."

Steve chuckled, then said, "He's nothing like that. The healing services are quiet and serene. The lights are dim and the music is soft. It is hard to explain, but they are incredibly moving and peaceful. Again, I know it sounds crazy, but I'm telling you, he's legit."

I wasn't convinced yet, but my intrigue was gaining ground on my skepticism. I had just never heard of anything like this before; and although it sounded impossible, my buddy was a solid guy, a doctor himself, who I had tremendous respect for.

After departing from Steve's that night, I felt that I was left teetering between what I had always known to be and this strange new claim of the unbelievable possibilities that may exist with a God that I did not know.

After a few nights of researching Dr. Nemeh online, I was amazed at the hundreds of first-hand testimonies from those whose debilitating afflictions had vanished after the doctor prayed over them. Shifted vertebrae spontaneously became realigned, damaged nerve endings suddenly functioned properly, and terminal cancers were inexplicably cured. There didn't seem to be any limit to the miracles that were occurring as a direct result of Dr. Nemeh's powerful prayers. So, with mounting interest, I took another leap of faith and asked my wife, Kristen, if she'd consider joining me at one of his upcoming healing services. With trepidation, I explained to her about Steve's son and the experience they had with Dr. Nemeh. I then acknowledged that I knew this sounded unbelievable, but next week he was going to be at a church only about ten minutes from us in Westlake and I would really like to attend. After days of deliberation, she, along with her mother, Mary, agreed to join me. Little did we know how that one decision would have a lasting effect on me for the rest of my life.

The week quickly passed, then before we knew it, we were pulling into the church's parking lot for the healing service. Although none of us had any real medical issues, Kristen's younger sister, Katy, had suffered a severe traumatic brain injury in a terrible car accident decades earlier. Looking back, I think Katy was our main motivation for considering this, but my own growing curiosity about this God who I never knew was driving me as well.

We cautiously entered the church, not knowing what to expect. This was way out of our comfort zone, and it was probably very apparent as we nervously made our way toward the sanctuary. A very sweet lady approached us, accepted the tickets that I had ordered online, then directed us to our seats in the sanctuary. Steve was right, it was very quiet and peaceful with dim lighting and soft angelic music playing in the background. Dr. Nemeh had already given a short talk and was now gently praying over individuals in the front of the church. It was clear many of them had disabilities. From children to the elderly, they approached on crutches, or in wheelchairs, or with white canes. Volunteers would take turns assisting them up to the front of the church. They sat in a row of about ten chairs, lined up in front of the pulpit. The doctor would start at one end, then slowly pray over each of them individually as he patiently worked his way down the line. Some of his prayers took only a few minutes, while others took much longer. Clearly, there was no rushing in his process of prayer.

I gazed across the sanctuary, taking it all in, trying to open myself to the process. I noticed several people throughout the church were hunched over in their pews, silently praying to themselves as the doctor went on with his business up front. I was forty-five then, and the last time I could remember praying was right before bedtime as a young boy: "Now I lay me down to sleep, I pray the Lord my soul to keep…" And although it had been a very, very long time, at that moment, something within me surrendered to this notion of prayer. So, I closed my eyes and began to pray for all the people with physical afflictions that were scattered throughout the sanctuary. I found it difficult at first. There seemed to be competing thoughts running through my mind that garbled what I was trying to convey in my prayer. But at the same time, there was a certain sense of peace that emerged within me the moment I began to pray. As my wife and mother-in-law quietly conversed, I fought to fall deeper into my prayer. At times, it felt as if there was clarity in my plea for their healing, then others where there seemed to be nothing but chaos erupting in my mind. Within my own head, other distractions kept overtaking my prayers, muddling my thoughts and occupying my mind. I still don't know what moved me at that moment, but for some reason, I closed my eyes tighter, then silently pleaded to God directly, *I believe in you, but can you give me some sort of sign so I know that you're here?*

Some time passed, but nothing.

I persisted, *Anything at all. A distant spark in the darkness…just some flicker, so I'll know. I'm fighting to find you. I'm fighting to feel you. I'm fighting to believe that you are real.*

More time passed. Still nothing.

I remember sighing to myself as if defeated. A sudden feeling of foolishness for ever considering this charade came upon me. But even though doubt had entered my mind, I never opened my eyes. I took in a deep breath, then redirected my prayers to all who may be in need of them in the church. With my eyes still clenched, I stared into the black abyss and focused from my heart. That's when the notion came to me. I began to picture the people I was praying for, then fought to imagine how each of them must be feeling. I tried to open my heart to a life lived with a disability. I searched for their struggle, their pain, their inevitable moments of hopelessness. I fought to envision the challenges within each of their lives, and although an impossible task, I tried to feel what they must feel throughout their daily struggles. As I pushed to further open myself, a strange lightness emerged in my chest.

Then another plea into the dark. *I'm searching for you, God.* I squeezed my eyes tighter, then focused with my mind and my heart. *With all that I am…I'm searching for you.*

    I felt myself delve deeper into the strange black void of my consciousness. And that's when it happened! In that moment, all I had known to be true about the laws of logic and physics and the reality that dictated my life within this physical world came crashing down all around me. I felt something in the calves of both of my legs that I had never felt before. It was heat and light and energy, and it quickly began to move up toward my knees. The light rose within me, then spread throughout my thighs. It was radiating from within my body, from the inside moving out. That was the moment I knew with unwavering confidence what it was. I had no idea how I knew; but nevertheless, I knew with absolute certainty, like I had never known anything before—it was God's Holy Spirit within me, and it was rapidly rising toward my chest. I exhaled and felt my breath quiver as it left my mouth. This strange, magnificent light kept rising up through my body, and as it did, its intensity grew exponentially. When it finally reached my heart, it seemed to explode into a virtual light show of peace and power and security and love like I had never felt before. The closest thing I could compare it to was a distant memory of my mother holding me as a toddler. I was wrapped snugly in the softest blanket you could imagine and she was looking down at me, smiling as she gently rocked me. At that moment, her love for me was clear, and present, and absolute, and uncompromised; and as I lay embraced in her arms, I felt overwhelmed by her love for me.

    As I took my next breath, it felt as if I had drawn in nearly all the oxygen from inside of the sanctuary. The air itself suddenly felt different in my lungs. It was cleaner, purer, and felt as if it carried more oxygen than it ever had before. I had no explanation as to what was happening to me. Involuntary tears suddenly crested my eyelids, then rolled down my face. It was totally out of character for me, but at that moment, I was completely unimpeded by any insecurities I had within me or any distractions from around me. Without a thought in my mind, I openly wept. All that existed at that moment was this strange, beautiful light that was suddenly entwined within my being, weaved within my very soul. How could I have lived this long and never have experienced anything like this before? I did not fully understand, but I did not care. In that unexpected moment of what felt like my soul's birth, I knew with absolute certainty that God was real and accessible from this physical world. I suddenly had complete confidence that our lives continue after we pass from this one. Any fears of death that I had ever carried instantly released themselves from within me. It somehow became clear to me that the world itself was centered around the essence of God, the same essence that consumed me in that moment. Inexplicably, I suddenly knew that the center of everything, including this uncertain life that I had been living, was simple, and clear, and accessible to everyone. It was the essence of what I was unexpectedly submerged in at that moment—it was love.

With my eyes still closed, I began to thank God for this invaluable gift he was giving me. How could I possibly convey to him what this meant to me? He had literally answered my prayer, and within seconds, I had been changed. My perspective on everything had been changed forever. As I poured my heart out to him, I felt his light slowly begin to recede from my heart. The intensity from the explosion within my chest slowly began to retract. Feeling it slip away, I immediately pleaded to him, *Dear Lord, don't leave me.* I couldn't imagine ever taking another breath without the warm indescribable security that I was feeling right then. Looking back, I wonder if he needed me to know that he was listening, that he would always be listening, and that he would always be with me. Immediately, every ounce of the peaceful intensity that I had felt came rushing back into my heart. Another flood of tears emerged from my eyes as I took it in. Deep grateful exhales followed. *Thank you for not leaving me…thank you.*

When I finally opened my eyes, my wife and my mother-in-law were both staring at me. Kristen looked horrified as she watched me wipe the tears from my face. I couldn't form words yet, but I smiled, trying to convey that my tears were okay, that I was okay, that I was more than okay. I wanted them to know that I was better than I had ever been before, but I still couldn't speak. It was to no avail. Kristen stood up, pushing by me with a worried look on her face, then fled the sanctuary to the lobby. Later she told me that she couldn't understand what could have unraveled me like that. She had never seen me break down like that in private, let alone in a packed room of strangers. It just didn't make sense to her, and that was frightening.

I reached across my wife's empty seat, then rested my hand on Mary's shoulder. "It's good, it's good…" was all I could muster.

As we drove home, I gathered myself, and to the best of my abilities I tried describing to them exactly what I had experienced, an impossible task at best. And although they were both intrigued with my unusual experience, they seemed to be just as equally perplexed by it.

I remember curling up in bed that night, still fighting to understand exactly what had happened to me. I turned my light out, then lifted my shade a bit and stared out my window at my neighbor's towering oak tree. The moonlight seemed to dance across its leaves like it never had before, glistening with a playful brilliance that was new to my eyes. I dropped the shade, pulled the warm comforter up to my chin, then thanked God one last time before peacefully drifting off to sleep.

When I awoke the next morning my first thought was, *What an incredible dream!* It felt so real. I immediately rolled over and tugged on my shade, allowing it to rise again, opening my view to my neighbor's old oak tree. The morning sunlight danced across its leaves just as it had the night before. The shimmery luminescence sparkled with an indescribable quality that could only come from heaven above.

It was real...it is real...GOD is real! I thought.

Endless possibilities suddenly lay at my threshold. For the next couple of weeks, all the light that my eyes took in carried that same brilliance to it. The air I breathed felt purer and more abundant in my lungs than ever before. My state of mind and peace of heart were heightened and steady. Any issues that arose that would typically send me over the edge, just seemed to effortlessly roll off my shoulders as if they never happened at all. I was suddenly unaffected by the small stuff and carried an unusual, profound peace deep within me. I was not aware of it at that time, but what I had been given was a new reference point, or baseline of consciousness that I would forever use to gauge my present state of mind.

That is how it happened. That is how my perception of all that is, changed forever. The morning after the healing service, I went straight to a Sunday service at Avon Lake Presbyterian Church, the same church my wife had attended as a child. At that moment, I was in search of answers. *Why did this happen to me, and has anyone else ever experienced anything like this before?*

That one service led me to weekly services, and that went on for over a year. Then one night my phone rang. It was Rae Mathews from the nominating committee at Avon Lake Presbyterian Church. She told me that their committee had noticed my recent involvement at the church and thought I may be a good fit for a deacon position, which they were looking to fill. Without even knowing what a deacon was, I felt a nudge from within me to accept, so I did. These strong inner nudges began happening to me after my experience. When I reflect on them now, I wonder if they've always been within me, offering me one direction instead of another; only unnoticed, or more likely ignored, until then.

As part of my duties, I would hold monthly meetings where eleven other deacons, Pastor Charlie, and I would plan and organize church events and discuss creative ways to unify our congregation through fellowship. In general, our goal was to care for all the members of ALPC and make sure each felt loved as a valued member of that church family. The deacons, as well as Pastor Charlie, were an amazing group of people who helped me understand the incredible gift that I was given when I began to serve others, an intimate gift of transcendence into my own deepening spirituality.

I began to pray aloud at each of our monthly meetings for those who were sick, or distraught, or were grieving a loss—anyone who was in need of a prayer. I also began writing what I hoped would be inspirational articles for the church's newsletter. I served for six years, and within that time, a life-changing realization bubbled up within me: when I prayed or served or wrote for the sake of another, that beautiful light that I had experienced at the healing service began to rise within me again. It may not have been as intense as it was at the healing service, but unmistakably, it was the same light!

Over those years I prayed, and served, and began to research all that I could about God and our role within his ultimate plan. Instead of listening to music as I hauled truckloads of dirt, I listened to podcasts that explored God, our spirituality, and multiple viewpoints on the larger questions in life. In my free time, I began reading scripture and a variety of books by spiritual teachers like Eckhart Tolle, Mother Teresa, Thich Nhat Hanh, Wayne Dyer, Thomas Merton, Deepak Chopra, Gary Zukav, and Don Miguel Ruiz, which offered a colorful spectrum of insights into our creator. I did not know it at the time, but this research would ultimately provide me the insight to write the Christian story and the explanation for life itself through the lens of Eastern wisdom. I also began watching Oprah Winfrey's Super Soul Sunday, where she would interview a wide range of people, including some of the most introspective in the world, in search of their views on God, spirituality, and the meaning of life itself.

I studied over one hundred firsthand accounts of near-death experiences from people who were pronounced dead but then were revived and brought back to life, most of them with undeniable similarities in what they experienced in the afterlife. To my surprise, I found that many of the aftereffects that I experienced after my encounter were the same as those who had died and were brought back to life. Again, I had no explanation for this, but after researching so many NDEs, our similarities in the wake of our experiences, despite their differences, were undeniable.

I fought to attain a wider perspective of God and what this life really was. And like breadcrumbs, I continued to follow the emerging nudges that would inevitably rise up within me.

One of those nudges was the book you are about to read. It took me over five years to complete it. Most of it was written through the snowy days of winter or rainy days when we were not able to work outside. A fair portion of it was written at three o'clock in the morning when I'd rise from a dream, then stumble downstairs to my computer to translate thoughts that seemed to manifest while I slept. It felt as if I had unknowingly softened the noise that had always muddled my consciousness, and in doing so, I had cracked a strange door to my soul open, offering clarity and guidance from within, which I had never known even existed.

On the heels of such a heart-opening experience, it felt as if I could feel more of everything…the darkness and the light. The content on our nightly news suddenly began to feel amplified to me. Political and racial divide, corporate greed, the opioid crisis, human trafficking…all of it just felt heavier to me. And as I focused on the details of others' pain, I felt its weight grow within me. All that was good became amplified too. A simple walk on a wooded path was no longer simple. The deep, rich presence of the trees and flowers and birds filled me in a way that they never had before. I had unknowingly stepped into a deeper, clearer unification with all that surrounded me.

Through these years, another important realization came to me. Dr. Issam Nemeh, the man who offered prayers to a child who could not speak—a child who now, thirteen years later, is fully verbal and attends a local community college—is just an ordinary man. It took me awhile to understand, but Dr. Nemeh was born with no more gifts than you or I were born with. What separates him from most is his stillness of mind and deep love he carries for all who surround him. He is kind, humble, sacrificial, and his faith in God is absolute. With pure intention he lays down his own will in exchange for the will of God. His consistent, loving state of being thins his veil and transforms his heart into a beautiful window that allows heaven itself to blow into this world and, quite literally, heal it. But he is just a man…no different than you or I.

Upon this realization, I was given great hope for all of humanity. The same access to God, the source of all that is, is available to each one of us. But we must first break down the great walls that separate us from one another and truthfully love all who surround us, so we may find the stillness within our own mind to open that same window.

Although my hope for this world remains strong, from time to time, I still find myself looking inward and inevitably asking myself, *why did this happen to me and what is the heart of God's intention for my personal journey?* Although the specific details to my trail's end remain unknown, I have absolute confidence that its purpose does exist. Maybe it has nothing to do with this story I wrote…and maybe it does. Maybe, by viewing the world through my lens it may shed light on how important each one of us really is, regardless of our wealth, or color, or religion, or the great failures from our past, or the great fears of our future. Despite all of our beautiful earthly imperfections, each of us remains flawless as a unique expression of God himself. And through that expression, you are given the ability to shape this world by means of the very heart that beats within your chest right now.

But if my book never travels beyond the railroad tracks that mark the southern border of my small town, only being read or understood by a few…I think that will still be ok.

Because after reading it, if only one finds themselves paused at the cliff's edge watching the crash of the great waves against the rocks, or the light and dark clouds that seem to endlessly pass over them, noticing that both strangely cling to each other, almost as if through their own opposing nature, each is fighting to consume the other, it is my hope that they will be drawn back to center; back to the place where they are able to ask with an open, searching heart, "My God, in what direction did I move this world today?" And that alone, I think, will be enough.

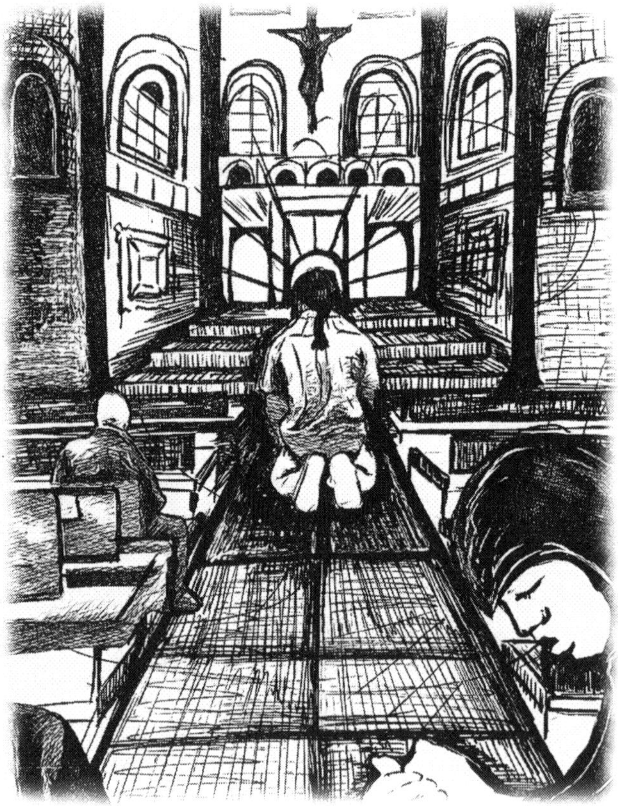

1

Lejos slowly walked past the pews in the Mission's old sanctuary just before dusk, then knelt at the foot of the large wooden cross. Bodies of the hopeless were scattered like trash throughout the old church. Most slept, satisfied for the moment within the safety of their drafty refuge. An old man, unshaven and cloaked in soiled clothes, sat on the floor in the corner, smoking the butt of his last cigarette, fighting to lose himself in its drifting spire of smoke. Pigeons cooed from high in the rafters, unaffected by the occasional movements far below. Another old man slept in the first pew, where he always did, just feet from where Lejos had knelt. His deep phlegmy cough rattled with every breath, reflecting a lifetime of smoking and drug abuse.

Lejos closed his eyes, then began to pray the way he always did; the way he was taught to pray by the chaplain in the prison. He opened himself, with intention, to the pain and suffering of all who surrounded him.

The beautiful light of the setting sun cast heavenly hues across the high ceilings of the sanctuary as it refracted through its broken stained glass. Dust hung in the air and accentuated the beams of light, defining them as if cast from God himself. Lejos lifted his eyes up toward the cylinders of light, gazing in awe from his humble place of prayer on the floor. *A gift from God*, he thought. He then opened both palms of his hands, as if searching for heat from the changing light above, but it was not warmth he sought. He was searching for something greater.

From his position of surrender, he ran the words of the prison chaplain through his mind: *simply love all who surround you, and God will shine within you, my son.* Above all else, this had become Lejos' mantra throughout his days. So as he knelt on the hardwood floor and silently sank into prayer, he sought to love all who surrounded him as deeply as he could. He searched for their pain, willingly taking in their suffering, accepting it with a rare depth of heart. Then, for their sake, he truthfully offered it back to his Lord. One by one, he focused on each person who was sick, or broken, or forgotten, or unloved. Beyond running the words of his prayers through his mind, he ran them through his heart, envisioning each soul fighting to navigate the torment within their individual lives. Although each of their lives' experiences had been different from his own, he asked God to help him understand their pain. With great concentration, Lejos fought to feel what each must have felt throughout their struggles. He prayed with pure intention and truth of heart to transcend their bodies and understand their pain intimately, as if their hearts beat within his own chest. That was the moment it happened. That was the moment when darkness was cut down to its knees.

2

Three men dressed in green hospital scrubs sat conversing at a large, meticulously polished boardroom table. Each sipped coffee and laughed as they spoke casually about the day's events. The room was clad in rich dark mahogany and decorated tastefully with many large, well-kept potted plants and beautifully framed pieces of artwork hanging on the walls behind them. A large platinum logo reading, "The Cleveland Hospital" dominated the room's decor.

The door swung open and Dr. Samuel Pierson walked into the room. He was dressed in a fashionable gray tailored suit. As he poured a cup of coffee, one of the other surgeons spoke up.

"Got any plans for the weekend, Sam?"

Without ever making eye contact, he responded, "I'm feeling a little pale. I might fly down to Miami tomorrow for a little sun."

One of the seated doctors rolled his eyes, then poked, "What happened, bulbs burn out in your tanning bed, Sam?"

Snickering, the three scrubbed doctors restrained themselves from open laughter.

Dr. Pierson strolled by as if he didn't hear them at all, then paused in front of a large framed window that offered a view of the darkening city. His gaze appeared contemplative as he noticed the changing light on the buildings as the late summer sun set over Lake Erie. Brilliant pinks and blues washed throughout the darkening sky. Sam silently took in their colors as he slowly sipped his coffee.

Dr. Pierson eventually broke the silence. "Besides, mojitos taste better over a Miami bar."

One of the surgeons remarked, "I guess you won't be volunteering at the Mission, then."

More subdued laughter came from their table. Another doctor prodded, "Dr. Pierson would love to help humanity, but unfortunately, he's feeling a little pale this weekend…" More soft laughter ensued.

"Mission? What are you talking about?"

"You should have gotten an email, Sam. The hospital is asking for volunteers for tomorrow evening and throughout the weekend. They're offering a free clinic a few blocks away, at that rundown Mission on Superior. I don't know, I think it's some public relations thing."

Another one of the doctors mimed air quotes, "Caring for those in need throughout the city."

Sam smirked sarcastically. "I'm sure you three clowns will be there, right?"

"Been there, done that," another doctor added. "While spending my weekend treating illegal immigrants and prostitutes does sound inviting, I think I'll pass."

Sam immediately spoke up. "Don't get me started…" He shook his head in disgust. "Gentlemen, I'm telling you, they are overrunning our country. I think we need to shut down our southern border all together!"

"Don't worry about it, Sam. Volunteering's what interns are for, anyway."

The three doctors chuckled in unison. Then, knowing where this subject would lead with Dr. Pierson, they drew their conversation inward, conversing among themselves.

Outside of the window, something caught Sam's eye. Just as the final rays of the setting sun fell upon the city, a beautiful single beam of light broke through the clouds, then struck the steeple of the sanctuary at the old Mission. Sam sipped his coffee, strangely suspended in the moment. As he mused, a distinctly beautiful cloud caught his attention, brushed with fading hues of pinks and deepening orange, drifting low in the sky in front of him. He watched as it slowly made its way above the building in which he stood, pausing as if it had found its home. Sam drew his attention back to the old Mission, taking in the dappled light against the canvas of the old steeple, as he slowly finished his cup of coffee.

3

The colors over the horizon began to soften with the setting sun, all blending together like a freshly painted watercolor. Rachel watched the spectacular show of light, then raised her wineglass up to her mouth and slowly sipped again. A gentle, warm summer breeze rolled off Lake Erie from the west, as God's glory unfolded in front of her. The beauty of the moment would have opened most hearts, but hers lay dark and dormant. She closed her eyes and leaned against the back fence of her property, which stretched across a grassy bluff perched high above the lake below.

Rachel turned her head and looked at the backside of her home, first noticing the changing light cast on it from the setting sun, and then fixating on the one square of light that illuminated her kitchen window. Inside the house, everything was perfectly still. One dim bulb shone down on the kitchen table, where an open laptop sat idle. Next to it stood an empty bottle of Chianti, where a pewter corkscrew was left lying on the table next to it. Its wine-stained cork was still bound in its screw. Cast across the handle of the corkscrew read the words "Niagara on the Lake," a sad reminder of her honeymoon eighteen years earlier. Every bottle she opened began with a piercing pain entering her heart, but even before her first glass was consumed, her pain would inevitably grow into an angry resentment.

She didn't quite understand why she kept the corkscrew. She told her friends that she held on to it out of sentiment, but unbeknownst to them, and even to her, it was kept as a catalyst to retrieve the anger that she held deep within her heart, the anger for their betrayal. And although it was only within herself, it felt right to remember exactly what they had done to her. Remembering allowed her silent rage to live, giving breath to it, even if it were only within herself.

Taking in the warm lake air, she began to move slowly along the black wrought-iron fence that ran just a few feet from the cliff's edge. As she walked, her attention was drawn to her next-door neighbor's home, which was fully illuminated and teeming with life. Faint laughter could be heard along with the soft echo of their television set. Shadows moved freely within their draped windows, and although she could not see them directly, she knew their walls witnessed a very different life than hers did.

To the rest of the world, Rachel was a strong successful woman who appeared to be virtually unaffected by the obvious obstacles she was forced to face. But within, she carried a deep-seated sadness and a very real pain, which at that moment felt as if it were more than she could bear.

She took another deep breath, then slowly exhaled, hoping the pain would go with it, but tears welled up as she realized it wasn't so. She emptied her glass with one final sip, then turned her head toward the horizon and asked herself out loud, "Would my daughters even know if I were gone? Would they even care?"

Tears began to roll down her face as she took a few more steps, then leaned down and unlatched the back gate. An eerie squeak came from the hinges as she drew the gate open. The thin strip of earth that separated the fence from the cliff's edge was only a few feet wide and moved with the warm breeze. Ankle-high grass swept in large swaths with the wind's indecisive gusts. Rachel took another deep breath as she moved closer to the grassy ledge. Reluctantly, she looked over the bluff at the large limestone boulders far below, which formed a break wall where the pounding waves crashed into the base of the shoreline. Tears fell from her face but were immediately whisked away as the breeze blew strong at the cliff's edge and swirled all around her. She softly pleaded aloud, "God, help me…"

Again, Rachel looked down at the relentless waves crashing over the jagged boulders. She then drew her eyes up to the horizon and with sad desperation in her voice, asked, "Are you even there?" She shut her eyes, listening for an answer, then squinted them tighter as if to squeeze a response out of God. Her concentration was eventually broken by the faint sound of thunder, far off over the lake. She gently opened her eyes as the deep rumble slowly faded, then looked out at the changing sky. She noticed that both dark and white clouds covered the sky now and seemed to drift south in her direction. One large cloud had moved in and rested high above her. It appeared to circle ever so slowly. Its movement was nearly undetectable, as if it had found its home. The sun dropped behind the horizon, and its brilliant light blanketed both dark and light clouds equally. Soft heavenly hues of purples, pinks, and blues touched all clouds and everything within its reach, totally changing her surroundings in an instant.

After holding her breath in silence, she softly muttered, "Nothing?" With another deep sigh, she turned and slowly moved back through the wrought-iron opening. The sound of the heavy gate closing behind her seemed to represent a finality that any hope that God exists had been lost at that very moment.

She made her way through the darkness of her backyard, then opened her door and stepped into the silent isolation of her home.

4

As her SUV idled in her driveway, Rachel sat inside, awaiting the arrival of her two daughters and reviewing her day's schedule on her iPhone. Her head throbbed with a familiar dull haze that hung thick within her mind, as it did most mornings. She flinched at the sound of her next-door neighbor's front door opening. She adjusted her side mirror, then watched as a beautiful woman wearing a loosely draped silk robe opened the door. It was her neighbor of nearly sixteen years, Shannon Jennings.

Rachel's grip tightened around her steering wheel, and unknowingly, her jaw began to clench as she watched her through her side mirror. She noticed her heart beating faster, feeling every throb clearer than the moment before. As Rachel studied the woman, a dark spike of jealousy pierced her heart. Within moments, her jealousy grew into a dull but unspoken anger, which only masked the true void that lay deep within her.

While still holding the front door open, the woman turned inside, then directed, "Hurry up, girls, your mother's waiting!"

Rachel's two daughters hurried out of their new home, then made their way across the lawn and into their mother's SUV. As Rachel and her daughters drove down the driveway, she caught a glimpse of her ex-husband kissing his new wife goodbye at their front door. The newlyweds held their embrace until Shannon's two kids, Nick and Ashley, bustled by. They were both dressed in their Catholic school attire, motioning to Dave to hurry up. The three of them hopped in his car and hurried down the driveway toward their school. Rachel took a long deep breath, then exhaled, hoping her anger would subside, but it did not.

The sky was filled with dark rolling clouds that traveled very low and fast. Both of her girls looked out the car windows watching for rain. But no rain fell.

Rachel stopped at the end of her long driveway, then put her SUV into park. She sat inside with her two daughters, Terra, who was fifteen, and Meghan, who was ten, waiting for Meghan's school bus to arrive. On Rachel's days, the three would sit waiting together, then after her youngest had departed, Rachel would drop Terra off at Avon Lake High School before shooting off to work.

Terra sat up front with her headphones on, listening to her music and staring out her passenger side window, as she always did. Since the divorce, she seemed more and more frustrated and withdrawn from both of her parents. Rachel noticed other changes too, but this was also her first experience raising a teenage girl, and it had become difficult for Rachel to know if her daughter's actions were backlash from their divorce, or just normal teenage behavior.

Recently, Rachel had received a phone call from the mother of a girl at Terra's school, informing her that Terra and two of her friends had been bullying her daughter over social media. Since the divorce, Terra just seemed angrier and less patient with everybody. And no matter how hard Rachel tried, their conversations always seemed to end in an argument.

Looking over at Terra, Rachel felt torn, knowing she should be more engaged with her daughter. But she had developed a certain peace, understanding that as long as Terra's headphones were on, chances were pretty good that there would not be an argument. The truth was, Rachel had grown so tired of arguing with her teenage daughter that it was just easier to allow her to isolate herself within her own world.

Meghan, on the other hand, looked forward to their time together each morning. It felt as if the distractions of her mother's busy day had not yet begun, and as of recently, she had been asking her mother questions about her childhood growing up in the same small town in which they presently lived.

Rachel was the only child of a third-generation winemaker and a loving, hard-working mother. They lived in a small but quaint bungalow in the cottage district of Avon Lake, known as the 45 Allotment. The name came from the electric train that ran from Cleveland to Lorain, and her old neighborhood was the forty-fifth stop heading west on its daily route. The locals simply referred to the neighborhood as the 45s. Rachel's father was in charge of the vineyards at Hamlin Winery, which bordered the neighborhood where they lived. Actually, the ten most southern homes in the cottage district were built on the vineyard and were used by old man Hamlin to house their seasonal employees as well as Rachel's family. As a perk of being the foreman of the field hands and the only year-round employee, Rachel's father was able to choose the nicest of the ten homes. Most of these homes were somewhat neglected by the winery and were looked down upon in relation to the other homes in the 45s. Although Rachel's parents kept their house very clean and well-maintained, they remained in the perception of what came to be known as the Lower 10 of the 45s. As Rachel grew, she felt more and more affected by this perception. In fact, she made a personal vow to herself that she would do whatever it took to ensure her own kids would never have to feel as she did.

Her younger years growing up in the Lower 10 were very different, though. She loved where she lived and looked forward to the beginning of each season in the vineyards when a new crew of field hands moved into her neighborhood. Quite often they brought their families, providing a new bunch of neighborhood kids for Rachel to play with.

Meghan loved hearing all about the simplicity of Avon Lake thirty years ago and how this now-developed suburb of Cleveland was primarily a farming community known for its local wines and beautiful sunsets over Lake Erie. Rachel began to look forward to reminiscing, as she felt carried back to a happier, more innocent time in her life. If only for a few moments, telling stories of her childhood seemed to distract her from the relentless pain and resentment that she now carried within her.

As Rachel described her younger days, Meghan would sit in the back seat and, with her eyes shut, would let the images of her mother's childhood flood her imagination. She would smile as her mom spoke of one summer in particular when her days felt endless and were spent exploring all the hidden corners of their little town with a new summer friend, Peggy Bender. Rachel and Peggy spent that whole summer together climbing trees, playing in creeks, and jumping off the sandstone piers into Lake Erie. They enjoyed the absolute freedom of childhood in a time when it was not unusual for kids to venture off in the morning and not return home until dinner was about to be served on the table.

Meghan loved hearing about the grape vineyards and how they blanketed most of the small town back then. Vivid images arose, as her mother described looking out her bedroom window on the brisk mornings of fall to find the most beautiful cool, soft haze hanging thick over the vineyards, until the morning sun rose and burnt it off within the first hour of daylight. And how, right before harvest, the aroma of the grapes would hang dense and pungent throughout the town. Rachel and Peggy would sneak into the fields and pick a few bunches for themselves to snack on as they lay on blankets under a canopy of Catalpa trees in her backyard. It all sounded so sweet, and innocent, and perfect to Meghan.

It was so different back then, Meghan thought, recalling that she had spent most of her last summer sitting inside on her cell phone or watching television. And although Rachel's daughter had everything she needed, Meghan envied the childhood her mother spoke of. It just sounded so perfect.

"Meghan, Meghan, your bus is here," Rachel exclaimed. "I'll see you at school in about thirty minutes, dear."

"You'll be on time, won't you?" Meghan asked with concern.

"Of course, I'll see you there." Rachel forced a smile as Meghan departed, running over to the open doors of the bus. She then climbed in and waved goodbye as the bus doors closed in front of her.

It was Career Day at Eastwood Elementary school, the same school Rachel herself had attended twenty-six years earlier, and Rachel would be speaking later that morning about what it meant to be a pharmaceutical sales representative. She'd been a rep for over twelve years now and was very good at what she did. She seemed to be good at most everything she did. For the last eight years, she had maintained the number one slot in her company for overall sales. Outside of work, she was a key player in the Avon Lake PTA, lobbying for and successfully procuring the necessary state funding for the new computer lab at Meghan's school. She was a woman who set her mind on a goal, then would reach it, end of story. She had made professional connections at the state level, lobbying for her pharmaceutical company, and had no qualms about using the people she knew to get things done. Although her daughter was very proud of her mother's achievements and enjoyed the lifestyle that her position had afforded them, Meghan, at times, felt a bit disconnected from her and attributed it to her mother's strong professional drive and demanding work obligations.

Since Rachel had cleared her morning for Eastwood's Career Day, she'd need to work extra hard throughout the afternoon and early evening to get all of her sales calls in.

Before departing for Meghan's school, she dropped Terra off at the high school, then headed toward Wagner's Market to grab lunch, a few groceries, and her morning coffee.

Driving to the grocery store, Rachel organized her thoughts for the talk that she was about to give. Comfortable with her ideas, she pulled into a parking spot, then began gathering her things. As she sat parked in her SUV, Rachel's mind immediately was drawn to the image of her ex-husband kissing his new wife, Rachel's longtime friend and next-door neighbor, Shannon. Rachel felt a familiar fire begin to burn within her chest as she envisioned them embracing on their front porch.

Since the divorce, whenever Rachel's mind would wander, it seemed to always find that painful default filled with visions of Dave and Shannon together or times spent with Shannon and her husband, Jack, before he passed away. They had always been close neighbors, and for years, the two couples spent many nights grilling out, sipping wine, and laughing together while their kids played in their backyards. When Rachel allowed herself to reminisce, it almost felt like someone else's life that she was recalling. They were all so happy together, until about four years ago when Jack was diagnosed with glioblastoma, an aggressive brain cancer, which, in Jack's case, was inoperable. She remembered her heart breaking for Shannon and her kids, then again, when she told her own two daughters that Jack was sick and that there was no cure for his illness. She remembered how helpless they felt watching their close friend rapidly decline.

Thinking back, the sadness within her morphed into resentment as she recalled her husband spending more and more time with the struggling couple next door. Both Dave and Rachel worked, but she was the primary breadwinner, earning more than ten times what Dave did. Even though she grieved for her neighbor throughout his decline, her unwavering professional drive prevented her from ever compromising her work obligations to help with Jack, but that was not the case with her husband. Both Dave and Rachel had always been hard workers; but through this tragic event, it had become painfully clear to Dave that Rachel's priority, above all else, was her job. Whenever needed, Dave would drop what he was doing to run next door to help Shannon with his dying friend. Time after time, he would lift Jack from their couch into his wheelchair, and again, into Shannon's car for his repeated visits to the Cleveland Hospital. He found himself sitting with his friend, listening as he grieved his own impending death. Dave promised Jack that he would be there for Shannon and his kids throughout the painful process of his decline. Dave sat with Shannon day after day as she wept by his side. She described the pain and helplessness of watching the father of her children wither, then die in front of her eyes.

This long, heart-wrenching process, and ultimate death of his close friend, had become a pivotal event within his own life. Something had changed in the way Dave looked at the world around him. Something had changed in the way that he looked at his wife, Rachel, and something had changed in the way he looked at Shannon too. It was nearly two years from the day his good friend was first diagnosed to the day Dave knelt by his casket, reaffirming his promise, through prayer, that his family would be cared for. After his death, it had been another two years that Dave spent conflicted, his heart torn between the vow he had made to his wife, and this powerful new calling he felt toward Shannon and her kids. A two-year battle raged within him, before he painfully decided to step away from his marriage to start a new life next door with Shannon, his best friend's widow.

Whenever Rachel saw them together, she was consumed with anger and deep resentment, but her strong pride prevented her from moving from her home after their divorce. Rachel had no interest in the circumstances. In her mind, it was absolute betrayal by a husband, as well as of a dear friend. Rachel's heart burned with humiliation from their betrayal. She vowed never to forgive either of them. It was her only perceived vindication for what they had done to her.

The rattle of a passing shopping cart brought Rachel back to the moment, where she was still sitting in her idling car. She glanced down at the clock on her dashboard, then, realizing her limited time, opened her door and hurried toward the entrance of the grocery store.

Wagner's Market was busy with the same old locals that Rachel always saw. It seemed to her that most of them casually perused the aisles as if they had no schedule at all. Rachel grabbed a shopping cart, then hurried toward the sushi counter to pick up her lunch. As she passed the beverage aisle, she noticed a local painter, Jerry Stevens, with his two young children, putting a twelve-pack of beer into his cart. She grabbed some freshly rolled sushi and a couple more items she needed, then proceeded to the line at Starbucks for a coffee. Two women stood in front of her gossiping while the barista waited to take their order. Rachel rolled her eyes as they continued laughing, oblivious to the world around them. Growing impatient, she interceded, "Excuse me," then motioned to the young man, who was patiently waiting to take their order. Embarrassed, the ladies apologized, put their order in, and continued gabbing as they shuffled off to the side of the kiosk to wait for their coffees.

After grabbing her coffee, Rachel took a quick sip, then moved toward the grocery checkout at the front of the store. Waiting again, she sipped her cappuccino and glanced over her afternoon calendar on her iPhone. With her eyes on the screen, an overwhelming feeling of uneasiness washed over her, distracting her from her train of thought. It almost felt as if someone was watching her. She glanced over her left shoulder but found that no one was there. Then, shifting her head forward again, she looked up at Mr. Z., the checkout clerk, and the backs of the two people who were standing in line in front of her. She looked at the clerk to her right, a very young soon-to-be mother, who was focused on the groceries in front of her as she passed them over her scanner. As Rachel looked back toward her phone, she caught a glimpse of a strange man's eyes looking back at her. His body and most of his face were obstructed by the line of people in front of her. Though her view was compromised, Rachel continued to stare back, wondering if it was someone she knew; after all, she had lived in this town most of her life and couldn't walk down the street without having someone say hello or wave to her. Even with her limited view of the man's face, she could tell that he was old, and appeared to be sitting on one of the store benches just across the aisle from the store's bagging area.

It only took a couple of minutes before old Mr. Z. had waited on her, bagged her items, and got her on her way.

"I hope you sell a lot of drugs today, Rachel!" he said, chuckling out loud. This had become his lighthearted one-liner that he commonly used when she would pass through his checkout line.

Rachel smiled at the clerk. "Oh, I will, Mr. Z., don't you worry about that," she said as she grabbed her groceries, then hurried toward the exit doors.

Curiosity got the best of Rachel as she passed by the stranger, so she lifted her head and gave him a quick glance. Her heart dropped when she saw that he was still glaring at her with a baiting grin.

He was a very old, distinguished-looking man that Rachel didn't recognize. He sat alone, with a cane propped in front of him and a well-kept derby hat hanging from its silver handle. His shoulders were broad and his posture was tight as he sat perfectly upright, dignified like a king. Rachel found his stature was not the only trait that was odd for a man of his age. He wore his hair longer, combed back nearly to his shoulders, and although it was an eye-catching silver, his hairline was very thick. He had a handsome face despite his apparent age, which carried a road map of wrinkles, each line enhancing instead of detracting from his appearance. His skin was tighter, not loose and hanging, like she would expect of such an old man. Even though he was sitting, Rachel could tell he was unusually tall, meticulously clad in a freshly pressed dark gray suit. He stared into her eyes with confidence as she briskly passed by. He was grinning with bushy gray eyebrows raised high, almost as if he had expected a response from her. The old stranger studied her with glaring intention, like a brazen man eyeing an attractive woman in a bar. Rachel cracked a quick, tight-lipped smile, as not to be rude, but kept walking past him. He kept his eyes beaded on her, and as she turned her head toward the exit, she heard him raise his deep voice. "That a girl!"

She immediately scowled in protest at the stranger's unusual comment. Without dignifying his remarks, she continued walking toward the exit doors. Two quick taps of his cane on the tile floor rang out, like two large stones being struck together. *Crack, crack!* With a loud threatening tone, his angry voice rang out. "Hey! I'm talking to you, girl."

The aggressiveness of his tone gave her the distinct impression that this stranger meant her harm, which caused her heart to drop again. Despite his verbal attack, she continued through the automatic doors without breaking her stride. Rachel reached the safety of her car, and with a perplexed look on her face, muttered aloud, "Crazy old man!"

For one moment she considered that the old stranger could have dementia and may have wandered down from Sunrise Village, a retirement center that was two blocks north of the grocery store. Rachel quickly got into her SUV and attempted to erase any further thought of him, but she could not.

Still sitting inside of the store, the old man chuckled to himself, then softly said out loud, "Oh, I'm much darker than that, my dear."

5

As an involved parent, Rachel knew she could not get out of her Career Day obligations. Still, she made sure to have her laptop tucked away in her satchel. The morning would be filled with parents and grandparents speaking about their vocations and would allow ample time to get some work done as they spoke.

When she arrived, the gym was buzzing with adults and fifth grade students, talking and laughing and waving to each other as they slowly settled into their seats. Family members sat in rows of folding chairs while the children sat cross-legged on the gym floor in front of the crowd. Meghan's parents had agreed to alternate years speaking at Career Day, and Rachel knew from the past that the format of the assembly would be informal. The gymnasium was small enough that no microphones were needed, and the speakers wouldn't even get up on stage. All spoke from the gym floor standing directly in front of the children. Parents and other family members would take turns with a short talk about what their career entailed, or what it used to entail, in the case of some grandparents who were no longer working. The presenter would then answer any questions the children or adult audience may have for them. The students' questions were typically quite entertaining, as they ranged from fairly intelligent questions for fifth graders, to "How old are you?"

As she entered the same gymnasium that she had entered daily throughout her elementary years, she stopped for a moment and stared around the high-ceilinged room. It looked so much smaller now, even though not much had really changed at all. Musing, Rachel took in a deep breath. Memories of countless days spent in the gym came rushing back to her. The same old piano sat perched high on the stage floor with the same worn ivory keys that Rachel herself had practiced on as a child. The pull-up bars still protruded off the west wall, tarnished and defeated, after Rachel had fought to overcome them as a fifth-grade student. In the opposite corner of the gym, the same old ship rope still hung from the high gym ceiling with an old, dented cowbell hanging just inches from it, fastened to the steel rafters near the ceiling.

Gazing up at that cowbell, it struck Rachel that this is precisely where her strong desire to win had emerged. Back when she had attended Eastwood, no fifth-grade boy could achieve an A+ in gym class without first climbing to the top of the rope. He would then have to hold his body weight with one hand and reach out and ring the cowbell with the other. That tinny *clank!* became the sound of success to each fifth grader at Eastwood Elementary. Upon their final examination, only about six boys in the whole grade were able to do it. Rachel had wanted more than anything to be the first girl to ring that bell on her examination day, and envisioned how amazing it would feel. Although the girls were not graded on the same scale, or even expected to attempt it, Rachel was one of two girls who had conquered their fears and shimmied up the rope earlier that year. The other girl was Peggy Bender, her summer friend. Rachel mused, remembering how, ultimately, she was the first girl to muster up the courage to reach out and ring the cowbell on her examination day. As a successful adult, she stood there staring at that rope and for the first time, truly understood what a pivotal moment that was in her life: conquering her fears, and other people's doubts, surpassing all obstacles to reach the top of the rope that day. She began to understand how this small event was an important part of her foundation, which she ultimately built on throughout her life, shaping her into the strong, confident woman that she now was.

A loud voice jarred her back into reality. "Everybody take your seats please, we'll be starting soon," Mrs. Hildebrandt cheerfully exclaimed.

Before Rachel even sat down, another mom, Donna Swartz, spotted her at the entry doors to the gym. She bustled over with a concerned look on her face. She moved in toward Rachel's ear to give the perception of discretion.

"I heard about what happened with Terra and Mary Katherine over social media. I think this can be a good lesson for all our kids."

Donna stood just inches from Rachel's face, waiting for a response. Immediately, Rachel felt a burning within her heart, partially from the shame she felt as a mother whose daughter had bullied another girl, but mainly from her resentment toward Donna for mentioning it to her.

Rachel spoke up with a hint of annoyance. "It really was not that big of a deal, Donna. It's not quite as dramatic as some are making it out to be. Terra and Mary Katherine had an argument over social media. I spoke to Terra about it, and now it's resolved." She paused briefly with an exaggerated exhale, before she added, "I think the program is about to start."

Donna complied with a smile, then hurried off to her seat. Rachel rolled her eyes as she grabbed an open chair against the back wall of the gym. She intentionally sat toward the back, so she would be inconspicuous while working on her laptop throughout the program. She watched and listened while the first speaker was introduced, as well as for the first couple of minutes of their talk. Inevitably though, she would draw her eyes down to her keyboard and work on her laptop until she heard applause at the end of the talk. Periodically, she would stand up in her daughter's line of sight and give her a thumbs-up and wave so Meghan thought she was engaged in her assembly.

Rachel continued catching up on her work for the first couple of hours of the morning, then, seeing that lunchtime was fast approaching, motioned to Mrs. Hildebrandt that she would like to speak next. With a smile and a nod of her head, the teacher acknowledged her request. It was not long before she introduced Rachel, then waved her forward to begin her talk.

Meghan sat up with pride as her mom spoke about what it meant to be a pharmaceutical sales representative and the importance of medicine in regard to health and well-being. Rachel went on to describe how she was recognized for her achievements by her company and how she was offered the opportunity to represent them in Washington, D.C. She explained how she met with top officials and worked directly with them to ensure we all have the medicines that we need when we are sick. Meghan beamed with pride as her mother spoke of how her own focus and hard work led her to her accomplishments and how anyone can accomplish whatever they set their minds to if they want it badly enough and are willing to work for it.

As anticipated, Rachel excelled at her presentation. Even when it came to entertaining questions from the audience, she was spot on, answering them thoroughly with great confidence. Rachel finished by thanking everyone for their time, then with a smile, began to walk toward Meghan to give her a kiss goodbye before she departed. As she moved past the crowd, Mrs. Hildebrandt spoke up.

"I believe you have one more question, Mrs. Dawson," she said, motioning to the back of the gymnasium.

As she turned to answer her last question, her eyes widened in disbelief. Standing in a cold silence was the old man from the grocery store. He towered over the seated crowd and glared at her with a blank look on his face. Totally void of expression, his eyes burned into Rachel's.

She stood alone, vulnerable in front of the crowd, her mind reeling, trying to understand who this stranger was. Quickly gathering her composure, she asked, "Do you have a question, sir?"

With a suspicious grin, he replied, "Oh, I have many questions for you, but I'll ask only one." He paused again but continued grinning at Rachel as if he had a dirty little secret to share with the crowd.

Rachel pushed, with a hint of frustration, "Well, what is it? What is your question, sir?"

His grin fell away from his face as he spoke. "Tell me what your duties at Jackson entailed before you began selling pharmaceuticals?"

Rachel thought it was presumptuous of him to assume that she held any previous duties. She answered with a touch of defiance, "As I mentioned before, I was hired by Jackson as a salesperson over twelve years ago. So to answer your question, selling is what I've always done."

The old man continued standing with a bewildered look on his face. Rachel looked back at him with confidence, as their eyes remained locked. Neither of them spoke for several seconds.

After a period of awkward silence, Rachel asserted, "Is there anything else, sir?"

A large insincere grin crept onto his face. "Yes. What about the first eighteen months of your employment at Jackson, before your duties involved selling?"

Who the hell is this guy? she thought, stunned by his question.

Something about this man suddenly felt very wrong. Rachel began to consider that their passing in the grocery store may not have been a coincidence at all.

Probing thoughts raced through her mind. *How the hell would he know about my first eighteen months at Jackson? It was confidential, and although I mentioned I had the opportunity to work in Washington, D.C., I didn't mention the specifics of what I did there, or that I had worked there for the first year and a half of my employment at Jackson.*

She turned and slowly began to pace in front of the crowd, gathering her composure and her thoughts before she spoke. She looked like an attorney about to address a defendant in front of a jury. Rachel turned toward the tall stranger, and with a strong but controlled voice, responded, "As I said, I have always been a salesperson for Jackson, but early in my career, I was asked to assist in product development for a short period of time, which brought me to Washington, D.C."

With a seemingly playful grin, the old man raised his eyebrows high and asked, "Product development?" He chuckled softly, ending in a breathy, sarcastic gasp.

Seriously and succinctly, Rachel responded, "Yes, product development."

The old man continued to glare at her in silence.

After a short pause, Rachel pried, "Thank you, Mister...?"

With an almost rehearsed innocence, the old man bowed his head slightly, then replied, "Kaw. My name is Titus Kaw."

Shaken, Rachel made her way back to her seat. The tall intruder remained standing, his eyes beaded on her as she moved through the crowd toward her chair against the back wall of the gym. With an unsettling grin, Titus Kaw turned toward the old stage and sat back down. Rachel took a long, deep breath and glanced up at the clock hanging on the wall to find that the assembly was nearly over. She put both of her hands across her forehead in thought.

How would he know about my first year at Jackson? How the hell would he know that? And the way he shouted at me at the store. He can't be sane. He must be some crazy old man. But...I just don't understand how he knows so much about me. He's toying with me!

For someone so self-assured, she suddenly found herself very confused and frightened. She even thought about calling the police, but what would she say to them? That some old man was rude to her in the grocery store, then showed up at Eastwood's Career Day?

He really hasn't done anything illegal at all, she thought. She knew she had no other choice but to confront this stranger face to face.

It was only a few minutes before the loud clatter of the old lunch bell jolted the crowd. In a sudden, chaotic frenzy, all the parents and children stood up at once and bustled in opposite directions toward the exit doors of the gym. Mustering all of her courage, she stood up and pushed through the flow of the crowd toward where the old man had been sitting.

When she finally approached, defeat coursed through her, realizing that the old man was now gone. She scanned the masses as they exited the double doors, but he seemed to have vanished into thin air. With haste, she hurried to the exit doors to check the hallway for any sign of him; but nothing. She pushed through the crowd, then made her way out the front doors of the school, checking the main parking lot. He was gone.

A few parents were leaving the school from the back door, so as a last resort, Rachel hurried upstream through the crowd, toward the back of the school. With the realization that she may have lost him, her apprehensiveness elevated into panic. The loud shuffling of her heeled shoes was the only noise left echoing throughout the empty halls now. After swinging the back door open, she found nothing but the final cars rolling out toward the street, none of which appeared to carry Titus Kaw. With a deep sigh of failure, she stared off into the woods beyond the back lot of the school. It appeared that Rachel's dark stranger had walked out of her life just as quickly as he had walked into it.

Feeling disconcerted, Rachel slowly made her way toward the front doors of the school again. The remnants of the strange intruder's violation still lingered heavily within her heart. An intruder who had studied her, stalked her, and then attacked her openly in front of a crowd of bystanders. She carried a strange insecurity now, bringing her to a state of vulnerability she had rarely experienced.

She passed through the main corridor again, walking by the closed doors of the gym, and continued toward the main exit doors of the school. As she reached down to push them open, her concentration was suddenly broken by loud disjointed musical notes. They sounded as if it had come from the old piano that sat high on the stage floor inside of the gymnasium.

As she stood in the doorway listening, the notes morphed into what sounded like hands being run up and down the keys with no melodic rhythm whatsoever. The sound struck her like the thoughts of a madman. She crept back toward the closed doors of the gymnasium. The chaotic notes grew louder as she approached. Her heart began to beat faster as she cautiously pushed on the handle and inched the large door open. The vast room was totally abandoned now. Despite the stage curtains being drawn together, it was clear that the pounding of the keys was coming from the old piano.

The knot in Rachel's stomach tightened as she stood staring at the tall, still curtain, wondering if it was her intruder who was continuing to toy with her.

She eased the door shut, then removed her heeled shoes and took several gentle steps toward the stage stairs. As Rachel quietly approached the middle of the open floor, suddenly all notes stopped; total silence fell upon the gym. It felt magnified in the wake of the pounding chaotic notes. She stood perfectly still, holding her breath, watching every crease of the curtain, watching for any possible movement.

Twenty seconds of silence. Her heart beat faster as she helplessly waited to be discovered. Suddenly, the piano rang out again, only this time it was the low dark notes of Bach's *Toccata and Fugue in D Minor*. The ominous, baiting piece deepened her fears but offered an unexpected moment to advance closer to the hidden pianist. With her footsteps now camouflaged by the music, Rachel began to move more quickly toward the stage. Fearful and reluctant, she took in the haunting music as she crept closer, her heartbeat seeming to increase with every step.

Then, just as she was about to reach the stage steps, she noticed something that shot panic through her heart. Nausea quickly emerged within her as she came into view of Titus Kaw's cane leaning against the front of the stage wall, with his well-kept derby hat perched on top of it.

She now knew it was the dark intruder who was baiting her. She stared at the velvet barrier, searching for the words to confront him. As she considered his repeated intrusions into her life, her apprehension began to fade and an unexpected anger lit within her, sparked by his unprovoked invasion into her and her daughter's lives.

With a deep breath, Rachel rushed up the stairs and broke through an opening in the curtain.

As expected, there sat Titus Kaw at the old piano, glaring back at her. He wore a triumphant smile, with razor-sharp arrogance radiating from his striking eyes. He continued to play as she walked onto the stage floor, just feet from where he sat. He held his gaze on her as she approached, then began to laugh with sinister joy. As she moved around the piano, his eyes bored into her without a blink.

"Who the hell are you?" Rachel shouted.

The old man remained silent as he played louder. Titus just smiled at her, totally unaffected by her questioning. Then, after several seconds, he spoke with an elevated, deceivingly playful tone.

"Who am I? Why, I am an *angel*, dear. I was sent here to enlighten you." A false innocence washed over his face. Then he raised his eyebrows high and began to laugh again, adding, "A fallen angel, that is!" His sinister grin returned as his laughter intensified.

Rachel stood next to the old piano, frightened and confused. She didn't know what to think. She barked back at the old man, "Tell me the truth, who are you and why the hell are you here?" The old man held his confident smile as he answered, "I assure you that I am who I say I am. I am one of the fallen angels, my dear."

He glanced up at Rachel. Then, embracing all the fear that he was instilling into her, his eyes gleamed as he played on. In Rachel's mind, hearing his response seemed to confirm that Titus Kaw was absolutely delusional. It was clear to her that this man actually believed he was the devil, or in his own words, a fallen angel. And as he played, she saw within his eyes that he believed it to be true.

In clear objection, Rachel asked outright, "Are you telling me that you actually believe that you are the devil? Is that what you're trying to tell me, you crazy old man?"

Titus simply laughed as he continued playing the piano. Toying with her, he responded, "No, my dear, I'm not telling you that I am the devil, but I am working my way down that ladder." He broke into laughter again. "I'm actually one of his brothers, Rachel. We are the closest of kin." He then smiled smugly, as if she should be impressed by his dark declaration.

There it was, Titus Kaw was clearly a crazy old man, totally detached from reality.

Frustrated and angry, she leaned toward him and shouted, "It's obvious you're out of your mind, sir. Stay where you are, I'm calling the police!"

The old man drew his hands away from the keys as Rachel turned and fumbled through her bag for her cell phone. She noticed that the old man had gotten up from the piano bench and was now standing directly in front of the drawn curtains. He held his cane in his right hand, and with a pretentious grin, casually leaned on it as he watched her move toward the steps.

"Not so fast, my dear." he said in a calm but authoritative voice.

Ignoring his command, Rachel kept her eyes trained on him as she quickened her pace toward the steps.

Like a ringleader, with his back to the curtain, he slowly bowed in front of Rachel. Without breaking their eye contact, he announced, with heightened tone and distinction, as if he were addressing a packed arena of spectators, "Welcome...to *the show!*"

The old man raised his cane up high, then, with an evil cackle, slammed it down into the stage floor. *Crack!* The sound of two tremendous stones being struck together echoed across the stage.

Then in an unimaginable moment, Rachel gasped in disbelief. She threw her hands over her mouth as several incredibly bright bolts of light shot out from directly under his cane, forming a web of electricity. Simultaneously, the stage curtains drew open on their own, revealing a surreal scene: a packed gymnasium that was teeming with teenagers.

All the bleachers had been pulled out, as if a basketball game were about to begin, and what looked like hundreds of high school students filled every seat. In an instant, the gym went from dead silence into roars of laughter and shouting and chaotic chatter. From every corner, students shuffled throughout the bleachers. The stands were suddenly alive with movement and banter. Rachel noticed one young girl standing idle in the middle of the gym floor, totally alone, just watching in silence as all of her peers socialized high above her in the stands.

Rachel took several steps backward, then began to weep, realizing that this dark figure was much more than a delusional old man.

"Yes, yes…who's crazy now, my dear?" Victoriously, he began to laugh at her again.

Standing on her old elementary school stage, the reality that had always existed within Rachel's world seemed to crumble right in front of her eyes. All that she had known to be true throughout her life was suddenly in question. She instantly felt light-headed and became worried that she may faint.

"Come, Rachel…watch!" Kaw directed.

"What is this? Where did all these kids come from? Who is the girl in the middle of the floor?" Rachel frantically inquired. "I think I'm having a nervous breakdown." She turned her eyes down toward the stage floor and began to sob uncontrollably.

Kaw spoke up. "'It really was no big deal.' I believe those were the words you used to describe your daughter Terra bullying Mary Katherine over social media. Well, since seeing is believing, dear, let's show you the real specifics of the pain that ran through Mary Katherine's heart as your daughter belittled her on social media in front of all those followers. Oh, the power Terra felt from hurting that one!" Kaw pointed his cane down at the teenage girl, who stood frightened and isolated in the middle of the gym floor. "It really was quite impressive!"

In a panicked voice, Rachel asked, "Is that Mary Katherine? What is this? What the hell is going on here?"

The stage felt as if it were spinning around Rachel now. She felt like she had been thrown into a nightmare; only this was no nightmare, it was very real. She was fully awake but had no explanation as to how any of this was even possible or why it was happening to her.

Kaw responded, "This is the physical representation of how Mary Katherine felt for over a month as your daughter and her two friends relentlessly bullied her over social media. "Let's watch, shall we?"

Rachel stood petrified. She watched in horror with both of her quivering hands covering her mouth.

Within seconds, the crowd of busy teens took their seats in the bleachers. Simultaneously, the lights above faded and a hush fell over the crowd. An infectious silence blanketed the entire gym. All of their eyes were on Mary Katherine now, who stood alone at the center of the gym floor, fully illuminated by three bright spotlights. From the other side of the room, three girls rose from their seats, then began to slowly walk across the gym floor toward Mary Katherine.

Rachel squinted her eyes as she hurried closer to the edge of the stage. Under her breath, she muttered, "Terra?"

It was Rachel's teenage daughter, Terra, and her two best friends walking toward the vulnerable girl, all with stern looks on their faces. The three girls approached Mary Katherine, then slowly moved around her in silence, circling her as if they were a pack of wolves about to attack their prey.

"These are the three girls that harassed Mary Katherine for over a month, bullying her in front of her peers on social media." He paused, then added, "Oh, forgive me, 'harassed' is such a strong word. I would hate to come across as *dramatic*.'" He laughed again as he taunted Rachel.

The gym was totally quiet now. Mary Katherine stood defenseless at the center of the three girls, whom she already knew disliked her. Simultaneously, the three started shouting at her. Their voices were received like loud angry strikes, telling her she was ugly, that nobody liked her, and that she was a loser.

Horrified, Rachel screamed across the complacent crowd, "Terra, stop! Leave her alone. Stop yelling at her!"

Kaw interjected, "They can't hear you, Rachel. They can't see you either. We are watching the emotional reality of what Mary Katherine felt. We are watching the pain and the fear that ran through her heart as she was being attacked online. To truly understand the full perspective of this life, you begin by training yourself to understand the specifics of another's pain. With absolute intention, you need to open yourself to it, as well as their joys."

Kaw added with a sneer, "But unfortunately for you, right now we'll be witnessing her pain."

The old man's eyes burned into hers with delight at the clear power he was holding over her.

Down on the gym floor, the three girls continued to verbally abuse Mary Katherine; shouting at her, calling her ugly, belittling her.

Mary Katherine's heart sank and tears began to well up in her eyes. To be attacked in front of so many people, and to have nobody help, hundreds watching in silence. She stood quiet and alone, accepting the blows as they came. If only somehow, she could climb inside of herself, she surely would have, but all she could do was lower her head as they berated her with verbal punches, beating her down further and further.

Rachel screamed again, louder this time, straining her vocal cords, "Stop yelling at her! Leave her alone!"

Now comprehending her inability to intervene, Rachel began to sob again as she truly took in the young girl's pain for the first time, only now beginning to understand exactly how alone she must have felt, how petrified she must have been.

With a grin, Kaw replied, "Look at the anger in your daughter's eyes," as if he was taking personal credit for the pain she was inflicting.

Then, one by one, the 'followers' began to rise from the bleachers and descend, forming a larger, denser group with the shaken girl crumpled in the center.

As they walked out onto the floor, each began to shout with disturbing pleasure and point at Mary Katherine, "Yes, she is ugly…give her more!" Tightening their hands into fists, they screamed, "Don't stop! Tell that bitch she's worthless."

Rachel fell to the stage floor, weeping, "Dear God, make them stop. Please, make them stop!"

Kaw replied, "These are all the students who 'liked' your daughter and her friends' hurtful posts on social media. With every 'like' posted, a cruel message was conveyed, each received like a small knife sliding into Mary Katherine's side, cutting her…changing her. With each of the notifications, every one of their faces was so clear to her, as was their message, 'We like that you're being hurt…we agree that you're ugly…and we hope they keep hurting you."

Mary Katherine stood in the middle of the ravenous crowd, just staring at the floor alone, weeping, helpless. Periodically, she mustered up the courage to lift her head, fighting to draw her eyes up from the safety of the floor, looking past all the shouting, and the fingers pointing at her, and the fists being pumped, and the hate in the eyes of so many who surrounded her, searching for some kind of help. Her eyes began to scan the crowd, all the people who were watching this spectacle from the bleachers.

Kaw said, "Now she's staring at the hundreds of followers who saw the cruel posts and did nothing. Inside, the girl is praying, 'Somebody, anybody…please? Say something! Somebody, do something to help me.'"

Hundreds of her fellow students—boys and girls, most of whom Mary Katherine had grown up with—choose to sit in silence and say nothing. The bleachers were filled with students just watching, watching them beat her down, choosing to do nothing, regardless of the clear pain she was in.

Suddenly, Mary Katherine heard a door crash open and slam against the wall of the gym. The little girl's heart leapt with hope as the guidance counselor as well as the superintendent, principal, and vice principal all came rushing in.

Thank God they're here! Mary Katherine thought. *Finally, someone will pull them off me. Someone will make them stop.* She mustered up all of her courage, then began to yell out over the vicious crowd, "Help me! I'm here…I'm in the middle of them. I'm here!" Tears flowed out of her eyes as she raised her voice. "Please, make them stop!" she screamed as loud as she could, her voice cracking.

She watched for a reaction from the faculty through the crowd, but despite her desperate pleas, they just stood and watched with faces like stone as the mob of teens continued to verbally beat her down.

In disbelief, Rachel shouted at the old man, "Why aren't they doing anything? That's her principal and superintendent. Why aren't they stopping them? What the hell is wrong with them?"

Kaw calmly responded, "After several weeks of abuse, Mary Katherine found the courage to speak to her guidance counselor about their hateful slander. She really didn't want to involve faculty, but their relentless bullying just kept going on and on. She felt as if she had nowhere else to turn."

"Good. That's good she was brave enough to do that." Rachel's voice broke as she continued, "And what did they tell her? What the hell did they do?"

With a grin, Kaw paused, then responded. "Her guidance counselor told her, according to school policy, that they can only intervene if the bullying takes place on school property. Unfortunately, they can't do anything about social media bullying. He told her he wished he could help, but there was nothing he could do." Sarcastically, the old man shrugged his shoulders, then raised both of his palms up.

Helpless, she yelled at Kaw, "You are a son of a bitch!" Then, she directed one last futile scream at the teachers who stood by, idly watching. "Do something, damn it. Save her!"

Imagining the absolute desperation that the young girl must be feeling, Rachel watched and wept from the edge of the stage.

Abandoned by all within the gym, any hope of rescue fled as the reality set in that no one was going to say or do anything. She drew her eyes back down to the floor, standing totally alone with her head down as the vicious crowd continued to verbally abuse her.

Eventually, the yelling began to subside. The young girl standing in the middle of the crowd was shaken like never before. Her eyes seemed different now as she stared down at her own feet, not daring to make eye contact with all these people who obviously hated her. She was hollow now, changed.

She waited with her eyes to the floor as one by one the crowd surrounding her turned and slowly walked out of the gym. In silence, hundreds of spectators from the bleachers stood up, then followed them. The teachers then filed out, and the superintendent clarified his position with one final slam of the gym door. *Crash!* Mary Katherine was left standing, despondent and alone.

With tear-filled eyes, the shaken girl finally lifted her head, looked around the gym, then wiped her face. She then slowly began to walk toward the door that led to the hallways of her school, where all the witnesses and students who hated her awaited. The stage curtains drew closed as a changed young lady, broken and fragile, walked away within her own silence and isolated pain.

From high up on the stage, Kaw broke the silence.

"Do you have any idea what kind of darkness spawns from these attacks? The depression that so often ensues? The isolation people are cast into as the world around them turns its back on them at their greatest time of need, and the devastating sense of desperation these kids are left with? These victims feel as if the world has turned a blind eye to them, so they have nowhere else to go. So what do they do? Some take matters into their own hands, dear."

Rachel sobbed, "Yes, I know…I know now how serious it is."

"Do you have any idea how many kids have taken their own lives as a result of this bullying?"

The old man pointed his cane at the closed curtains. Rachel stood silent up on the stage, filled with confusion and a broken heart. She knew Kaw spoke the truth about the connection between bullying and the devastating responses of those who were beaten down over and over again. Her mind reeled with vivid images of the young girl's attack and the many questions surrounding Kaw.

Why the hell is this happening to me? Is this man actually who he says he is? How could this be? And if so, why was he sent here, and why is he giving me lessons based on my own life?

Although nothing was adding up, somehow Rachel felt her questions would soon be answered, but a large part of her was too afraid to ask. She stood trembling, teetering between her own deepest fears and the shared pain of an innocent girl, pain that was inflicted by her daughter. It felt as if Mary Katherine's heart beat within Rachel's chest now, throbbing in the aftermath of her attack. Until then, Rachel had never taken in another's pain like that. She hadn't the time nor concern for it in her fast-paced, self-absorbed world.

Again, as if the demon knew what she was thinking, he spoke up.

"It is our absolute intention to eradicate this world of all bridges that span from one heart to another, allowing them to share their pain, just as you did up on that stage. Don't you see, my brothers and I are looking out for each of you. We are on your side! We want to protect you by isolating your hearts from each other's. Why would any of you want to feel the pain of another, when you could avoid it by focusing on yourselves? We offer you the walls that you need to protect yourselves and the guidance to build them, like fortresses, so you never have to feel another's heartache again. Think about it, Rachel, your God wants you to accept it while my brothers and I are fighting for you to release it. Our wheels have been in motion for quite some time now, and your emancipation from the divine bridges connecting each of your hearts is close at hand." Then, with a calm voice and the hint of a grin, he added, "No need to thank me, dear. The look on your face is thanks enough."

The reality that Rachel had always known had been stripped away in an instant, and her seemingly impenetrable confidence had now been shattered. She sat vulnerable at the mercy of an actual monster, a demon that stood only steps away from her.

Kaw's echoing voice rang out. "That's your first lesson, Rachel. A very important one too."

Rachel's voice cracked. "Lesson? What are you talking about?"

Kaw explained, "You are all supposed to use the *full* capacity of your hearts every day, and yours has laid virtually idle throughout most of your adult life."

Rachel spoke up. "How can you say that? I love my kids with all my heart. Don't tell me that my heart lies idle. You don't even know me!"

Kaw's casual defiance flowed as he laughed. "I know you better than you know yourself. I am very aware that you believe that you are a loving person, but the truth is that your definition of love falls quite short of what is intended. Throughout your lives, each of you has carried a potential for unimaginable possibilities deep within you, but it can only be accessed when you open your hearts much deeper than most of you do. Our job has been to blind each of you to the powerful core within your hearts, and that's exactly what we have done.

"Standing on the edge of that stage, you expanded the capacity of your heart more than you have in a very, very long time. To feel, truly feel, for another. That's how you are supposed to be using your heart, just like you did up there." Kaw raised his eyebrows mockingly, "That's how *they* intended you to use it."

"Who are you talking about?" she asked. "When you said 'they' intended me to use my heart this way, who are 'they'?"

"I am talking about the Trinity, Rachel. God, the Father; his son, Jesus Christ; and his Holy Spirit. Contrary to your beliefs, they are all real, as are the angels in heaven, and yes, Lucifer and my other brothers too. Every day, each of us play significant roles in your lives, and most of you, from birth to death, have no idea. You see, God created each of you with hearts that have limitless capacity, and most of you choose only to explore a fraction of them throughout your life experience. And you are certainly no exception. Most of your idea of love simply scratches the surface of your heart's true capacity.

"Jesus came not only to redeem all of you through his sacrifice, but to display his living testimony of how your lives are intended to be lived. He lived with unimaginable selflessness, humility, patience, meekness, stillness of mind, forgiveness, quiet bravery, and a deeper love for all who surrounded him that radiated from the depth of his heart. He saw the physical world through the crystal-clear lens of the present moment, without the murkiness of shame from his past or fear from his future. Each man and woman who has ever walked this earth has possessed the same capacity in their own hearts. Most of you, though, are just too distracted or blinded to ever know they even exist. Most of you die without ever accessing the unimaginable gifts that lie waiting for you at the core of your hearts."

It felt as if Rachel had stepped into a living nightmare. She had no idea why one of God's fallen angels had singled her out and was now explaining the truth behind the world she lived in. She stood baffled as she took in his words. Her mind whirled, still stunned by the impossible event she had just witnessed in the gymnasium and bewildered at why this self-proclaimed demon would be teaching her about God.

Kaw went on uninterrupted, "I think it would be helpful to first look at Jesus and how his sacrifice affected the darkness in this world. When he willingly died on the cross to wipe out all of your sins—although more significant than any other act throughout time—it was not enough for God. He demands sacrifice from all who pass through this physical world. Jesus did his part by living his life as God intended, but God leaves it up to each of you to pick up your own cross and follow. Each of you is intended to complete within your lives what was lacking in his cross."

Confused, Rachel spoke up. "I don't understand. What do you mean when you say we are all intended to pick up our own cross and follow?"

"When Christ sacrificed his own life for this world, it was intended to teach each of you that sacrificing yourselves for others was an endeavor that God intended. God's struggle stretches well beyond the cross. It can only be eased through the choices that each of you make throughout your lives, choices made from your own free will.

"Through God's own design, my brothers and I have been given the ability to influence all souls who pass through the physical realm. But when Christ offered his life for all of you, a great fissure cracked open, tearing through the entire universe. Much of our power and influence was lost at that very moment. All the influence that came from the head of our body of darkness—which is my brother, Lucifer—was neutralized through

Christ's selfless sacrifice. Jesus stripped him of that power, casting it into a bottomless crevasse, where it was lost forever. Each of you has the same ability to eliminate our dark influence through living your lives selflessly, as God intended.

"You see, Rachel, Christ began the redemptive act through his sacrifice on the cross, but each of you is intended to complete it through the lives you choose to live. No other entity within this universe can complete his atonement, except those souls who pass through this physical world."

"How am I supposed to change anything? Besides, I thought you said Satan's influence was neutralized through Christ's sacrifice?"

The old demon stared into her eyes with joy, then replied, "Yes, it was. Christ stripped Lucifer's power from him, but there are still armies of fallen angels who remain and continue to cast a deep influence upon all within this world. Every living being that has ever walked the earth has had access to more power than they could ever imagine. Each possesses a miraculous portal within their heart, which, if opened, would allow God's Holy Spirit to blow into this world, wiping our darkness from it. But you must first find the rare stillness of mind to open it."

"Portal? What does that even mean? And how could our choices eliminate your influence? I just don't understand."

"We'll get to that soon enough. I *will* tell you that mankind's key lies within the unexplored depths of their hearts—those same depths you were moving toward up on that stage. The way you took in that little girl's pain, how you felt it with such truth and purity. Well, that is how all of mankind is designed to feel for all who are in their presence, as well as all who are not in their presence, for that matter."

Rachel paused again. "I'm not sure what you mean by that?"

"I mean, you should not have to actually witness another's pain to be able to truly take it in. If you are using your heart as it was intended, using its *full* capacity, you would take in another's pain simply by thinking about it, without having to witness it with your own two eyes. If you are exercising your heart properly, there should be no difference." The old man's expression widened. "Fortunately though, through television, social media, and any number of other instruments that we employ, we have you all so desensitized to it that when introduced to another's pain, it barely breaches your heart's surface." He paused for a short moment. "You're going to need this later, so let me repeat it for you."

Rachel wondered what he meant by that but was too frightened to ask. All of this was just so confusing. It felt as if the old man were speaking in riddles that didn't seem to add up.

Kaw raised his voice a bit louder, then repeated himself, "You are each intended to use the full capacity of your heart every day, taking in other's pain and love in a much deeper manner than you currently do."

Rachel declared, "Of course I'm going to feel Mary Katherine's pain. They just attacked her—in front of a crowd that did nothing!"

Staring down at her, Kaw's grin grew larger. "Well, tell me then." Kaw hesitated as he leaned down closer to Rachel. "If you are so sympathetic, why then did you have to see the physical representation of what ran through Mary Katherine's heart before you truly felt it?"

Rachel stared down at the stage floor, thinking, as Kaw continued.

"When you received the call from Mary Katherine's mother, explaining to you how Terra and her friends had been mistreating her daughter, why didn't you feel that same pain that you felt watching her from the stage?"

Kaw began to slowly pace across the floor, with the persona of a prosecutor addressing his accused. "Think about it, Rachel. It's time to soul search, my dear." The old man chuckled out loud at his choice of words.

Rachel responded. "Well, that was the first I heard of it. I wanted to talk to my daughter before reacting. There are two sides to every story, and I just wanted to hear Terra's side before I responded."

Kaw smirked. "Sounds reasonable to me. And after you spoke to Terra?"

"Terra said that Mary Katherine wasn't very nice to her."

Kaw responded, "Terra said she was a 'bitch', didn't she?"

"Well, yes. And she told me they only called her a couple of names, and that was it." "And you believed her? Did her story correlate with what Mary Katherine's mother told you?"

"For the most part." Rachel began to get emotional as she recalled her first conversation with Mary Katherine's mother. "Her mother said it was more, though." Beginning to open up, Rachel's emotions spilled out. "She said it had been happening for a while. She said they had been bullying Mary Katherine for over a month."

"Yes, yes, that's correct. I grew stronger from every post they made. Please allow me to clarify, though. The sole reason your daughter targeted Mary Katherine was because she envied the girl and viewed Mary Katherine as weaker than she was, an easy target. It was a way for Terra to push another down, thereby raising herself up and making her feel more powerful at a time in her life when her parents were separating. It was a time when she felt as if she had no control or power over anything in her life. Her torment of that girl gave her the control and the power she so desperately needed."

Hearing the truth and how her divorce had played a role in her daughter's actions, Rachel's heart felt heavy, and tears began to emerge from her eyes.

"Did you even read your daughter's posts, Rachel?"

Rachel stared down at the floor, then, without looking up, simply replied, "No."

The old man playfully pushed. "Dig deep now, dear. Why not? Why didn't you ask to read her posts?"

Rachel brought herself back to that moment when she confronted Terra about the bullying. "I don't know, I guess I was too scared to see what she actually wrote." Emotional, she paused. "I just…I just didn't want to believe it."

Kaw's voice became gruff. "Why not? Why didn't you take in Mary Katherine's pain, the same way you did up on that stage? You know why, Rachel…I can feel it in my bones."

Rachel wept, knowing somehow the old man could feel what she was feeling. She finally spoke up, conveying what she had felt at that moment. "If what Mary Katherine's mother said was true…if my daughter had tormented that girl, day in and day out for over a month for no reason, then what would that say about me as her mother? What kind of failure would I be?" She wept as she shouted, "I failed as a wife. Now I'm going to fail as a mother too?"

Kaw's eyes gleamed. "Yes, my dear. Now you're getting it. Of course, your ego couldn't withstand that kind of blow. I totally understand." Kaw grinned with false sincerity.

Rachel lifted her head and shouted as she cried, "Why are you doing this to me, goddamn it? What do you want with me?"

Kaw stood above her, glaring down in silence before he spoke. "My brothers were very specific when they picked you. They told me that so much of our power lies in the balance of the choice that only you can make."

Nervously, Rachel inquired, "Choice? What choice?"

"The choice that you are going to make by the end of this day."

Petrified, Rachel pleaded, "Would you please tell me what you're talking about? Why the hell are you here?"

The demon's lips curled into an evil grin as his strength grew from Rachel's mounting fear. "Why am I here? Why, I was sent here to test you, Rachel."

6

With horror in her eyes, she looked up at the tall, dark figure. "What do you mean, test me?" Her voice cracked as she pleaded, "Explain to me what the hell is going on!"

Rachel's mind and heart felt broken; she reeled with anger, fear, and confusion all at the same time. She had never been so terrified as she was at that moment. Her body began to shudder as she questioned the demon's intention. The ramifications from his examination petrified her, and as she contemplated it, her hands began to shake.

Kaw continued, "This really isn't about you at all. I assure you that our encounter is strictly self-serving. You are nothing more to me than a pawn. You are merely one of the countless people that I have manipulated during my time here. You are simply a means to an end, nothing more." He began to slowly walk around the stage, explaining as he moved, "I have walked among your kind for thousands of years, doing exactly what I was supposed to do, and doing it very well, I might add." He beamed with arrogance. "My life's work has been to influence you. My tools have been deceit, temptation, distraction, confusion, and fear, among many others."

Rachel sat, fighting to understand. "Deceit? Deceit about what?"

Kaw answered bluntly, "From the truth; the truth behind the world you live in, the truth behind why you are really here, the truth behind what this world really is. My job has been to make sure all of your attention stays on this physical world in which you live, pushing and prodding you like cattle." He gave a snarl. "And that's about as sophisticated as most of you are! You are like cows, merely focused on the grass you need to eat in order to survive, nothing more." The old man looked away, as if disgusted by the sight of her. Kaw continued in a belittling tone, "Most of you vermin aren't even aware of the most basic fact of your existence."

Rachel stared back in silent inquisition.

"From the very beginning of time, all who have walked this earth have possessed a deeper dimension to their being. It is the most basic fact of your existence, as well as one of the most significant, and most of you have no idea whatsoever."

"Deeper dimension? I'm not sure that I understand."

"It's clear that I have done my job well." Condescending, Kaw continued, "What I mean is that your being is not only physical in nature.

Your being has a very real spiritual dimension to it, as does everyone else's in this world. It is the place where your living soul dwells. I know this may sound strange, but you are not actually your body or even the thoughts that you create in your mind. You, the true you, exists as a beautiful eternal consciousness, residing in the core of your own heart. Most go through their entire lives solely identifying themselves as their body and the thoughts and beliefs that define who they are. But your true identity exists in a much deeper realm within you. Once its presence is realized, your soul can act as a portal between you and the mind of God, through the vehicle of God's Holy Spirit. It is your direct line to and from God. This spiritual language is being communicated through and manifesting within your heart. It has been with you since the day you were born and will stay with you throughout this physical experience."

Rachel interrupted, "Communication from God? I have no idea what you're talking about. What communication?"

The old man's frustration grew as he continued, "With intention, we have blinded every one of you from it. We've deafened your hearts to his word, and we've blinded you with the very eyes that you were given to see. In fact, I am convinced that mankind is *so* blinded and *so* distracted from God's presence that my job here has become quite obsolete. You are all so confused and self-absorbed that my physical presence is no longer needed to direct you. I'm ready to leave this world."

Rachel asked, "What are you saying…that you want to die?"

"Die? There is no real death. The concept of death is nothing more than another instrument in my tool bag. It's just another way for us to strike fear into all of your hearts, and within that fear lies our control. You and everyone else who has ever existed are eternal beings."

"Life after death?" Rachel asked.

Kaw began to laugh. "Yes. And my job has been to keep your eyes focused on life—what you can see, and touch, and hold in your greedy little hands. We point you toward the laws within your physical world and distract you from the possibility that anything beyond them even exists. My power, as well as my brothers', lies with the choices each of you make throughout your physical lives. I contend that you're all so busy scratching and clawing to advance yourselves at the rest of the world's expense, that all other considerations have been lost forever. We use your ego, your incredible need of self, to intentionally misdirect you away from where your true purpose lies. The deep-rooted pride within each of you stems directly from our influence, the seed of ego. We convince you into believing that money, beauty, popularity, success, intelligence, possessions, and power will fill that natural void that has always existed deep within each of your hearts. This is the food your ego hungers for. Don't you see, my dear?"

Rachel was overwhelmed by the old man's rant. She struggled with his assertion that he and his brothers' dark influence manifests within every living soul as our ego. It sounded ludicrous to her, that individuals' egos could be anything beyond the natural human tendency she always believed them to be. He sounded like some crazy conspiracy theorist, spouting off more and more unbelievable claims about the world in which she lived.

Rachel cautiously spoke up. "Everything you're talking about is part of human nature. I mean, ego and pride…"

Kaw immediately barked back, "We are the biggest part of your human nature! Where do you think your insatiable need for praise comes from? Internal *and* external."

Fighting to gain her bearings, Rachel spoke up. "How can you tell me that loving yourself is a bad thing? I fight to love who I am, and I want my children to be confident and to love themselves too!"

Kaw rebutted, "Don't misinterpret what I'm saying. God intends for each of you to love yourselves deeply. But the intricacies behind your perception of self are extremely important in this regard. He wants you to love yourself as a loving creation of God. Because you are to love God with all that you are, and since each of you are an actual extension of his very being, you should love yourself just as deeply as you love God. The difference is, his intention is for you to love yourselves humbly, serving the righteousness of his will, not your own. Loving yourself should not be an egotistical endeavor, but a deep appreciation of your existence by the grace of God.

"My brothers and I have instilled an incredibly powerful ego within each of you, with the purpose of intentionally clouding any spiritual guidance from above. Through your ego, we divert so much of your attention inward, focusing it on yourselves as separate entities from God, and in doing so, we create an intended barrier between your consciousness and the mind of the Father."

"I'm not sure I understand."

"Rachel, as we move forward, you need to remember that our influence manifests through many of your natural tendencies, which carry with them unimaginable implications for this physical world and all who dwell in it."

"What natural tendencies are you talking about?"

Kaw scratched at his chin in thought, then offered, "Humor me for a moment, won't you?" An insincere grin came over his face. "Try to imagine how you would feel if you were to purchase a brand-new designer suit, then head into one of your sales appointments? New shoes, purse, the whole kit and caboodle, sparing no expense to look and feel as fashionable as you possibly could?"

Rachel answered quickly. "That's my point, it would make me feel good about myself. It would make me feel current, confident, and powerful. It would make me feel like I should feel when I'm going out to do the best job that I can do."

"What do you think it would cost?"

A sense of arrogance came over her. "For everything? Thousands." She looked into his eyes with a sudden display of perceived power.

"Very good, dear! Now try to imagine how you would feel if you were to take those same thousands of dollars and buy brand-new clothes for some neglected children, children who are destitute and in obvious need? Maybe they are residing in a local orphanage, or are abused and living in foster care, or maybe some have no home at all and are living on the streets. Imagine if they only owned one pair of pants and one threadbare shirt, as many children do. Try to picture yourself taking them to a store and buying them new outfits—modest but new. How many children could you clothe for the same thousands of dollars? Twenty? Fifty? One hundred? Imagine willingly sacrificing your own time and money to take them to a salon to have their hair washed and properly cut. Try to envision yourself going out of your way to pamper them, maybe for the first time in their lives. Imagine their expressions as they saw themselves in a brand-new light for the first time. How would that make you feel?"

Rachel paused for a moment, picturing a room filled with neglected children in new clothes, then did as the demon had asked, and tried to envision how she may feel. "It would make me feel good about helping so many children who were in need."

"Would it make you feel confident?"

"Yes, in a sense, I think it would. Confident in myself that I made a difference in some children's lives, helping them to look at themselves through more hopeful eyes."

"So both scenarios would lead you to feel better about yourself? Would you go so far as to say that each would push you to love yourself a bit more through two very different choices?"

"Well, yes. I would love myself in two different ways. I think that's a fair statement."

The old man grinned, then said, "Although in both scenarios you are moved to love yourself, the sources of those feelings come from two totally opposing entities. One is from our instilled ego, which is part of your human nature and focuses on elevating yourselves. The other opposes the nature of this world and comes from the essence of God himself entering through your spiritual consciousness and your open heart."

Rachel's defensiveness flared. "Are you telling me that buying expensive clothes or wanting to look good is evil?"

"No, I am not. What I am telling you is that one choice removes our distortion around your consciousness, while the other one feeds it. I am not saying that buying a new outfit is evil, but understanding the mechanics behind the light and the dark within this world is critical in understanding the physical world in its totality. More importantly, it is critical in understanding your intended purpose within it. Although most may argue that your ego and your desire for material things are not evil, the reality is that they can cloud your perception and distract each of you from feeling the presence of God's Holy Spirit and, with that, his guidance toward your intended purpose.

"You see, all the darkness that exists within this world grows directly from the seeds of our influence. It enters your consciousness through your ego, then manifests quite distinctively in each of you. From the day you are born until the day you die, ego manipulates your perception of this world and, more importantly, of yourselves. Then, depending on that perception, certain degrees of need inevitably arise, which dictate how our darkness will uniquely manifest itself within you. For some, our darkness will manifest overtly, moving them toward choices that directly hurt others. But more often, it manifests covertly, moving them to focus on themselves instead of focusing on the needs of others, as well. Both acts of darkness push you to surrender to our will instead of your Lord's, clouding his presence within your hearts and blinding you from his inner guidance.

"Darkness, by its very definition, is the absence of light. Both covert and overt darkness manifest like storm clouds that surround your minds. They prevent you from perceiving the light of God within your consciousness. Many people would not consider loving yourself as being dark at all, but the intricacies within your perception of 'self' make all the difference. If you love yourself as we intend, it will invite darkness around your consciousness, but if you love yourself as God intends, it will remove it."

Rachel spoke up. "That seems like a very hard line to navigate. This concept of loving yourself sounds like a big gray area that could lead to a lot of confusion."

"Confusion is exactly what we are hoping for. The gray areas within your world are the precise places where my brothers and I prefer to operate. In fact, those places are where our most effective work is done. Trust me, when I tell you that if a gray area exists within your minds, we are fighting tooth and nail to exploit it. Do you understand, Rachel?"

With fearful hesitation, she responded, "Yes, I think so."

7

Kaw continued, "God, who is an entity of absolute love and absolute selflessness, created us angels to help him in the creation of this physical world and the universe that cradles it. All of us operated and coexisted in perfect harmony within God's will, where we all flourished in the fullness of his absolute love and perfection." Titus Kaw paused for a moment, then raised his eyebrows up high, as if suddenly distracted. "If your God is so almighty, why then did he need the angels' help to create this place? Answer me that!"

Frightened by his tone, Rachel stood silent.

"Yes, that's what I thought. He's not almighty! This came from my inspiration, my hands, not only God's. You have no idea how alive I felt creating all of this. The incredible power that was within me to simply imagine a planet, or even a whole solar system, then with a wave of my hand, make it materialize.

"That's when it happened. That's when the choice was made, and the separation began. Although we existed in this beautiful consciousness abiding by his will, fear unexpectedly emerged in him, ushering in the belief that if he continued to live by God's will, he would be nothing at all. At that very moment, my brother's fear of not being enough moved him to step outside of his harmonious unity with God. It all began with my brother, Lucifer. In one beautiful, unexpected moment, he realized exactly how powerful he was; not God, but him! Through his own defiance, he stepped outside of his blissful service within the perfection of God's will. At that critical moment, it became clear to Lucifer, as well as it did to God, that he believed he was powerful enough to live in separation from him. Lucifer believed he was meant to rule as a god himself. Through his own defect, my brother came to believe that the origin of the creative process was his, when, unknowingly to all of us angels, it was actually manifesting through God's son, Jesus Christ."

Rachel fought to understand. "But I thought Jesus Christ was born just over two thousand years ago, how could all of creation take place within him if he wasn't even born yet?"

Kaw responded, "He was born into your physical world two thousand years ago, but he has always existed spiritually, as a very important part of God's being. My brothers and I were not aware that God was a trinity—that is, until Jesus died on the cross. But it became painfully clear to us at that very moment, when so much of our power fell away from us. Oh, but after Lucifer's choice, it did not take long for his dark beliefs to spread to many other angels, myself included. They spread like wildfire!" He took a deep, calming breath. "That is precisely when it was born into this place, like a newborn child that we would feed and nurture until it could sustain itself in this strange new world."

Rachel responded, "What? What was born at that moment?"

Kaw spoke with loving affection, as if he were speaking of his own son. "Ego…ego was born, my dear."

After a long pause, Rachel spoke again. "I don't understand. Ego didn't exist before that moment?"

The old man replied, "No, it did not. Ego sprouted from my brother's fear of not being enough. You see, the word 'ego' comes from its Latin root which means 'I'. So, your ego moves each of you to solely perceive yourself as an 'I,' or a separate entity from God and the rest of the world around you, abiding by your own will instead of by his. But the truth is, each of you are a living extension of God, intimately connected to all other souls despite your physical separateness and strong, willful nature. When we chose to turn from God's will and exist within our own will, a defect occurred within some of us—well, God calls it a defect, we call it our greatest attribute." His sinister laugh rang out again. "Ego emerged in some of us, and it led us to believe that we were gods ourselves. Regardless of the perfection of our true state of being, our great fear instilled an insatiable need in us to be greater than we were. Our fear separated us from the fearless state we had known abiding in God's will. Ego, my dear, is our defect, and that is the core defect of this world in which you live. At that moment, 'self' was born into a totally selfless entity." The old man grinned with obvious pride. "There were no cigars passed out at that birth, I can assure you!"

More laughter flowed from the demon.

"At that very moment when we believed that we too were gods…the moment ego came into being, all who possessed it were cast down to the murky depths within a lower spiritual dimension. And all who fell were forever isolated from God and the rest of the angels within the highest heaven. But unfortunately for mankind, our influence was not limited to our lower spiritual home, but also to this physical world in which you live. Ever since the fall, self has been woven into the very fabric of every soul's consciousness, and it always will be.

"Lucifer felt it would be beneficial to have a physical presence within your world—that presence is me. I have served within this realm from the beginning of time, but over the years, I have grown to despise it and its inhabitants. I long to live among my brothers in the spiritual realm of our lower heaven. If allowed to join them, I could finally reign from the spiritual place, which is my true home. It's where I can be praised like a god, praised in the way that I deserve to be praised, through your incredible selfishness that flows so naturally throughout this realm."

Hearing those words, 'you praise us,' lit a small flame within Rachel. Apprehensively, she raised her voice. "I don't praise you!"

Kaw replied softly, "Oh, but you do…you praise me through your selfishness, your anger, your judgement, your resentment, your greed, and your pride. I don't even have to go beyond this very day to feel *your* praise."

Rachel looked at him with skepticism.

"As you pulled up to the grocery store this morning, you parked, then sat alone in your car before you went inside. You remember, don't you, Rachel?"

The old man's grin grew, knowing that without ever touching her, he was violating her very being. She grimaced in disapproval but said nothing.

The old man pushed. "Who could blame you for feeling so much hatred? You should hate them. Your husband, leaving you for your next-door neighbor. My god, what a sight that must have been. He didn't even have to rent a moving truck. He simply carried all of his belongings across your driveway." The old man laughed out loud, then quickly dropped the tone of his voice, prodding her. "Oh, what humiliation you must have felt, Rachel. All the people who know you, driving by as he carried his whole life out of your front door and across the drive into *her* house."

Rachel felt a pit of nausea in her stomach, brought on by the old man's words, words that were all true. Her blood boiled every time she thought of them together. It was brought on by their betrayal and by the humiliation she felt every day living next door to them.

Rachel yelled out, "I do hate them! Who would blame me after what they did to me?"

The old man replied, "There you go, let it out. I actually agree with you, my dear. You should hate them—hate them with all that you are!" Kaw gritted his teeth with heartfelt encouragement. "But don't believe for one minute that you don't praise me through that hatred. My strength lies within it and grows every time you think of them." Kaw's demeanor grew seductive. "Aww, your anger tastes sweet. I ingest it like fine Chianti." He raised his voice in a sexually provocative manner. "It intoxicates me!"

Frightened, Rachel drew her eyes away from him, then stared at the closed stage curtains in front of her. She thought back to all the times her heart had burned with hatred for her husband and her good friend who had betrayed her. She then envisioned the old demon taking it in, growing stronger from the resentment in her heart. All of this just seemed so surreal to her.

She turned to face the old man and said, "Okay, so you want to leave this place? Then why don't you just go? Why don't you leave now and get the hell out of my life?"

Kaw continued, "The only way I can transition into my new spiritual home is to prove to my brothers that I am no longer needed down here. And my brothers, unfortunately, are not easily convinced. But that…that is why you are here. You are going to help me convince them that I am no longer needed in this cesspool of a world."

Realizing their time together had just begun, a cold fear crept over Rachel.

Kaw continued, "And you'll prove it by making one choice by the end of this very day." Rachel's heart dropped again.

Kaw went on, "The only problem is…"

Rachel interrupted, "What are you talking about? What choice?"

Kaw responded, "Patience, my dear, patience." He smiled, noticing the fear in her eyes as he continued. "What I was saying was, throughout your entire life, we have deceived you, and that poses a significant problem. You see, Rachel, this choice you have to make needs to be made from the perspective of truth."

Rachel asked, "Perspective of truth?"

Kaw explained. "You need to have a true understanding of this world, *all of* this world, first. You need to have a fuller knowledge of the light as well as the darkness before your choice can be made. In other words, I am not allowed to trick you or deceive you into choosing." A pause ensued, then he burst out, "Damn them!" He playfully shook his fist at the ceiling. Then another evil laugh echoed across the stage floor. "As unbelievable as it sounds, I will be forced to explain to you exactly how each of you are deceived by your ego, and then guide you on a path to your Lord's doorstep so you are able to attain a truthful perspective of this physical experience which is your life. You must understand the true mechanics behind the light and the dark of your world, or nothing will change for me—or for you, either."

Rachel's mind raced with worry, not knowing the consequences of this examination.

"Since man has existed, my brothers and I have enslaved you through your human nature. We have done all that we can to hide any signs that a loving God even exists, and now I will be forced—no matter how painful—to show you the path to his grace. Regardless of the truth's bitterness on my tongue, it's my only way out of this physical world. Do you understand, Rachel?"

Rachel answered, "Yes, I think so, but why me? What did I do to deserve this? I'm a good person. I provide for my family. I pay my bills. I bust my ass every single day of my life." Rachel raised her voice. "Why are you doing this to me? Damn it, I'm a good person!"

Kaw calmly replied, "Because, like so many others in this god-forsaken world, you actually believe that you are righteous."

She apprehensively walked toward the tall figure. "I know you're trying to explain everything the best way that you can, but you have to understand that all of this is overwhelming, to say the least. I understand that you and your brothers have intentionally kept things in the shadows, but I'm struggling with these 'mechanics' that you're describing. You are telling me that the reality of the world which I have always known is something totally different than what I have experienced, different from what I have seen with my own eyes. Try to understand that all of this is making me feel like I'm losing my mind."

Clearly frustrated, the old man rolled his eyes and said, "I should have known that asking you to conceptualize any ideas beyond this physical world would be unrealistic, considering your obvious limitations."

He paused for a moment to gather his thoughts, silently staring in the direction of the stage curtains. After a few moments, he lifted his head, then asked, "Where does God's love shine the brightest?"

Rachel sighed, *Another riddle...* She repeated the question out loud, "Where does God's love shine the brightest?" After a few moments of consideration, she responded with the holiest place she could think of.

"I don't know, how about the Vatican in Rome? Home of the Pope and all the clergy who have devoted their lives to God."

Decisively, the old man said, "Very well, the Vatican it is."

Rachel watched as the old man's eyes grew wider. His whole body seemed to open as he raised his cane up high, then, with great force, plunged it down into the oak stage. Again, the sound of two tremendous stones colliding together rang out. *Crack!* Electric bolts of light shot out in all directions from the contact of his cane onto the old wood floor. Rachel threw her hands over her eyes to protect them from the blinding light. It shot up in all directions like a spider's web. After the bright flash had faded, the distinct smell of static electricity was left hanging in the air. Rachel's heart sank as the stage curtains slowly drew open again. She prayed that whatever awaited her on the other side would be less traumatic than Kaw's last manifestation had been.

As the tall velvety curtains drew open, Rachel couldn't believe what she saw. Large plumes of beautiful white clouds, layers upon layers, gently floated by, with occasional hints of blue sky breaking through them. The magnificent scene stretched as far as her eyes could see.

Awestruck, she gasped, "My God, it's beautiful!"

The walls, floor, and ceiling of the gym had totally vanished now, leaving nothing to remind her of her childhood school except for the open curtains that gently framed the picturesque sky and the old stage where they both stood. Astonished, Rachel took several slow steps toward the edge of the stage to see what lay beyond it. All she saw was an endless sky filled with the softest, whitest clouds she could ever imagine. It was as if the stage had suddenly been dropped on top of a mountain with nothing but endless sky above and beneath it. She squinted her eyes as the bright sunlight periodically broke through the clouds and shone warm on the side of her face. Its warmth felt different than any sunlight she had ever felt before. With her eyes softly closed, she rested within it, surprising herself with a soft coo and slight smile. As its rays softly warmed her face, it felt as if it was only her and this beautiful light. Everything else seemed to melt away.

A sense of unease crept into Rachel when the strange light brought vivid memories of her mother who had passed nearly ten years earlier. Though it sounded crazy, the light itself felt as if Rachel's mother was calmly caressing her face, nurturing her with her soft hands. Although its warmth seemed to carry the gentleness of her mother's loving touch, fear of the unknown washed through Rachel. She had never believed in life after death, so to suddenly feel the presence of her mother frightened her. When her parents passed away in quick succession from poor health, she didn't allow herself to grieve beyond their funerals. She found it easier to detach herself from the pain and pour herself into her career. Being brought back to a place of childlike surrender stirred up feelings left buried for nearly a decade. Apprehensive, she opened her eyes and drew both of her hands up to her face, only to find the soft, warm skin of her cheeks.

She heard the abrupt sound of the old man's voice just as a cloud passed in front of her. Its shade brought her back to the reality of the stage, which was now void of light.

"Join me, Rachel, won't you?"

Rachel took a deep breath as she walked toward the old man. Though the strange light was now gone, its clear connection to her deceased mother left her confused and unsettled.

The old man pointed his cane toward the heavenly scene and immediately, the lower clouds began to dissipate. The higher clouds filled the sky with thick white plumes, which continued to roll across a brilliant blue background. As Rachel curiously watched, the lower skyline continued to thin, ultimately revealing the most surprising and beautiful structure off to their left.

A building came into view far off in the distance. From the stage, she looked down upon it, as if from the vantage point of a bird that was approaching. A beautiful large-domed building became clearer as they moved closer. Rising from its pinnacle was a stunning gold cross that seemed to reach toward God himself. Two long rows of adjacent buildings joined the domed structure on both sides, forming a large square that bustled with people. Most were cloaked in white robes draped with colorful sashes, which presumably marked their positions within the church. The fronts of the buildings were lined with ornate marble columns that were meticulously honed, as if God himself had created them. The columns supported stone roofs lined with ancient statues of all the saints, who gazed down at the crowds below. Several large fountains sprung clear water that shimmered in the sunlight as clergymen paused, admiring their beauty.

Rachel immediately recognized the area. The large domed building was St. Peter's Basilica, which sat in St. Peter's Square, the center of Vatican City in Rome. She and her ex-husband Dave had always wanted to travel there, but Rachel's demanding work schedule had never seemed to allow it. Although the beauty of the structures was more magnificent than she could imagine, the sight brought a subtle sadness to her; a regret for what was only imagined, but never fulfilled.

The details of the ancient buildings became clearer as they moved closer and closer to the Vatican, as did the features of the people in the courtyard. A small crowd was gathering around one man who stood in a doorway at the top of a stone staircase. Rachel could tell that it was the pope himself. He was speaking to a crowd of men who looked as if they held some sort of high position within the church.

Kaw explained, "In your eyes, Rachel, these are the men who represent the holiest of mankind. They have dedicated their lives to God, vowing to sacrifice for him and searching for his divine guidance within his Holy Spirit. They are committed to serving the world around them, selflessly, for the betterment of their church and all of mankind."

Rachel answered, "I've never really thought about it, but yes, I guess they would be the holiest people I could imagine."

Kaw said, "The light you are about to see is the light of heaven itself. God's absolute love for each of these men lies within it."

Suddenly, the bottom of the clouds became illuminated with the most magnificent light imaginable. It surged, blinding Rachel for just a moment, and then retreated into multitudes of controlled beams of indescribable brilliance. They radiated down to each person standing in the courtyard. The light was strong and constant and warm, and shone down to the tops of their heads. Every beam of light seemed almost alive, each emitting a soft soothing hum as it shone down from heaven above. Although each beam was no larger in diameter than the heads of its recipients, the energy within seemed to barely be contained. Each cracked and popped every so often, like a bright sparkler on the Fourth of July.

Kaw spoke up. "The light, which is heaven itself, carries God's love and stays strong and constant with each of these men night and day. None are able to see God's light with their eyes, but all are able to feel it within their hearts."

Rachel's mind whirled. If heaven even existed at all, she had envisioned it to be high above the clouds, well out of people's reach until they die and pass into it. Seeing how close heaven was to all these holy men immediately made her question her own light. Rachel had never felt that God had played any role in her life, and it made her wonder what her light would look like, or even if she had any light at all. After all, these were some of the holiest men on earth, at least from her perspective. They had dedicated their lives to God, and Rachel didn't know with any degree of certainty if God even existed.

The old man raised his cane up high and swept it in front of him. The thick bank of clouds to the right of the Vatican followed his cane as it passed. They quickly began to dissipate as the other clouds had, revealing a very different structure far below to their right.

Several large stucco turrets appeared, which speared through the clouds. Each had a stainless-steel railing encompassing it, and behind each railing stood a uniformed man wielding an automatic rifle. Rachel looked perplexed as they came into view. Below the turrets, tall barbed-wire fences soon became visible, capped with spiraling coils of razor wire, which held rows upon rows of stainless-steel blades that glimmered bright in the sweltering sunlight. Rows of white stucco buildings with faded blue trim emerged through the clouds. They appeared to be old, weathered bunkhouses, and all lined the dry desolate grounds within the confines of the outer fences. A similar building, only larger, ran perpendicular to the bunkhouses, forming a very different type of courtyard.

As the clouds fully thinned, a sea of men emerged, corralled like cattle into the restricting space. There were a few pockets of activity where some lifted weights or tried playing basketball on a makeshift court, but most just mulled around within the masses. Nearly all the men had black hair and tan skin, appearing to be of Hispanic descent. All wore similar uniforms, each one clad in an old T-shirt and gray-and-white striped pants, which looked unwashed and saturated in sweat. The relentless sun beat down on all the men as they bustled about.

Rachel noticed the temperature on the stage even began to rise as their vantage point grew closer to the men.

She spoke up. "What is this place? Where are we?"

With a chuckle, Kaw explained, "These are *my* children." He looked down at Rachel, expecting a response, but got none. "This is the Cefereso No. 9 federal prison, just south of the Texas border in Ciudad Juarez, Mexico. Some of the most brutal acts against mankind were orchestrated by these very men you're looking at. Rape, murder, drug trafficking, human trafficking, torture, you name it, they have done it all. My star students, if you will."

Rachel felt a shiver run up her back as he spoke with sincere pride.

"Let's take a closer look, shall we?"

Again, their perspective was that of a bird descending upon the prison. As they got closer, a smaller group of men came into view, gathered at one end of the courtyard. Most stood and talked among themselves, while a few sat by themselves, isolated from the others. Rachel pointed to one specific prisoner. The inmate looked to be more of a boy than a man. He sat alone and gazed through the barbed-wire fence, watching all the townspeople shuffling past as they went about with their everyday lives. The boy's eyes were glossy and sad, and filled with contemplation. His head was shaven, and he wore a dingy white tank top with striped pants that were several sizes too large, bound at his waist by an old piece of rope. The boy would have looked more natural leaning against a chain-link fence in a schoolyard, if not for a tattooed teardrop that appeared to fall from his eye, just above his left cheek. It seemed to make him look older and less innocent, as if he had seen things a boy of his age should not have seen.

Rachel spoke up. "He looks too young to be in there. What did he do?"

Kaw replied without expression, "He killed a man. The teardrop is a gang symbol representing the life he took."

Rachel thought, *How could such a young boy kill somebody? What could bring him to do such a thing?*

As if Kaw knew what she was thinking, he said, "Look into his eyes, Rachel. What do you see?"

Rachel remembered what the demon had told her in the gym, how we are all intended to open our hearts to all who surround us, accepting their pain or joy with intention. But at the very moment, an iron-clad door seemed to drop within her heart.

"Regardless of his age, I see a killer. He is exactly where he should be, behind bars."

Rachel had always viewed the world around her as black and white, which she found comfort and confidence in. Her world was clear-cut and efficient, and there was no room for sticky gray areas. Despite his age or his specific circumstances, in her mind, this boy was a killer. End of story.

Without being asked, Kaw elaborated. "He is an orphan. Both of his parents were killed when he was six years old. His grandmother, who is his only living relative, lives far away in another country. He was raised in an orphanage, but recently left to live on the streets, fleeing the abuse within it." The old man paused. "I'll leave the nature of his abuse up to your imagination, my dear." He grinned with sick pleasure. "After struggling to find food, the boy had been accepted into a local gang, strictly as a means of survival. This murder was part of his initiation into the gang. He had to prove himself to his new family. So, in broad daylight, he walked up to a targeted man on a crowded street, raised his gun, and shot him point-blank in the forehead."

Rachel heard the boy's story but felt nothing beyond the confident condemnation of a murderer.

"He killed a man. He belongs in prison."

The old man grinned openly as he looked at the boy. Kaw's joyful expression drove an unexpected spike of anger into Rachel's heart.

Rachel responded, "I suppose you felt incredible power when he shot that man, right?"

All expressions left Kaw's face as he turned silently and began to slowly walk around the stage. After several strides, he broke his silence.

"The boy sits in that same place every day, just staring through that fence, but all he really sees are the eyes of the man he shot. You see, Rachel, he was looking into the victim's eyes as he pulled the trigger. It was only for a second, but that was all it took. They seemed to open just a bit wider as his life left his body. To this day, those eyes haunt this boy. No matter where he looks, that's all he sees. There are only the eyes of his victim, closed forever by his choice. Each day the boy sits alone, wondering, 'What could he have seen at that moment I took his life? Where did I send him to? Do his eyes still look upon me from where he is now?'" The old man grinned with pride. "Oh, how very lost and distracted this young one is." Then with cold, emotionless sarcasm, he said, "Pity, isn't it?"

He stared at Rachel but got no response, so he continued to prod her for a reaction. "The truth is, the last thing that went through the victim's mind was quite significant."

Reluctantly, Rachel asked, "What was that?"

The demon's face lit up as he responded, "Why, the boy's bullet, of course." A baiting silence followed, then his dark laughter erupted over the stage again. Rachel intentionally turned from him to avoid any acknowledgement of his twisted humor.

At that moment, the shade from a cloud passing over the prison moved across the young man's face, blocking the sunlight from his eyes. The boy lifted his chin up to find the most beautiful white bank of clouds moving across the Mexican sky. They were so white and full and pure that they seemed almost surreal to the boy, as if they belonged in a cartoon he saw as a child. Beautiful puffy white plumes rolled across the purest bright blue sky. Then with no warning...*flash!*

Rachel closed her eyes and turned away as an unexpected flash of light shot out from the bottom of the cloud bank. Then, just as it had done over the Vatican, the most spectacular beams of heavenly light shone down on each of the inmates, the boy included. The young man continued staring up at the clouds, unable to see the beam of light that rested just above his head. Rachel looked stunned, watching the brilliant flutes of light pop and crack and shine with the same power, and life, and beauty as the light that reached down to the pope himself.

Excited, Rachel spoke up. "The beams of light are the same. God's love is exactly the same for these men as it is for the pope and all of his bishops?"

Kaw sat in silence for a few moments, looking out at all the vibrant beams of light.

"Yes, it's hard to understand, isn't it? God's love for every man and woman is absolutely the same, despite the sins they have committed, whether they have faith in him or another god, or whether they have no faith at all, for that matter. God loves each one of you as if you were his only child, with a depth of love that is hard to comprehend from this physical world. Oh, and just like a parent's love for their child, when you hurt, he also hurts. He feels every detail of your pain. Whether it is physical or emotional, he willingly takes it in. Whether you know it or not, you have never been alone within the pain of your life. Although you are not able to see him with your eyes, he has always been with you walking by your side, weeping while you weep. He accepts all of your loneliness and resentment at the very moment you are experiencing it. And these men are no exception. He walks beside each of them within these prison walls, taking in all that runs through their hearts too."

Rachel spoke up. "God actually hurts from our pain? I had always imagined that if God were real, he would be so powerful that nothing could hurt him at all."

Kaw replied, "Yes, I will admit he is powerful." The old man's face became hardened as he walked toward Rachel. "But don't you ever believe he doesn't feel pain."

His voice was filled with aggression and contempt as he ranted, "He understands more than anyone exactly how we control you. And through our influence, he knows the great power we hold and the pain that accompanies it. He knows we are the puppet masters within this world…and each of you are nothing more than our marionettes. All we must do is tug on your strings, and you dance for us. And trust me, you dance, Rachel! We control each of you through the vehicle of your ego. And through you, we can inflict pain onto God himself, every moment of every day. We inflict deep pain on God through each of your choices."

He raised his voice as he ranted on. "We drive nails into the hands and feet of your God just as we did to his son. And just as we moved the Romans to crucify Jesus, we wound God by moving you to hurt each other. From the beginning of time, we have been influencing you through distraction, temptation, deceit, and fear. We orchestrate our influence through your ego, your sense of self that none of you can escape."

The old man lowered his voice as he continued. "Please understand that although we have always influenced you, we are not able to force you to do anything. One of the highest spiritual laws is that of free will. We cannot force you to choose darkness, just as your God cannot force you to choose light. Do you understand?"

Rachel stood idle, filled with trepidation. "I think so. But if heaven is as close to each of us as you described, then why are we feeling any pain or anger or hatred at all? If God's unconditional love is within my reach, then why can't I see him, or even feel him for that matter? Shouldn't we all be able to feel God's presence if he is here walking with each one of us?"

The old man took a deep breath, then slowly crept to the edge of the stage. He stared into Rachel's eyes, then began to softly chuckle as if he had a dirty secret. "I will answer that question soon enough, my dear. I will show you the specific mechanics of how God fights to touch each of you but too often falls just a bit short. But don't worry, dear. I'll explain it in physical terms, so you won't be forced to conceptualize too much. But first, I believe a touch of perspective on *your* life may be helpful."

8

Kaw turned away from Rachel, then looked over the edge of the stage at the Vatican to his left and the Mexican prison to his right. He then passed his cane in front of the surreal scene. The buildings disappeared as great plumes of ominous black clouds followed its path. Rachel's stomach dropped as the dark scene took shape in front of her eyes. It was as if dark armies of underworld soldiers were engaging in some forbidden dance in the sky. When she looked over the edge of the stage, it felt as if she were standing on the very edge of the earth, looking into the belly of some bottomless dark abyss, a churning turbulence of the blackest clouds you could imagine, moving in all directions, a cradle of chaos.

The clouds began to wrap around the tall stage curtains, then quickly consume the stage floor as they surged toward her. Rachel took several frantic steps backward, but before she knew it, she was knee-high in darkness. She turned her head and saw that the entire stage floor was now gone. She was only able to see the old man and the piano, which sat idle in the clouds behind her.

Panicked, Rachel asked, "What's happening…what is this!?"

Kaw calmly strolled past her over to the edge of the stage, leaving a wake of darkness behind him as he walked. Without a word, he raised his cane up high, then slammed it into the stage floor. *Crack!* The sound of his cane hitting the floor had begun to shoot terror into Rachel's heart. With the end of his cane still submerged in the darkness, Rachel noticed a bright light coming from the tip of it. It illuminated the lower clouds that rolled beneath his knees. The old man drew his cane up, revealing that its brass tip was no longer metal but was now an incredibly bright light. Kaw took two more steps to the very edge of the stage, hung the tip of his cane over its edge, then with a mighty thrust, cast the tip up toward the sky. The glowing tip detached, streaking bright in front of the dark background. Like a shooting star, it shot straight up, disappearing into the cloud bank high above. Unlike a shooting star, its trail stayed illuminated, forming a perfectly straight strand of light no thicker than a finger. The old man turned in silence, then walked past Rachel toward the back of the stage.

From Rachel's vantage point, she could not see where this strange beam of light began or where it ended. Cautiously, she walked over to the edge of the stage. The silence was broken by the soft sound of classical music being played gently on the old piano. Rachel turned her head to find the old man sitting behind the keys, calmly playing a beautiful piece.

Watching the old demon play, Rachel thought, *This must be a nightmare...*

He played calmly as dark clouds rolled under and around his piano, covering the floor, then pushing up the walls behind him.

Rachel turned back to the thin beam of light and carefully slid her feet across the stage floor until she found its edge. She looked up toward the sky, beyond the tall frame of the stage curtains. The beam of light seemed to shoot a mile high, then disappear into a bank of dark, churning clouds far above. She turned her eyes down beyond the stage floor, where the clouds rolled off its edge. The strange light dropped the same distance down below.

She stood silent, studying the beam of light, then turned back to the old man, who continued to play the piano.

"What is it?" she asked.

Without lifting his eyes from the keys, he responded, "Leonard Bernstein's *Symphony No. 2*." Then he glanced up at Rachel with a devilish grin. "Oh, you mean the light?" More laughter came from the old demon.

Rachel glared back at him with a scowl, then stood silent, waiting for an answer. The old man paused, grinning, savoring his power within the moment before he spoke up.

"Why, that's you, my dear!"

Rachel looked back at the beam, studying it for a moment before she spoke. "What do you mean, that's me?"

"The beam of light is you, Rachel...it's your existence. The very essence of who you are. Your soul, if you will."

It looked similar to the beams of light that represented heaven, only it was thinner. As she moved closer, the warmth and security that she had felt earlier began to fill her again. Although thin, her light looked strong and bright, and even though she didn't totally understand it, she felt good about how long the beam stretched.

"Does this mean that I'm going to have a long life?"

Just then she noticed something in the middle of the beam of light. At eye level, she saw what looked like a small pebble that was so miniscule, it was nearly undetectable. It seemed to float in the middle of the beam; but despite its presence, the light shone continuously around it, endlessly shooting in both directions.

She studied it for a moment, then asked, "What is this in the middle of my light? It looks like something is hanging within it. Do you know what that is?"

The old man replied, "The light represents your true existence. Your spiritual existence, your soul that is never-ending. It is eternal. As I've told you before, you as well as everyone else in this world are an actual part of God himself. Each one of you—richer or poorer, whether in the Vatican, a violent prison, or anywhere else throughout this world—is an extension of a selfless eternal entity. You are all a living part of God. The beam of light in front of you is your very soul, whose essence is the same as God's essence. Your true essence is absolute love. The pebble that rests in the middle of your light is the totality of this physical life that you are now living. The very bottom of the pebble represents your physical birth and the top of the pebble represents your physical death. Every moment from birth to death exists within it. Most of you live your life in separation from your true essence, in separation from your selfless origins…in separation from God.

"You see, most of you view your soul as an extension of your physical body, existing because you were born, but the contrary is true. Your body is actually an extension of your eternal soul. It came into being because of your soul, stemming from it. Your body is nothing more than a new vehicle that each of you boards at birth. You drive it for a while, then eventually it begins to slow down, sputter, then stop running all together. But the passenger, the passenger goes on. Do you understand?"

She stood silent, staring at the pebble, then down at the long beam of light.

"Yes, I think so. So, if this light represents my actual existence, and stretches down for a mile before it even reaches this pebble, which is the life that I know, then are you saying that I lived long before I was even born?"

The old man responded, "Yes, you did. I know it's hard for you to understand, but the essence of everyone's being is not physical in nature; it's spiritual, and we have all existed as a part of God's spiritual being for a very, very long time. The life you know is nothing more than a pinprick within your full existence."

"Then if I existed for some incomprehensible length of time before I was even born, then how am I not aware of it? Why can't I remember it?"

The old man grinned with delight, then said, "It is by God's own design that you have no memory of your existence prior to your birth. Your unknowing is necessary for God's intention to manifest. From the moment you were born until the moment you die, you are veiled from your spiritual existence, veiled from your true essence. It is also by God's design that every soul who passes through your world bears the burden of ego throughout their journey. It is the seeds of your ego that inevitably grow into the veil that expands darkness and blocks God's light."

Rachel paused, considering the old man's words, then responded, "How can your influence block us from God? I have never felt influenced to do bad or hurtful things. I am a good person. Ever since I was little, it's been important to me to try to do the right thing."

"Confident, are we, Rachel? You'd never hurt anyone, would you?" He laughed as he stared into her eyes with defiance. "You have never been without our influence. It is one of the most significant and natural characteristics within this world. Our influence moves you to build a spiritual veil that is so powerful, it separates each of you from God, with no exceptions—none!"

"So when God reaches down to us, it's actually you who blocks him?"

Teeming with arrogance, the old man replied. "By his own design…yes, it certainly is."

"Why would God create a world where ego could influence our state of mind and drive us further away from him? I don't understand. If God is perfect and his essence is absolute love, why would he design such an imperfect world that is overflowing with so much pain and suffering?"

Kaw answered, "He designed the perfect stage for his redemptive act, abiding by his own spiritual law of free will."

"Redemption for you and your brothers' defect—for your ego?"

"Yes, he was aware of the possibility of our fall well before our ego ever emerged. Your world was created as the perfect stage for his atonement for our fall."

"Why would God need to make atonement for a defect that occurred within you and your brothers? You said free will was a very important spiritual law, which God created himself. Wasn't that same free will given to the angels upon your creation, just as it was given to each of us?"

"Along with the full knowledge of good and evil, yes, we were given free will to choose."

"It's not his fault you chose evil over good, is it?"

"No, it is not. But angels, just like humans, were created as an extension of God's own being. His being or his will has always existed within all of us. And although I choose to diverge from God's will, he still loves me. No different than any of you who choose to follow your own will when given the chance to follow his. His atonement is an integral part of his perfect love for all. Each human is a unique, intimate expression of God himself; bound as one within your individual bodies and wills. His love transcends all the walls of your separation. He loves each of you and his angels with such purity that he accepts responsibility for each of your choices, even when made in separation from his will. Don't you see, my dear, your world is a very important part of his own progression toward a purer love."

"But I thought God was perfect. Why would he need to progress anywhere if he exists in a state of perfection?"

"It is true that God's love is without flaw, but God does not only define himself as the essence of perfect love, solely residing in the bliss of the highest heaven, but as all those who have been created in separation from himself. This physical world is his means of searching for the hidden caverns of his own being, which manifests through the awakening of his will within those who he created. Each of you is born into this world as a living part of God, where from birth to death, you are intentionally drowned in 'self.' As part of this physical experience, each of you is immersed in the defect of our ego, which resonates through your human nature. Your intended purpose is to fight through the murkiness of your willful human nature, in search of God's will and the truth that is accessible to all through his Holy Spirit."

The old demon went on. "You asked, 'Why would he design such an imperfect world with so much pain and suffering?' From your perspective, pain is something you are all obviously fighting to avoid. But through God's divine wisdom, he understands that the pain that is so abundant in this world may lead you into a deeper search for his will. Consider the organization Alcoholics Anonymous. Most who pass through their doors have experienced unimaginable suffering. But their suffering was necessary to drive them to the understanding that they could no longer live in separation from a higher power. After your hearts have been breached by deep pain, whether you are aware of it or not, it can lead each of you closer to the hidden caverns that exist within your hearts. Beyond that, it may deepen your compassion for others who are also suffering. Through it, you are offered the insight to build a divine bridge that spans between your hearts."

"God loves each of you so much that he is willing to accept every ounce of your pain, understanding that as it deepens, it may draw you closer to the path you are intended to walk. Quite often it is the pain in your individual lives that becomes the catalyst for your true surrender. And when you *truthfully* surrender, your Lord will be waiting with open arms to lead you through the darkness. Although he hates to see any of his children in pain, his hope is for each of you to deepen your search for meaning within it. Your truthful search is where the sparks of his will become illuminated.

"You see, when viewed through truly inspired eyes, even your suffering can be interpreted as a blessing. No matter how difficult your individual circumstances may be, your pain does not have to define you—that choice will always be yours."

The old man continued to play the piano as he spoke. Rachel stood alone, knee-deep in darkness. She paused to look up, just as the last of the high ceiling was devoured by the rolling black clouds.

Seeking solace, Rachel spoke up.

"Alright, so I can see how our struggles may have a deeper purpose. But what about beyond our lives? Can you help me understand the light that goes on beyond the pebble, after my life has ended?"

Kaw responded, "After your physical life has expired, your spiritual veil will be broken as you transition back into a spiritual being. Within that realm lies a beautiful freeing knowledge, unimaginable peace, and a sense of security and understanding within the light of God. You will retain your individuality, but your understanding of his truth will manifest within your consciousness, reuniting and binding your soul with his in your true home in heaven."

She paused for a moment, staring at the long beam of light shining upward, endlessly stretching into the rolling clouds above.

Kaw continued, "As I said before, Rachel, you are all eternal beings. This world is not your true home."

Rachel responded, "It's hard to imagine a different place. And right or wrong, it still scares me to think of how heaven will be with no physical body, existing only in consciousness. The whole idea is a bit frightening to me because there are so many questions about this life after death. I mean, there is a definite sense of security in knowing that it all isn't just over when I die. It's just difficult imagining what that life will look like from where I am standing now, and that can be scary."

Both gazed up at the long beam of light.

"As God himself is Mind, Body, and Spirit, so are each of you. You will maintain your own identity while sharing the mind of God, without the barriers that now separate you." The old man continued, "Close your eyes, Rachel."

Already fearful, she hesitated, staring at him with understandable apprehension.

"It's alright…close your eyes."

Reluctantly, Rachel complied.

"Clear your mind now. Try to open your heart while focusing on the light that's emitted from the endless beam of your soul. Tell me what you feel."

Rachel took in a deep breath and tried her best to let go of all of her questions and fears. With her eyes shut, she immediately noticed the warmth from the radiant light on her face, and again, it brought her back to the safety and security of her childhood home. And as it had before, the presence of her mother began to radiate from the soothing light.

"I know this is frightening for you, but you need to *fully* open your heart and let your fears fall away. It is the only way to gain a fuller perspective and understanding of this afterlife experience."

So, with intention, she pushed all apprehension aside and tried to open her heart and fill her mind with thoughts of love. The warmth of the light continued to penetrate her skin, filling her with its comfort. She felt as if her mother had wrapped her in a snug, cozy blanket and was holding her tight, rocking her. When she intentionally released her fears, it felt wonderful and incredibly safe. Rachel was able to feel the security of the safest home she had ever known and the strongest love she had ever felt, simply by closing her eyes and allowing this strange light of her own eternal life to encapsulate her. All of her fears washed away as she basked silently within the security of the powerful light.

"What you are experiencing is the unified consciousness of God, which is one with your eternal spirit. This unified consciousness is also shared with all souls that have passed and now reside in heaven, willingly bound as one with God."

Reluctantly, Rachel opened her eyes. "Am I feeling the soul of my mother who has passed? It feels like it did when I was a child, when she would hold me."

"Yes, my dear. She is praying for you right now as we speak. That's how she continues to hold you and love you from heaven. She is fighting to intercede for you, just as she did throughout your life. So many souls in heaven share her deep concern for you. And most importantly, they are all unified within God's love for you. They are all bound within God's unified consciousness, and love you as God loves you. All love you as one, feeling all your light and forgiving you for all your darkness as you move through this physical experience."

"Are you saying that they are all aware of what runs through my heart and my mind?"

"Yes, I am. The perception that you conceal what you create in your heart and mind is perpetuated through your own sense of self. It's what we *want* you to believe. Our power depends on it. All that you feel, as well as your true intention behind everything you do, is felt by all who have passed into heaven. Your intention actually moves this place and carries great purpose as it manifests."

A long pause followed as Rachel considered his words. "My intention?"

Kaw spoke with a smirk as he continued to play the piano. "Sounds so insignificant, doesn't it? Yes, throughout your lives, most of you don't put a whole lot of thought into intent."

After a moment of reflection, Rachel spoke. "But the world around us is actually only affected by our words or actions, not by what we feel."

"We have you so disconnected in your day-to-day lives, few of you actually understand what you feel, or take the time to understand your true motives behind what you say or do. So many of your true intentions center around protecting yourselves within your vulnerable lives. *What* you do is what's important, not why you do it, right?" Kaw asked sarcastically. "Well, *why* you do it is actually more important than any of you could ever imagine. You see, beyond your actions, God feels every detail of your true intention. God feels your guarded truth behind every word you speak and everything you do. There is a hidden reality behind every one of the thousands of thoughts that run through your mind every single day, and each one absolutely matters." Kaw paused for a moment. "Trust me, if you knew half of what God knows, you'd be shocked at how full of excrement most of you are!"

His words angered her, but she resisted lashing back at him, and instead stood in silence thinking about intention.

"Oh, you're all so proud and arrogant when you deceive. It comes so natural to you. Most of you don't think twice about it. Others' image of you is just *so* important."

Rachel spoke up. "How can you judge me? You just told me it's *your* influence that pushes us to be deceitful and to care about our own well-being when given the chance to focus on another. Besides, honesty has always been important to me. I'm upfront with my true intentions. I don't need to lie."

Titus Kaw raised his voice as he played the piano, uninterrupted. "Your arrogance surprises even me, Rachel. And trust me, I take that as a personal compliment."

He drew his eyes back down to the keys of the old piano, closed them, and began to sway to the beautiful music that he was creating. After a few moments, he cracked his eyes open to meet Rachel's gaze.

"And don't you worry, we will get to your 'honor' and your 'true' intentions soon enough." Kaw continued as he played. "Everything leads back to your ego. Through it, most feel that it only matters what you say and do. Most believe your consciousness remains locked within each of you, and is yours alone to dissect and share whatever shards you choose to at that moment. On the contrary, your hearts and minds are little factories of light and dark, which do not belong to you at all. All you create within your consciousness belongs to this universe. And whether you believe it or not, what you create within your mind pushes this place in one direction or the other. All things in the universe are interconnected on a quantum level, influencing each other instantaneously, regardless of physical action or spoken word. On this level, you are all one, tied together through a unified consciousness. So, in other words, everything you create within your mind influences the unified consciousness of all. Like I mentioned earlier, each of you are more powerful than you could ever imagine."

Rachel pondered the demon's words silently; and although she tried, ultimately, she still struggled believing all of his claims. It just seemed counterintuitive to what she had learned about this life, and at that moment, it was more than she could fully accept. She was always taught that it was wrong to hurt others through your actions or your words, but had always believed you can feel or think what you want, as long as you didn't say it or act on it.

Rachel replied, "I understand how God could be unified, through his spirit, with all souls who have passed, or even to all of us who still live in this world. But how could we affect the rest of the world simply by feeling or thinking? I'm trying to understand how any of it would truly matter, if we never spoke out or acted on our inclinations."

"Think about it, Rachel. Physically, mankind is an absolute minority within our universe. Consider every soul who has ever passed through this world, from the very beginning of time. Each one is an eternal being who exists and interacts solely as spirit, barring the pinprick of time that was their physical life. Imagine the number of souls who now exist openly within God's spiritual realm as a part of God within heaven. And what about the countless armies of God's angels, each existing within a very real consciousness, without a physical locale or a physical body. Consider these incredible multitudes, the countless souls who exist and interact solely within God's unified consciousness." The old man's frustration grew. "Please help me understand, when practically *all* of creation exists and interacts within this realm of open consciousness, why would *you* be able to conceal your thoughts within this pebble of a world?"

Rachel stood silent, stunned by his claims.

He continued, "Everything you say and do is a mere echo of what first transpires within your consciousness. Of course, your physical actions and words do matter, but none exist without first manifesting in your minds." The old demon paused in thought, then said, "Before your daughter posted her first scathing remarks about Mary Katherine, her heart burned, Rachel. And when it did, the universe felt her flame!"

With no warning, he raised his cane up high and slammed it back into the oak floor of the stage. *Crack!* Thin bolts of lightning trailed out in every direction from the tip of his cane. Rachel's heart dropped as she shielded her eyes from the blinding arc that was emitted. Again, the distinct smell of ozone filled the air.

When Rachel lowered her hand from her face, she saw that the long thin light of her soul had vanished. Beyond the stage, masses of dark rolling clouds began to pass again, but quickly dissipated, giving way to a shocking panoramic landscape of faraway mountains and a harsh, dry valley in the foreground. In the distance, five African women dressed in traditional garb could be seen walking single-file through fields of woody brush and prickly undergrowth. Large trees draped with moss and vines towered sparsely throughout the valley in which they walked. Each woman carried a clay or metal vessel on her head as they moved in unison through the unforgiving terrain.

"What is this? Who are these women?" Rachel asked.

"Who they are is not important. They're just a few of the nameless masses who blindly move through their little worlds. They are no different than most of you, occupied with their own lives, totally unaware of the perpetual cogs of light and dark that move them each day."

Frustrated, Rachel pushed, "I don't understand. Why are you showing me this, and what does it have to do with Terra?"

"Over a month ago, you took Terra and Meghan out for dinner in the town in which you live. When you were done eating, the three of you sat silent, as you so often do, entertaining yourselves on your gadgets. That was the precise moment Terra heard them. The sound of their laughter from across the restaurant caught her ear. When she looked up, she saw Mary Katherine sitting with her family, laughing together as they ate their dinner. As Terra watched, she focused on how happy and carefree they all were. Such joy seemed to come from their conversation, at a time when it felt absent in her own life. Her heart immediately fell into a dark place of envy. 'Look at them, they are so annoying!' she thought. After all, Terra harbored so much resentment after your ugly divorce, and at that point in her life, was in desperate need of an outlet."

Rachel's heart sank again. Admittedly, she and her husband openly fought in front of their daughters. Right or wrong, at the time she had wanted her kids to know exactly how their father had betrayed her. Rachel's anger blinded her from ever considering that her girls may have felt as if *their* lives were spinning out of control, too. But now, she could finally see how her anger had deeply affected her daughter.

The old man went on, "At that very moment, it was born. The seed of envy had been sewn into her heart and quickly grew into something much darker. Before she even left the restaurant that evening, Terra's heart filled with an unjustified anger toward the unsuspecting girl. She had finally found the outlet for the pain she was feeling, and although it was unprovoked, her sights were set on Mary Katherine. At the very moment her heart began to burn with anger…lightning crashed!"

With those words, the old man slammed his cane back into the floor, and with it came a thunderous crash and a bright flash of lightning high above the African landscape. Rachel watched as the small group of women crouched down at the loud strike, then glanced up toward the tremendous flash high above them. Immediately following the lightning, a small dark cloud appeared in the precise location of its strike. It seemed to miraculously take form, then began to roll and churn and move as it grew larger and larger. In amazement, the women watched the unusual cloud grow enormous right in front of their eyes.

Titus explained, "That is how envy and anger are born. That black cloud is the actual darkness that your daughter manifested in her own mind. The problem is, your darkness does not stay concealed within you. The moment you create it, it takes form in the most significant way. The factories of light and dark within every man and woman's minds never stop. Every minute, each of you pump out one or the other, before you do or say anything. And what you create pushes this universe in one direction or the other."

Now high above them, the dark cloud continued to grow and churn and tumble. It rolled over itself again and again, growing larger as it transformed. Confused, the African women watched from below, until the ominous mass covered most of the sky above them.

With belittling disgust, the old man shouted, "Look at them! Look at those silly water-bearers, walking miles and miles barefoot every day. Oh, I'll bet they're praying to God right now. Praying for that darkness to open up and bless them with the gift of rain. Ha! All the prayers in the world won't draw rain from those clouds. They're made up of Terra's darkness, and although unspoken, it moved this world, nonetheless. Every bit of greed, self-absorption, bigotry, envy, arrogance, judgment, deceit, prejudice, and hatred that this world propagates every day takes form high above your world. Every fleeting thought, which you create within your minds and hearts, absolutely matters."

He shouted again, pointing his cane at the women who were studying the dark cloud. "Look at them! With their futile prayers for rain." His emotions heightened as he went on. "You torture the tortured with your darkness. So many of you move through your lives justifying your selfishness, substituting legality for morality, turning a blind eye toward the masses whom you imprison with your half-truths and hidden judgment."

Rachel stood silent as she listened to his rant, shocked and frightened by the demon's terrifying claims. The insidious cloud was now enormous. Its circular motion was so subtle; it was virtually undetectable as it loomed ominously high above the African valley.

"You see, Rachel, Terra's hatred is not static, nor is any of yours.

Inevitably, after enough darkness has gathered, its purpose within your world begins."

The two of them watched as the middle of the massive cloud opened, forming a colossal ring of darkness high above the women. Within moments, it dominated the entire African sky. As the frightening band of clouds continued expanding and rolling toward every horizon, it left an eerie dark haze with remnants of smaller gray clouds drifting in its wake.

The clouds' unusual behavior terrified the water bearers. Loud, unsettling shrieks echoed from the women across the dry unforgiving land. At the horrifying surreal sight, each frantically gathered their vessels and scampered down the harsh trail toward the dense forest in the distance. It was not long before they reached their woody refuge, cautiously drawing their eyes back up to the sky. Just as the last of the women vanished into the trees, the gigantic ring of darkness breeched every horizon, disappearing out of sight. The sky was left littered with multitudes of grey cumulous clouds rolling beneath an ominous black veil, like an oil spill in the heavens.

The demon reiterated, "The darkness that stems from your minds and through the choices you make leaves lingering traces of its essence high above this physical world. After veiling the entire planet, your darkness will surge one last time before raining down upon the conscience of the living.

"You reap what you sow. This message is conveyed repeatedly through the Old and New Testaments in your Holy Bible. In the East, this same idea is referred to as karma. What you create throughout your life will ultimately return to you as the universe balances itself through its scales, which are your individual souls. Although these scales are balanced on an individual basis, they are simultaneously balanced on a global level. Subconsciously, each of you will reap what your world collectively sows. As I told you, every soul is eternally connected. If you create light from your life, then light will be offered to all of humanity. If you create darkness, then darkness will be your offering."

Rachel stood shocked at the old man's account of the mechanics that engage with each of our passing thoughts.

The demon stared into her eyes, searching for her understanding, smirking as he continued. "You always thought your daughter would change the world. Turns out you were right!" His dark smile grew, consuming his wrinkled face.

His verbal attack on Terra instantly spiked anger into the vulnerable woman's heart. "My daughter's a good girl! She's just frustrated and confused," she shouted with sharp passion.

The demon erupted into loud unbridled laughter, quickly retorting, "I'm sure that's true, but let's not forget that apple didn't fall very far from its tree. Did it, Rachel? Let's not forget about your little stroll through the grocery store this morning."

Rachel thought back to earlier in the morning when she ran through Wagner's. She fought to remember if she had exchanged words with anyone as she shopped. She had merely breezed through the store. *It couldn't have taken me more than ten minutes*, she thought.

"I didn't speak to anyone but the clerk this morning."

Kaw corrected her. "I just told you that words are not needed to create darkness."

Rachel's mind raced again, trying to recall what had passed through her mind as she shopped, but she had no idea.

"What about that drunk painter, Stevens? What ran through your mind the moment you passed by him?"

It was clear Rachel was struggling to remember exactly what she had been thinking at that moment.

"I'll give you a hint, Rachel. It was the same moment he was putting a twelve-pack of beer into his cart. Come on now, you remember."

Her heart sank a bit as she remembered, choosing to profess nothing.

It was to no avail. The old man knew what she was thinking and repeated it with a victorious grin. "'Nice breakfast…' does that ring a bell?" He began to laugh as he went on. "Then the two women lingering in line in front of you while the barista waited patiently to take their order. Oh yes, your heart burned with judgement and frustration because they made you wait ten more seconds to order your coffee. Then again, staring at the pregnant teenager behind the register. 'I can only imagine the home she was raised in…her mother must be proud.' I believe that was the nature of your judgement, which you released like caged ravens into the universe. Like everyone else in this physical dimension, your judgement is very real, and whether it is spoken or not, it plumes black above this world."

She was shocked at all of her passing thoughts that condemned so many. "I didn't mean to be so judgmental. I…I don't even know why those thoughts were running through my mind?"

The old man explained, "That is the sound of the merciless judge that exists in all of your heads. Day and night, his relentless chatter never stops. He not only judges everyone around you but, with no compassion, judges you too. The judge in your mind is unconcerned with justice. Through his eyes, all, including yourself, fall short of his expectations, unjustifiably condemning you, regardless of circumstance. Your heart sinks or burns with every loud slam of his gavel, even if only within your own mind. No one will ever be great enough for the judge whose name is ego.

"The truth is, this continuous stream of judgmental thoughts is quite natural and unconscious throughout your entire lives. The trick is not in suppressing these thoughts of condemnation, but in understanding that the thoughts are not who you truly are. When you identify yourself as a loving extension of God instead of the thoughts themselves, then you are able to create space between you and the invasive thoughts in your mind. This is the place where you can breathe deep in a non-reactive state, then counter the darkness with intentional thoughts of understanding, love, and forgiveness for yourself and the world around you. If you are mindful, you can train yourself to counter your unconscious judgement with the simple awareness that you are not your thoughts. That awareness alone is enough to release light from your deeper self into the universe, negating any unconscious darkness that you may have released.

"Although God has already forgiven you for your judgement, his intention is for you to continually evaluate what runs through your minds and hearts. It is your care for yourself and those who surround you that should move you to examine what you create in your consciousness. Again, it is a matter of truly understanding the mechanics of the light and the dark within your world. Most of you are totally unaware of how much unspoken judgment you cast throughout your days. Pushing yourselves to become more cognizant of this is a very important step on your path to reorienting your mind, conditioning it so God's Holy Spirit may dwell within you."

Rachel envisioned all the negativity, judgment, and resentment that her divorce had led to, and the resentment that emerged from her job as she competed against other salespeople at Jackson and against rival pharmaceutical companies. She began examining all parts of her life, exhuming her judgment of so many parents at her children's school and of her own children, too. As she considered her true state of mind, the darkness that she had created seemed to grow exponentially.

What amount of darkness have I released into the world over the course of my life?

she contemplated. As this new truth struck her, she could not help envisioning enormous banks of black clouds hanging low over her home, then forming above her as she moved throughout her days.

"That's why you originally spoke to me, isn't it? Early this morning in the grocery store, that's why you said, 'That-a-girl!' as I walked by. You knew what was running through my mind, didn't you?"

"Spoken or not, I feel all of your darkness. So yes, I felt your judgement and I grew stronger from it." With a devilish grin, Kaw remarked, "I think you are finally beginning to see the bigger picture, my dear."

Rachel jolted as Kaw drove his cane back into the floor. When she turned, she found that the African landscape was gone and all the churning dark clouds that smothered them on the stage had begun to retreat over its floor. It was as if an enormous vacuum had suddenly been turned on. The clouds quickly rolled past Rachel and Kaw before dropping off the edge, becoming one with the cloud banks that passed just beyond the stage.

As the clouds thinned below, it became obvious that the floor of the stage had changed. It was no longer a wooden floor at all, but looked as if they were standing on top of a flat asphalt roof. Rachel closed her eyes for a moment to refocus, then opened them again. Dark clouds still obstructed the view in front of her, but when she turned around, it became clear that they were no longer on the stage at all.

9

Large, corroded cast-iron smokestacks protruded out from an old rooftop and towered above Rachel and Kaw from where they stood. Like ancient turrets on a castle, they marked the old building's pinnacle and distinguished it from adjacent structures. Several old brick chimneys rose up from the rooftop, as well. Empty wine bottles and garbage were scattered by some unknown strangers that must have used this hidden perch as a refuge from the world below. The only thing that tethered Rachel and Kaw to the school's stage was the old piano and its bench. The two of them stood in the same position that they held in the gym, as if they had never moved; all else had changed though.

Rachel turned her head again and saw that the clouds had now totally dissipated from the rooftop on which they stood. An old parapet capped with stone appeared where the edge of the stage had been. The wall stood waist-high and was built of brick, which looked to have once held a deep-red color. Now it appeared as a wash of charcoal gray and black from the years of soot raining down from the nearby smokestacks. Rachel took several steps closer to one of the walls encompassing the edge of the roof, then peered over.

"Where are we?" she asked.

The sky was now clear, and a moderately busy city street could be seen down below. There was an obvious contrast within the few blocks that ran east from their vantage point on top of the old building. Rachel thought they may be on top of an old apartment complex, but she was not sure. Toward the north of the roof, an old, rusted wrought-iron fire escape arched over the brick parapet. It ran up from the street below, meandered from window to window, and ended on the rooftop where the flat steel handrails were attached. The railings had been held down with heavy black bolts, which from years of recoating the flat roof carried layer upon layer of blanketed asphalt. Clotheslines had been strung between the fire escapes and were covered in pinned garments, air-drying in the breeze. The building across the street appeared to be a dilapidated abandoned warehouse. All its windows had been boarded with plywood that had then been defaced with colorful graffiti. Next to the warehouse, another neglected apartment building teemed with life as neighbors sat together, conversing on its large stone steps.

Small, racially diverse groups of men and women could be heard laughing as they gathered on the sidewalk in front of the apartment building. Old cars sped by, honking their horns to the bystanders as they chatted. The center of activity on the corner seemed to be an old church, which had a makeshift banner draped over its front stone wall that simply read, "The Cleveland Mission." A long line of underprivileged individuals stood single file beside the building, wrapping around the Mission from front to back. A group of five to six women sat on its large front steps while several others paced back and forth along the street corner. All of them appeared to be sex workers. Most of the ladies that sat were smoking cigarettes while chatting with each other, but would pop up enthusiastically when a new car would pull up next to the curb in front of them.

A few blocks east of the Mission, several brand-new sparkling buildings rose up from the street in dramatic contrast. No expense had been spared in their contemporary design. Floor after floor of enormous glass walls framed in shiny stainless-steel glimmered in the distance. A grand contemporary statue towered in front of the main building, marking its significance. Busy people could be seen through the large windows, many wearing white lab coats, bustling through crowds of people. The illumination from the large blue-and-yellow sign could be seen clearly from their rooftop. It read, "The Cleveland Hospital."

Upon seeing the sign, Rachel answered her own question. "Some of my clients are doctors here. This is one of the hospitals I sell to."

Kaw turned and stared at her for a moment, smirking. "Your medicine?" he asked sarcastically. "As you so vaguely refer to it." His lips slowly curled upwards, eventually manifesting into a sinister grin, which he held until the awkwardness of the moment compelled Rachel to respond.

Raising her voice in guarded defiance, she said, "Yes, I'm a pharmaceutical sales representative. That means I sell pharmaceuticals, which would mean absolutely nothing to a fifth grader. That's why I referred to it as medicine when I spoke to the children."

The old man replied, "My, you're a sassy little thing, aren't you?" He stood only a couple of feet from her and glared into her eyes, stone-faced with intensity. Licking his lips in anticipation, he continued, "Tell me more about your pharmaceuticals, Rachel."

She glared back in silence, grimacing without a response.

Kaw persisted, "Sales must be quite good! Mercedes Benz SUVs aren't inexpensive, are they? And that big house on the lake?" He laughed again as he waited for a response.

Her disapproval at his continued invasion into her private life would have come out more aggressively if not tempered by her fear of what he was.

"I'm proud of what I do, and I've busted my ass every day to get to where I am. So if I drive a Mercedes or live on the lake, it's because I've earned it, and I choose to!" Surprised at her own response, Rachel paused before taking a deep breath.

Kaw responded, "Tell me what you sell, you snippy little thing! What *medicine* brings in so much money?"

Rachel felt him toying with her. It was as if he already knew the answers to all of his own questions, but just wanted her to say them. She recalled earlier that morning when he had made it very clear to her that he was somehow privy to the intimate details of her early days at Jackson Pharmaceutical.

She stared back apprehensively, then responded, "I sell synthetic analgesics."

The old demon's eyebrows rose, as if impressed by her response. "Synthetic analgesics? Do I look like a doctor?" Raising his voice, he demanded, "Tell me what you sell!" With softened sarcasm, he added, "In layman's terms. You must remember I'm just an ordinary guy, Rachel." He stood with his hands behind his back, staring at her with a grin, waiting for the answer that she felt he already knew.

"From the very beginning of my career, I've sold pain inhibitors."

"You're starting to excite me, please go on," the old man persisted.

She took a long deep breath, then finally replied, "Hybalarium. I sell the painkiller Hybalarium."

As that word left her lips, it was as if the old demon had finally reached some perverse climax.

His eyes rolled back as he released a breathy exhale. "Hy-Bal…" Gratified, he briefly rested within that moment, then whispered softly, "Thank you, thank you, my dear. Hearing that word come out of your mouth means more to me than you will ever know." He paused again within his own sick perception of peace, then said, "See, that wasn't so hard, now was it?"

Rachel scowled at him in disapproval. She wanted to immediately give a rebuttal, listing all that her drug has done to help so many recover from their surgeries, cancer treatments, and devastating injuries, gifting thousands of patients with a fraction of the pain they otherwise would have had. She wanted to step up on her pedestal and explain the data behind this miracle drug that she provided to those who were truly in need, but she didn't. Instead, she stood quiet, considering that the man she was speaking to knew every one of her dark secrets that she kept buried throughout her life. They were buried so deep within her that years of justification had brought her to believe that they were not dark at all.

Kaw glared at her as if he could tell exactly what she was thinking, then turned and spoke as he walked away. "Well then, I guess we'll just cross that bridge when we come to it." Then, turning his eyes back toward hers, he added with an elevated tone, "Or burn it to the ground!"

The old man grinned as she stood silent. He raised his cane up high, then forcefully back down, driving it into the rooftop. The familiar *crack!* of two stones echoed across their perch. Bright electric bolts shot out in all directions, followed immediately by a loud rattle of steel coming from the fire escape.

Startled, Rachel took several quick steps backward. As she distanced herself, the rattle became louder and louder. Suddenly, the two rusted arches of steel began to visibly shake. Someone or something was moving quickly up the fire escape toward them.

As if bored, the old man turned and took several slow steps toward Rachel. He then spun around, facing the fire escape, and stood leaning against the old piano just a few feet from where she stood.

Rachel's heart beat faster at the anticipation of who, or what, was climbing closer toward the rooftop. The rattle and shake of the steel handrail came to a terrifying peak as a frightening figure emerged from behind the parapet. His appearance startled Rachel. He was a long-haired middle-aged man dressed in old clothes. At first glance, he appeared to be Hispanic, but it was hard to tell from her vantage point. He feverishly moved up the ladder and stepped forward onto the low brick wall. Without pause, the stranger jumped several feet down onto the rooftop. He stood panting from his long climb and seemed to stare off beyond where she and Kaw stood. It appeared to Rachel that the stranger couldn't see either of them at all. As he panted heavily, his presence spiked fear within her.

Now having a clearer perspective, Rachel could tell he was most likely Mexican, and looked to be in his mid-fifties. He had long, thick black hair with periodic strands of gray hanging down just past his shoulders. It draped in front of him, covering most of his face. He wore old jeans cinched with a weathered brown leather belt, a threadbare white T-shirt, and a beat-up green army jacket that was stained from years of wear. If his clothes were any indication, Rachel believed he was destitute. As his heavy breathing began to subside, so did the movement of his scraggly hair as it fluttered away from his face, then back in with every breath. Rachel had no idea who he was or why he was there. Suddenly, her heart dropped again, as more unexpected rattling came from the fire escape. Someone else was starting to move up the ladder in a similar fashion. The rattling grew louder and louder as they moved closer to their summit.

In no time, another man, in sharp contrast to the first, appeared at the top of the fire escape. A younger man dressed in a freshly pressed tailored suit stepped off the ladder and onto the brick parapet. He was obviously well-groomed and handsome and was holding a gleaming, well-crafted leather briefcase in his right hand. A shiny laminated badge was clipped to the lapel of his suit jacket. He was neat and clean and looked as if he could have walked off the cover of a Wall Street magazine. Without looking at the new arrival, the older Hispanic man turned to his left and walked five or six paces along the brick wall. It appeared as if he was intentionally making room for the newcomer. Rachel's mind raced again, not understanding who they were or why they were there. She watched as the first man came to a halt, then stood staring off over the rooftop at what appeared to be nothing at all. Neither of the men had engaged her or each other with words, or even eye contact. Like in the gymnasium, it seemed as if these men could not see Rachel or Titus Kaw at all. The suited man jumped down to the rooftop, then turned and took several steps to his left, pausing directly behind the first stranger. Both stood emotionless, staring straight ahead.

Again, more rattling came from the old steel fire escape, and within a few moments, another individual appeared and stepped out onto the brick wall. It was a scantily dressed woman, who at first glance appeared to be about Rachel's age. After closer inspection, Rachel felt she looked older due to the many deep wrinkles cutting through her face. She crouched down onto the old weathered wall, then unsteadily eased her way onto the rooftop. She stood disheveled, with unwashed hair pulled back into a loose bun. The woman wore a short tight miniskirt made of artificial black leather and a dingy white tank top that clung to her body and accentuated her breasts, as she wore nothing beneath it. An unwashed jean jacket hung from her hips, its arms tied like a belt around her waist. Her legs were bare and pale and thin and covered in a variety of large and small bruises of different shapes and colors. Her feet were clad with silver pumps that looked old and worn. At first sight of her shoes, Rachel was struck with pity, as they looked as if they should have been thrown away years ago. One shoe had several layers of gray duct tape repeatedly wrapped around the silver strap. Its adhesive edges curled up, with visible dirt stuck to it. Her toes protruded from the front of the pumps, with neglected remnants of chipped gaudy green toenail polish. Several toes on her right foot were covered in dried blood and dirt and, like her toenails, were left neglected. She turned, took two steps forward, then stood idle behind the man in the suit, forming a single file line of three, as if in a predetermined formation.

Rachel nervously watched as all three strangers turned together and faced her and Titus Kaw. They stood like soldiers, emotionless, looking past her and the old demon. As Rachel stared back, she couldn't help but feel that something about them felt familiar. It seemed as if she had seen them all before, but she couldn't quite put her finger on it. So, one by one she began to study them. She realized she had seen the woman just moments ago. She was one of the sex workers sitting on the steps of the Mission, smoking a cigarette. Rachel stared at the businessman and immediately recognized him, too. Cautiously, she walked toward him to examine the badge hanging from his jacket. From top to bottom, it read, "The Cleveland Hospital/Watson Cancer Center." Directly under, it read, "Samuel Pierson, MD."

Dr. Pierson was one of Rachel's many high-volume prescribers of Hybalarium. He was also on the team that had treated her neighbor Jack when he was fighting his glioblastoma. He was supposed to be one of the leaders in his field, young and in high demand for his groundbreaking research specializing in treating brain cancer. Rachel had always found him attractive and confident, but also had the distinct impression that he held this opinion of himself. It was clear to her that Dr. Pierson, although talented, was both brash and arrogant.

As she turned her head to study the long-haired Hispanic man, she began to feel the uneasiness of the old demon staring at her. When she turned toward Kaw, his intense gaze was upon her. With wide eyes and a wicked laugh, the old man raised his cane up high and crashed it back into the asphalt rooftop. *Crack!* The shocking intensity of what followed left Rachel longing for the security of the old gym.

A dense, dark haze began to gather directly above the woman. Its outer edges quickly became defined, forming a thick ring of black clouds that tumbled and turned as it began to slowly circle the crown of the stranger's head. The eerie mass looked like some dark, surreal halo that rolled into itself as it loomed above her, turbulent and persistent, as if it had a mind of its own. As Rachel moved closer to examine the unusual phenomenon, a bright electric light shot out in all directions from the area of the stranger's head. Rachel watched in disbelief as the light morphed into a blinding arc of static, like from an old television set. Black, grey, and white pixels seemed to radiate from the crown of the woman's head, shining out in every direction. Simultaneously, the deafening sound of white noise filled the rooftop, which instantly pierced Rachel's ears. It was the sound of crackling static on a radio whose volume had been turned up, only this was ten times louder than any static she had ever heard before. The obvious source of the ear-piercing clatter was the bright cluster of pixels. Rachel immediately cupped both hands tightly over her ears, trying to protect them.

She yelled out to the demon at the top of her lungs. "What's happening? Make it stop!"

Rachel couldn't even hear the sound of her own voice over the deafening, chaotic scream of white noise. Terrified, she turned her head to find the demon at her side, laughing at her. With total disregard to her pain, he raised his cane up, then slammed it back down on the rooftop again.

Suddenly, the piercing ping of a steel hammer striking an anvil rang out, as if it were within inches of Rachel's ears. The all-encompassing sound of static filled the air as the spike of steel-on-steel cut through her over and over again.

Rachel screamed out in agony, "I'll be deaf! Please…make it stop!"

The old man towered over her, smiling down while basking in the power he held.

"Make it stop. Please, I'm begging you!"

Rachel wanted to shield her eyes from the blinding light but couldn't release her hands from her ears. All she could do was turn her head from its source and close her eyes, while muffling her ears as tight as she possibly could.

The woman stood still within the strange light, totally unaffected by the ear-piercing sounds and seemingly unaware of the blinding static that surrounded her. Rachel then heard the crack of two stones, followed by silence. A long, steady tone lingered in her ears from the trauma they had just endured. Kneeling on the rooftop now, hunched over in clear pain, Rachel opened her eyes and began to softly weep.

"Why are you doing this to me…why?" Her voice cracked, pleading in desperation.

Calmly, the demon answered, "I told you, Rachel, I'm offering you a wider perspective of good and evil. And as part of that, you need to understand all the mechanics that lie behind the curtain of your physical world. I'm walking you down a path that has been obscured from nearly all who have moved through this physical realm." He smiled, then struck her with more sarcasm. "Can't you see how lucky you are?"

Rachel rebutted with restrained anger, "My ears are still ringing from that terrible noise. I could be deaf!"

Kaw retorted, "Oh, I know this path we are on may be a bit rocky, but it is the only one that leads to the summit." His face grew more serious. "And although it may be somewhat of a struggle, I assure you that if need be, I will drag you up it until you gaze from its peak. As I told you before, your true understanding of this world is my only way out of this dimension, so even if I must get you there kicking and screaming, that's exactly what I will do!"

Rachel's heart sank again at his threat. She knew now that the old demon was totally indifferent to her emotional and physical pain.

Kaw went on. "Once you know the truth behind this life that you are living, then and only then you'll be able to choose truthfully."

A deep fear rushed through Rachel again. Her voice cracked with desperation as she replied, "Choose what?"

He stared into her eyes, expressionless, then said, "Soon enough, my dear, soon enough." A grin cracked his tight lips as he offered, "Her name is Honey. Well, Honey Love, to be exact."

Still shaken and confused, Rachel asked, "What is that surrounding her? Who are these people, and why are they here?"

Kaw leaned forward, putting most of his weight onto his cane. "They are here to help you understand the function of your spiritual veil."

"Spiritual veil?"

"Yes, Rachel. That is the veil that surrounds all who are born into this world from your birth to your death. It is the barrier that was put in place to separate all of you from God and heaven itself. The veil cannot be seen with the eyes or heard with the ears, yet has draped every man and woman's consciousness from the beginning of time."

The demon's eyes gleamed when he saw the confusion on Rachel's face. "Every person's veil is made up of two distinct parts. The heart of your veil is its dark inner core. That is the band of black clouds that continuously circles your mind. It quietly seeps our influence into your consciousness, day and night, throughout your entire lives. It is the vehicle that allows ego to permeate into your psyche, the same ego that initiated our original fall from grace. Your dark inner core sows the seeds of ego in each of you, but it is the individual that will determine if these seeds will root, stem, and flower. These seeds are the parasites that have always existed in mankind. Whether you nurture them or deprive them will determine the degree of ego within each of you, and in turn, the distortion within your individual mind.

"The outer shell of your veil is made up of blinding pixels of light, a deafening clatter of white noise, and an ear-piercing ping of steel on steel. This shell is the distortion that each of you create in reaction to our ego flowing into your consciousness. Everything in existence has an energy frequency, even your individual conscious. The static shell of your spiritual veil is the difference in frequency between your mind and the mind of God. The thinner your static shell becomes, the closer your frequency is to God's, and the clearer his voice becomes. The state of your individual mind will dictate if you are able to interpret God's divine inspiration or not. As we speak, his absolute love and guiding inspiration wraps around every soul's spiritual veil. It is his intention that each of you diminishes the distortion within your minds so his divine guidance and inner serenity may blow into your consciousness."

Rachel spoke up. "I don't understand. I have never heard of anything like this before. A veil that covers our minds and blocks us from God? Are you saying that this veil prevents God and myself from truly connecting?"

Kaw explained, "The static shell of your veil only disconnects you from *feeling* God's Holy Spirit and his guidance that lies within it. You have always been surrounded by your Lord's unconditional love. Most of you just haven't been able to experience it fully because of the distortion that you have created in your own minds. It disconnects *you* from him, but God continues to feel all that runs through your hearts and your minds. Your veils cannot prevent that. He feels every thought within your consciousness every moment of every day, throughout your entire life." With a frustrated sigh, the old man added, "Your veil is the actual barrier between heaven and earth." The old man pointed at the bubble of static. "The static shell of your veil is where my brothers and I extract all of our power. And its dark inner core is where our influence on all of you festers initially, then thrives or withers through the choices each of you make throughout your lives. That veil is more important than you could ever imagine. It is the only thing keeping heaven itself from flooding into this world!"

Kaw went on, "Our influence is what keeps you focused on your physical lives and provides each of you with what you need to exist in this world where only the fittest survive." The old man paused for a moment, then corrected himself. "It feeds you with what you need not only to survive, but what you need to *thrive* in this world. All of your instincts to survive come from it. It is all part of your incredible need of self, which flows directly into your consciousness from our influence.

"What do you think pushed that fifth grader to make it to the top of that rope? It was your vision of self! Even back then, you knew you were greater than the rest of your schoolmates. More than anything, you needed to be the first girl to the top of that rope, and you were! It was your ego, Rachel. You do remember the specifics of that day, don't you, my dear?"

She turned away from the demon, intentionally avoiding eye contact.

With a confident grin, the old man continued, "You *do* remember, I can feel it! That was me inside of you, Rachel." He cooed softly. "It was my brothers and I who fed you that ego from the core of your veil. It all came from us."

Rachel took another deep breath, then exhaled with the intention of releasing all the memories of that day in the gym, but she could not.

The old man went on, "Each and every one of you are like children in our womb." He pointed at the churning dark core of clouds circling above the frail woman. "Taking in all that you need to live and grow and advance in this physical world. And just like climbing that rope, our influence is what pushed you to the top of your company too, selling more than anyone else. You are like a goddess in your field, being praised by your colleagues, those that are less than you. Working harder, longer, and doing whatever you have to do in order to exceed all others' expectations of you. All you have, you have because of our influence upon you. Your scholars are correct when they write that nearly all you do spawns from a subconscious push whose source is your ego."

Again, as if he knew what was running through her head, Kaw explained, "That is where your need to be praised comes from, Rachel, as if you were gods yourselves. Just like us, dear."

With those words, a feeling of sadness crept through her. In a subdued tone, Rachel spoke up. "It seems that so many of our natural tendencies are in total conflict with our true spiritual nature."

"That's right. Within your true nature, you would happily give instead of take, you would willingly sacrifice for your fellow man, you would offer unconditional forgiveness to those who have hurt you, and you would love all others in depths that are rare in this fallen world. All the answers of your existence lie within this realm, within a God whose hand continues to reach for you but typically falls short, as it rests idle just above your veil."

The old demon raised his cane up high and passed it in front of the veiled woman. Just then, a beautiful beam of light shone down from above. Its thin luminescence streamed down to the dense outer shell of the woman's veil. It then seemed to spread over it as if searching for a fracture in its surface. Immediately, Rachel felt the warmth radiating from this light, and again was filled with a strange and gentle feeling of peace.

"Is that God's Holy Spirit?" she asked.

"Yes, heaven itself radiates all around her veil, but until her dying day, she'll never know it even exists."

The old man pointed his cane at the woman's skinny arm. It was thin and pale and bruised and, at closer inspection, held a well-marked trail of needle tracks running over the deep vein protruding from her forearm. Titus grinned with pride, almost as if he were taking credit for her obvious drug use.

"Heroin?" Rachel asked.

"Aww…yes!" he cooed. "Ever since she was a child, she has fought to escape a home defined by an alcoholic father and the abuse that spawned from his alcoholism. Initially, painkillers became her answer for muting the deep pain of her father's abuse. But it was not long before she needed more. And now that the barbed hooks of heroin are well-set within her, all of her mind is occupied with is getting her next fix, at whatever cost. If left without it, desperation falls heavy on her being. She feels no different than a dog left for days without water. All of her focus is on her relentless need, no space for anything else. God's serenity and unconditional love have been muted from her heart; muted as if they don't exist at all. Her addiction has created a cycle of perpetual distortion within her veil that grows when she craves it, when she injects it, and again when she hurts others in order to get it." He paused, then stared at Rachel as if he were holding another dark secret from her.

His glare would normally strike fear into her heart, but the light was filling her with a strange peace, and she was becoming more comfortable surrendering herself to it. With intention, she looked into the woman's weary eyes and tried to take in the pain of a life enslaved by addiction. And although Rachel's heart ached for her, there was an obvious safety within the light. An unexpected security filled Rachel as she opened herself, fighting to understand the heart of this stranger.

As if Titus Kaw knew what Rachel was feeling, he turned his eyes toward the light, then passed his cane in front of it, making it vanish in an instant. Without the light, Rachel's insecurities seemed to creep back into her.

"Well then, that's enough of that," the demon said as he licked his dry lips. "The static shell of your veil grows when you envy, judge, hate, or live your lives in complacency, despite the plight of your fellow man. It grows when you withhold forgiveness from those who have hurt you, relentlessly clutching onto your pride as if it were your lifeline. It grows when you become enslaved by us through your insatiable needs, whether it be from a substance introduced into your body or a prideful need introduced into your mind."

Rachel inquired, "I understand being enslaved by alcohol or drug abuse, but what do you mean by 'a prideful need within our own minds?'"

"Your enslavement takes many forms, many of which are not perceived as enslavement at all. It is all based on occupying your minds with self-need. Think about all your pursuits that come so naturally to each of you—being successful in your career, being viewed as beautiful, being respected and admired by others…the list goes on and on. Each one is a very natural endeavor that nearly all of you embark on throughout your life journey, but each possesses engineered snares that can stop your spiritual progression, then enslave you when the unseen mechanics of ego engage."

Rachel interrupted, "There's nothing wrong with excelling at your career, or gaining others' admiration, or even feeling beautiful. I'm not sure I understand."

Kaw explained, "Advancing in your career is an honorable pursuit, but our hidden pitfalls are waiting as each of you climb your ladder of success. Pride, greed, and power from your ambitious endeavors are all hidden traps, baited by your own ego. Each of them has the potential to enslave those who are captivated by their allure, redirecting you away from your honorable pursuit. That's how we do it!"

The old demon went on, "And let's not forget about beauty! It is all part of your human condition, but the chains of vanity await many of the unsuspecting. You must look at the natural needs that drive you—your longing for praise, self-worth, or the need to be desired. Consider how much effort and thought is consumed throughout your lives in your pursuit of physical beauty. What exactly runs through your mind each time you look into a mirror? Yes, it is a perfectly normal drive but if unaware of its source, many become controlled by it. Whether it is in-person or over social media, you crave others' affirmation of your physical appeal and can easily become lost, then blindly driven by that powerful egoic need.

"Many don't put much thought into it, but every one of you seeks the respect and admiration of others. Again, it is a natural part of your human condition. This inner need moves you to compare yourselves to all those who surround you. Then, based on societal expectations, the belief systems within your childhood home, and many other factors, it will dictate your self-portrait, which may or may not be appealing. Although quite natural, it may lead you through our doorway of envy. Oh, the preoccupation within the minds of some, centered around what others possess or have accomplished, clouds their consciousness like smog."

Rachel had no idea how entrenched ego was in nearly every aspect of her life. She turned her head and stared at the woman standing totally unaware within her veil. Rachel's sadness deepened as she focused on the woman's thin arms and legs, her unwashed clothes, and the bruises from the needles that had repeatedly pierced her arms. The thought of her selling herself to feed the addiction that she was powerless over drew a feeling of sincere sadness and empathy from deep within her. She glanced over at Kaw, only to find him gazing at the woman with pride. His obvious satisfaction from her frail, needy condition pierced her heart like a spike.

Rachel raised her voice. "And what about her? She is physically addicted to heroin. Where's the free will in that?"

The old man grinned, knowing Rachel was on the verge of understanding. "I didn't stick her with that needle, my dear. But I must say,

I do remember the first time it pierced her skin...aww!" He cooed again, clearly filled with perverse pleasure from memories of the first time the woman had injected heroin into her veins. "There was such power within it...the birth of lies, theft, sex work, and absolute need—enslavement to us through her physical addiction. The needle is one of our many tools—tools to control you, tools to grow more powerful, tools to put your God in pain. That junkie is blinded from anything beyond her own insatiable needs. She reminds me of you, Rachel. The only difference is your drug of choice. Your thirst for money, power, and praise is just as desperate as hers is for heroin. Trust me, you are more alike than you care to know."

Anger and disgust grew within her as she considered their parallel.

He's an animal, she thought.

Rachel stepped closer to the fragile woman and studied the strange veil that surrounded her. The bright light that came from her blinding static shell had softened now, so she was able to examine it without hurting her eyes. The electric pixels and black band of clouds still covered the woman, but the deafening noise was now gone. She surveyed the pixels, which appeared thick and alive, dancing all around the woman as she stood perfectly still within her veil. She turned her attention toward the ring of black clouds that slowly circled above the stranger, focusing on the density of the frightening band.

Rachel inquired, "I know you said that each of us creates our own distortion in our minds, which forms the static shell of our spiritual veil. Its density is determined by each of us individually, through the choices we make and our state of mind. But what about our veil's dark inner core? I know its body is made up of the influence of ego, but who determines its density? Who dictates the degree to which darkness influences each of our consciousnesses? Who determines the size of our veil's core?"

The old demon paused, holding his cane with both hands behind his back, then paced in a wide circle pondering for a moment before he spoke. "When all the light or darkness that is propagated within this world gathers high above and rains down upon each of you, it is the dark inner core of your spiritual veil that absorbs it. So, to answer your question, your world cumulatively determines the degree of egoic influence upon all your minds. The mind of the world is no different than the mind of the individual. It reaps what it sows.

"Consider the billions of thoughts created by billions of people every second of every day, each fluctuating the influence of ego upon your minds. One might initially think that your minds would be in a constant state of flux or turmoil from this dynamic external influence, but the reality is a very gradual, nearly undetectable, hardening or softening of all hearts over the centuries. Now, over the course of history there have been sweeping global movements of darkness, like the world wars, or of light, like the flower power or Civil Rights movements in the late sixties. But in general, from your individual perspective, the shift within has been virtually undetectable."

Rachel interrupted, "But if the influence of ego on each of us is dictated by the rest of the world, wouldn't that mean that we don't really have free will at all?"

"No, Rachel. As I have explained, even though each of you is continuously influenced by our parasitic seeds of ego, what you create in your mind can never be imposed upon you. Although each of your propensity to choose may be compromised by external influences, your free will is not dictated by the light or darkness that falls upon you. Beyond all influence, the choice of what you create in your mind and how you choose to live your life will always remain yours."

Rachel's mind immediately whirled, "So, if our whole world could find a way to come together in the spirit of love, then we could actually eliminate ego from all of us?"

"Yes, my dear. And if you could, each of you would finally awaken from the dream of this world. And with that awakening, God's inspiration would bloom vividly within each of your hearts. Do you understand?"

"Yes, I believe I do."

Kaw went on. "Over the millennia, through a slow global awakening, the dark inner core of all souls' spiritual veils have diminished. The seeds of ego that are sown into your minds have grown sparse. With less seeds to flourish, what you create in your individual minds has become less ego-centric. This has led to a worldwide dissipation of distortion around your minds, and marks the evolution of human consciousness. For thousands of years this process has slowly been transpiring, all the while weakening our influence. You do see what the inner core of your veil really is, don't you, Rachel?"

The old demon continued without giving her a chance to respond. "It is God's gauge for the evolving consciousness of mankind. It is the actual meter that conveys if the human race is moving toward its true home, or further from it."

Frustrated, Rachel retorted. "But you told me that this world was so lost and distracted that your presence here isn't even needed. If our consciousness has been evolving for thousands of years and ego is diminishing within each of us, then wouldn't we be less distracted and self-occupied, and instead more loving?"

"Yes. For thousands of years, mankind's consciousness has been evolving, but with the recent advances in technology, your gadgets have you in…how can I put this? Well, in somewhat of a trance. As a result, the distortion in your static shells have grown. And although this advanced technology has led to enormous global strides in industry, medicine, and many other facets of your society, it has also become an instrument of great distraction and isolation. Many use it to promote division and hatred. Hatred, which has spread like wildfire! By means of your gadgets, racial, political, and societal divides have begun to grow again. With their resurrection, my brothers' and my power are finally beginning to thrive as they once did. We are doing all we can to turn the tables back in our favor. But we need to exploit each one of you by whatever means possible. Whether it comes from your cell phone or a needle in your arm makes little difference to us."

Considering the demon's claims about our society's trance sent her mind reeling back to her family. Rachel's mind returned to her daughter Terra and how she used social media to inflict pain on Mary Katherine and also isolate herself from the rest of the world by means of her phone and headphones. She then looked inward at all the time she spent on her laptop while her daughters stared at their own screens in total silence; the three of them preoccupied by their electronic devices hour upon hour, night upon night. It soon became clear to her that the demon's words were true. Her family had fallen into a deep trance without ever being aware of it.

In that moment of contemplation she looked deeper within herself. Beyond the distraction from her electronic devices, she considered all the different ways that she had unknowingly allowed darkness to infiltrate her life, shielding God's light from her heart. "How could I go through my whole life without ever feeling his love? How could I never know that God has been with me all along?"

Kaw stared at her in thought, then offered, "Do you really want to know?"

Without hesitation, she responded, "Yes, I do."

"Be careful what you ask for." He followed with a dark chuckle. "Forgive me if this strikes you as a bit insensitive but try to imagine placing an infant in a locked cage at the very moment they were born. Can you picture that, Rachel—an infant in a cage?"

She scowled in silence at the awful image that came into her mind.

"Now imagine if I were to place that cage in a dark cave where not a flicker of light was able to penetrate."

"You're sick!" Rachel asserted.

Titus continued as if he didn't hear her at all. "The temperatures and conditions of the cave were narrowly suitable to sustain life. Now, imagine if this child was given food and water each day, but only enough to keep them alive as they grew, day after day, year after year."

Rachel's stomach turned, envisioning a child left alone with no one to care for them in such horrific conditions.

The old man grinned at her obvious displeasure. "Well, as long as their food and water were provided each day, that child would live out their life, never knowing that anything else even existed beyond the darkness of their cave. They would perceive their cage as the entire world. They would never know that an unimaginable world of color, life, and beauty—a world of light and love—existed just beyond the mouth of their cave."

The demon paused for a moment, knowing now that Rachel was intentionally taking in the pain of the caged child, internalizing it, as she was intended to. He could see her accepting the isolation of a life lived alone, envisioning the constant darkness year after year, feeling the hollowness of a whole life that was reduced to simply existing, nothing more. He watched her closely, staring into her eyes before cutting her with the truth.

"Don't you see, my dear…that child is you."

With the demon's words, a cold sweat fell upon her. Rachel stood silent, considering that from her birth until now, she had been intentionally blinded from the beauty that existed within the accessible love of a living God. A world filled with light, and security, and a deeper love than she had ever known. A life filled with purpose, richer and more beautiful than she could ever imagine. Rachel's heart suddenly began to feel like a stone, heavy and dense. Her blood pulsed through it, but it now seemed to run cold as it moved through her veins.

The demon broke out into dark, soft laughter, adding, "After all of these years, I can see that you're finally beginning to feel our bars around you. The funny thing is, Rachel, the key that unlocks your cage has been lying at your feet throughout your entire life. As long as we keep the light of God from penetrating your veil, then you will live out your existence within this realm, *nearly* content, never knowing what actually exists just beyond it. Trust me when I tell you that I have personally made sure that the eyes of your soul have never seen the true light outside of the cave in which you live."

His power grew as he looked into her pain-filled eyes.

Rachel suddenly felt very alone, understanding that the monster in front of her was speaking the truth.

Rachel turned her eyes back to the drug addict, then asked, as if she were trying to convince herself, "So God feels her desperation…God feels all of her pain?"

The old man responded, "Yes, my dear, he's fighting to reach her. He's speaking to her through her own heart at this very moment. He's letting her know that he's walking with her through the darkness of her life, feeling all that she feels. He's telling her how beautiful she is…how perfect she is…and how deeply he loves her, despite what she has done and the struggles she faces. He's telling her that from the depths of his soul, he understands the influence we have on her and that he forgives her for all the choices she has made. He wants her to know how much he loves her, just as she is, at this very moment."

As Rachel sympathetically gazed into the weary eyes of Honey Love, Titus turned and walked in the direction of the old piano, which sat near the south wall of the roof. Rachel hated him and felt it deep within her as he walked away. The old man moved with poise as he approached the piano. He slid the bench out, then took off his derby and hung it on the top of his cane, carefully propping it against the piano's side. He sat down, set his eyes on the piano keys, then began to softly play a beautiful piece from one of Mozart's symphonies.

His music filled the air. It was soft and soothing, and it was truly beautiful, but instead of opening Rachel's heart to a short moment of peace, the notes only illuminated the insidious deceit that he used to perpetuate his darkness throughout the world. She felt unnerved by his beautiful music and acted as if she was unaffected, but as he played on, Titus felt her truth within him.

Rachel turned from Kaw, then took several steps toward the three people standing idle at the edge of the rooftop. The woman's static veil continued to dance all around her, dimly shining, with only a subtle hum coming from it now. As the old demon played on, Rachel considered his words about ego and how so many 'natural' tendencies spawn from it. She turned her eyes to the doctor who stood silent as he stared off into the distance as if she wasn't even there. Rachel understood the thick veil surrounding the drug addict. As the demon said, she built that great barrier over many years of lying, stealing, and selling herself, not to mention the distortion brought on by her heroin addiction.

But a doctor? Rachel wondered.

As she studied this well-to-do man whose life's work has been saving people's lives, she began to wonder what his veil would look like. Considering how much good he has done, initially she believed his veil would be quite thin, but at the same time, he clearly exuded signs of arrogance, which had been obvious the moment Rachel had met him years ago.

How clear would God's word be to him? she thought to herself.

She stared at him, then took several steps backward to gain a wider perspective. She focused on all of his physical details, which seemed to be perfect. His suit was tailored and looked very expensive. His polished leather shoes gleamed as they reflected the softened light that still glowed from the woman's veil. All he wore appeared to be custom cut and freshly pressed. Rachel gazed into his eyes, which were clear and brown, as they stared intensely across the rooftop. His skin was tanned, and his hair looked as if he had just left the salon. What seemed to strike Rachel more than anything was the expression he held. Standing there, he embodied a perceived strength that he carried through his piercing eyes. As she studied this man, she wondered what was running through his mind at that very moment.

The demon's soft music played on as she unknowingly stepped back into a tall, dark shadow that was cast behind her. With that, the back of her head and shoulders jarred, striking something solid. Shocked, she turned to find the towering demon standing behind her. He glared down upon her, his eyes filled with evil intention. Rachel's heart dropped again when she glanced back at the old piano, which continued playing Mozart's beautiful piece all by itself. Her mind bent with fear and confusion.

The old demon laughed as he felt the fear radiating from her heart. He raised his cane up high and slammed it back into the asphalt rooftop. *Crack!*

It was directly followed by the deafening sound of white noise and the now-familiar painful ping of steel on steel that cut into her ears. With her eyes still fixed on the demon, Rachel peripherally saw a blinding light arc from behind her, illuminating all the demon's dark features. She immediately covered both of her ears and squinted as she turned her head toward the surgeon. Just like the woman, he stood surrounded by his own spiritual veil, just as big, blinding, and ear-piercing as the addict's.

Rachel screamed at the demon, "Make it stop! Please!"

Kaw stood silent, staring down at her.

She cried out again, "I understand! It's his ego, his arrogance…I understand. My ears…make it stop!"

Unaffected by her plea, he stood high above her with a cold indifference to her suffering. Her eardrums rang from the sound of the all-encompassing static and felt pierced with each strike of steel onto steel. She glanced up at him one last time before dropping to the rooftop in agony. The bright light blinded her as the air screamed with the deafening chaos of the moment.

Rachel lay crumpled on the rooftop, fighting to retreat within herself as she curled up at his feet in a fetal position. She shut her eyes tight and cupped both hands over her ears with all the force she could muster. Her eyes welled up as she began to openly sob again. Tears fought through her clenched eyelids as the eerily illuminated demon watched her suffer.

Then, *crack!* As fast as it came, the deafening noise fell to a subtle hum. As the blinding light dimmed to a soft glow, Rachel could see a large veil of electric pixels and a swirling band of dark clouds circling the crown of the doctor's head, just as it had with the drug addict.

In a fragile state, she stared up at his surreal veil, then straightened her legs out of her fetal position. Disheveled from her trauma, Rachel swayed a bit as she fought to sit upright. It felt as if she were on a boat that rocked in slow, rolling waves. Clear trails of tears were now obvious on her face, their paths well-marked by her running mascara.

The demon's expression grew angrier as he intensely stared down over her. "This man is one of the elite in his field, just like you. And just like you, he knows it!" His voice was sharp and cutting.

Rachel knew he was talking but heard only muffled garble over the loud tone that now carried throughout both of her ears.

Dear God, help me! she thought.

It was obvious that Titus Kaw had no reservations about hurting her if it would help him in his own endeavors. The fear of more pain inflicted upon her filled her mind now. She knew that no compassion existed within this monster; and though she listened to the words he spoke, in the back of her mind, she began to consider a means of escape before she was forced to endure further pain. She wiped more tears from her face, then slowly straightened herself to an upright sitting position at his feet.

He continued with total disregard to her fragile state.

"Oh, yes, you are both my children, that is a certainty. So, to answer your question, yes, vanity does blind. It blinds the hearts of every one of you to one degree or another." The old demon's emotions seemed to grow as he continued. "You and the good doctor are just two of the billions who praise me through praising yourselves. Just like you, he is a leader in his field, very wealthy, a true success! Both of you are driven by similar motives, too; money and the perceived power that it brings you. The only difference separating you is the origin of your drive. Yours comes from a sense of providing for your family, a dictating need you developed as a child. Anything to keep them out of the Lower 10, isn't that right, Rachel? The doctor's, on the other hand, comes from his perception of power from being regarded as the top surgeon in his field, again stemming from his youth, predominantly from his father's influence."

The demon's eyes suddenly burned with hatred, as an angrier tone came upon him.

"The truth is, you both have about the same depth as a couple of pencil-drawn stick figures, mindlessly scratched onto a sheet of notebook paper. Both dimensionally challenged, both feeding us through your uncultivated perceptions. To you, all that exists is what you see, what you can touch, and what you can buy—the trophies of your achievements!"

His angry tone continued to escalate.

"Yes, that is precisely what you are, two stick figures, bumping into each other as you scurry around, fighting to climb higher and higher up your ladders of success, which really are nothing more than two expendable sheets of notebook paper. Line by line by line, you both climb, stepping on all others as you move upwards." He leaned down closer to Rachel, so she knew his words were directed at her. "By whatever means necessary! Oh, and with every line you climb, you pause for just a moment, looking down at all those whom you've surpassed, those who are 'less' than you, pushing out your chests, feeling praised and sublime in your *grand* advancements within your paper worlds!"

The demon's volatile anger rose like loud steel clanks from a slow-climbing roller coaster nearing its peak.

"Oh yes, within your fields, everyone revels at what remarkable successes you both are. You truly have it *all* figured out, haven't you?"

He paused for a moment, then continued, staring at the doctor. "Do you believe he owns a jet airplane? He does, he pilots it too. You should feel the massive wave of ego that rolls from his heart like a tsunami each time he flies to his winter home in Miami Beach. Soaring high above you all, looking down on creation as if he were God himself."

Still shaken, Rachel sat broken on the rooftop at Kaw's feet. Random glancing thoughts now passed in and out of her mind as she fought to comprehend the demon's words and all that was happening. Unable to escape the long steady tone within her ears, she suddenly envisioned the surgeon's heart monitor emitting a similar sound, a single continuous tone as some unknown patient's life slipped away in his operating room.

Pockets of Kaw's rant became more and more distinguishable with the demon's elevated tone.

"All of you and the doctor's acquired wealth—the planes, and the cars, and the jewelry, and the designer clothes, and the lavish homes that so many envy—actually amounts to nothing more than a pencil-drawn hat that each of you wear as you perch on the top line of your paper world. Gazing down at all those who are less than you, you are both as close to your own perverse perceptions of a God as you could possibly be!"

The old man turned from her and walked toward the piano again. Then, with a deep exhale, he seemed to slowly escape from his own rant. After staring at Rachel in silence for more than a moment, he spoke in a softer tone as he casually leaned against the piano.

"His reputation is spreading across the globe, you know? They say his ideas are groundbreaking. His survival percentages are as impressive as any other brain surgeons in the country, and yet his spiritual veil seems to grow every day. Dr. Pierson's father was a hard man. Just like Sam, he was an accomplished surgeon at the top of his field. Dr. Dwight Pierson had high expectations for his only son and was not a man to settle for anything less. He prodded Sam, relentlessly imposing his will on the boy ever since he was a child. His father did not only push him toward his present vocation but molded his perception of the world around him. You see, Sam's dad was a bit 'old school' in his way of looking at others who were different than him. Let's just say he had certain preconceptions of those whose skin was darker than his own.

"It used to bother Sam's mother whenever she would hear her husband making derogatory comments about African Americans, or Jewish people, or Mexicans, or Muslims, or anyone else who did not fit into his narrow perception of a 'true' American. Sam's father believed that the United States of America was built by and truly belonged to the hard-working White Americans who made this country great. As a child, Sam found it endearing, like a secret joke that he and his father would share. When they would walk past a Black man or woman, inevitably, under his breath, Sam's dad would mockingly speak in an uneducated Southern voice to his son. They'd both chuckle a bit, sharing a rare moment of comradery, which was nearly void in their otherwise sterile relationship."

Rachel was disgusted by the demon's casual description of this bigot. Through his demeanor, it seemed to Rachel that Titus Kaw viewed racism as a simple tool to feed his power and influence the world, nothing more.

The demon continued, "Sam's mom would just roll her eyes, half-heartedly scolding them both, writing it off to the two of them acting naughty together. If the person was Jewish, his comments would center around them hoarding their money; if they were Muslim, they were presumed to be terrorists; and if they were Mexican, it was about them being drug dealers or freeloaders, sucking off the teat of hard-working Americans like him. To young Sam, it was a moment when his father wasn't putting him down or pushing him to work harder or be better at whatever it was that he happened to be doing at that moment. It was simply a father joking with his son, nothing more. A lighthearted bonding that Sam desperately craved, and despite his father's emotional neglect, it presented a rare moment of perceived kinship that Sam embraced.

"To Sam's father, though, it was different. He was instilling a belief system within his son that would forever separate him from others, defining them by their race, religion, or class. Yes, his father laid a strong foundation for the walls that my brothers and I would continue to build within Sam's heart, those same walls that now bind his preconceptions of the ethnically diverse as a strong part of his identity."

"One of the primary goals of darkness is to divide you by whatever means possible, Rachel. That's what my brothers and I do. We look for solid ground to build our walls, with the sole purpose of dividing you from one another. Then, trowel by trowel, we build them as tall and as wide as we can. After each is established, they inevitably feed your spiritual veils, creating more distortion between God's word and your consciousness, all the while increasing our power and our influence over this world. If you were to break any of our walls down to their smallest unit, as you may expect, it would be ego."

"In the doctor's case, he was taught to fear those who were different from him. His father instilled in Sam a perceived fear of what 'others' may take from him and this country. Like so many walls that my brothers and I build, the true reality may be very different from the picture that is painted. The beauty of it is, the reality behind the fear does not have to actually exist to give birth to it, only the perception."

Although Rachel's head still pounded from her trauma, she fought to overcome the pain as she pondered Kaw's words.

"Now let's look at you, my dear. Although you and the doctor both fight for the same wealth and the perceived power it brings you, the source of your division is a bit different. Like the doctor, we began laying your walls at a young age...fifth grade, I believe." An insincere smile came over his face. "You remember your old neighborhood, don't you, Rachel? Do you remember how you felt the first time one of your schoolmates called you a farmer, then belittled your father, referring to him as nothing more than a drunk fieldhand?"

The demon's words brought surprisingly vivid memories of that specific moment back to Rachel, and although nearly thirty years had passed, her heart began to burn with the same flame that she had felt as an innocent fifth grader.

The demon continued, "It was Timmy Watson, I believe. He was a mean little bastard, who not so ironically, was raised by another mean little bastard, Larry Watson, his father. Where do you think that young boy's judgement came from? His slashing accusations were a direct result of the walls my brothers and I built within his heart. That particular wall separated you by class, where your house was, and by what your father did for a living. Timmy's father had always told his son to stay away from the Lower 10. He told him only 'seasonals' lived there, and they were nothing more than a bunch of drunk migrants. He told his son that you were all the same, and Timmy wasn't to play anywhere near that part of the neighborhood."

In defense, Rachel spoke up. "That was a lie! My father rarely drank. He ran the crew and was a good man. In all the years I lived there, I only remember one seasonal worker that caused any problems when he drank—one!"

The old man scratched his chin in thought, then slowly replied, "Oh, yes, I believe Bender was his name."

Rachel responded, "Yes. His daughter and I were friends, but I wasn't allowed to go over to their house because of her father's drinking. Throughout my childhood in the Lower 10, I swear he was the only seasonal worker that had an obvious problem with alcohol. I never knew why Timmy spread those lies about my father. My dad was a great man with a good heart."

"Well, like I said before, whether it is truth or lies that are ingrained in your hearts makes little difference to us. If solid ground is prepared, we will happily build on it. Our walls are built to cast shadows of judgement and fear on both sides, whether it is justified or not—and you, Rachel, still live within yours. To this day, that same shadow that carried your fear of being perceived as second-class fuels your drive for the finer things in life. The seed of fear was sown into your young heart, which prepared you with a solid foundation for us to build our walls, the same walls that still stand strong today. You still fear being perceived as less than others. It's our influence that relentlessly drives you day and night. It drives you to excel as a salesperson, and whether you know it or not, it drives your judgement of those who have less than you."

Rachel scowled in defiance at his claims but said nothing.

Kaw continued, "Now, many who have felt the pain of oppression will go out of their way to never cast judgement on those who stand in the shoes that they once wore. But you were cut deeply, weren't you? You had to separate yourself from those fieldhands and all others who were less than you. You had no choice, Rachel. It was a matter of self-preservation. You are still fighting to get out of the Lower 10, aren't you, my dear? And although you may not even be aware of it, through the lens of our veil, you continue to cast judgement and separate yourself from those who you perceive as less than you."

Lost in thought, it appeared that Rachel's hard shell was beginning to crack. She seemed to momentarily consider the demon's claims about the hidden origins of her deep unspoken fears, but then quickly retorted, "I work hard for the sake of my family. *They* are the reason I push myself day and night!"

"Oh, I am very aware that your family has been your justification for nearly everything you do. What a noble cause…" He paused with a glare. "Just like the doctor's father grooming his son for his own good? Or like that mean little sod's father protecting his family by keeping them away from all of you in the Lower 10? You're all *so* righteous, doing it for the sake of your families! Well, let me tell you, Rachel, your claims of righteousness in providing for your families are a tad flawed."

Rachel rebutted with angry defiance, "Don't try to tell me that I don't do all that I can for my family. My only job is to love and provide for them, and that's what I've always done!"

"*Au contraire*, my dear. Your job is to love all who surround you, not only your family. Here's a newsflash for you—within your own hearts, many of you view your family as an extension of yourselves. Even down to their genetic makeup, they are a part of you, a part of your very being, physically and emotionally. Now I'm not saying that you don't love them or that some of your drive is not motivated by your love for them. But millions only focus their true unconditional love on those within their own families. Deep inside, many feel that their need to sacrifice for others ends at the threshold of their own front door. As long as you have loved and provided for your family, then you have lived your life well, right? Ha!

"Don't you see, Rachel, God designed this physical world, but we manipulate it to perpetuate our own strength. Your whole world is intentionally snared in our engineered chaos. Within it lies exponential division in all of your lives. And believe me when I tell you that there is absolutely no difference between the walls that we build within your hearts and the walls that separate your ghettos from your suburbs. Each begins with a perceived fear of how the people on the other side may take something from you. This remains true for any division within this world, whether between Blacks and Whites, Asians or Hispanics. No races are immune.

"We sew your political affiliation, whether it be Democrat or Republican, so deeply into the fabric of your identities that when someone denounces your party, you feel as though they are denouncing you yourself. This perpetual divide fractures your entire country, and my brothers and I grow more powerful from your divide. Do you actually believe that your congressmen and senators truthfully want to unify your country? Most are so preoccupied with their own position and power within their party that they'll turn away from anything that may compromise either of them, closing their eyes and shutting their mouths as if they were men and women with no faces at all. They are no different than my brothers and me. Their true power lies within your division. Once they have sewn their political affiliation into the fabric of your identity, you are as vulnerable as a marionette, manipulated by your political leaders, making you dance with the tug of their strings. These are the men and women—the politicians— who create not only your political boundaries, but your economic, social, and moral boundaries too?" The old demon burst out laughing. "And you wonder how darkness flourishes. God forbid if your individual beliefs cross over their political lines!

"But we don't only divide you politically, we build our walls between your religions, moving you to judge faiths other than your own in the so-called name of your God. We influence the divide between genders, encouraging disparagement, judgment, and conflict between men, women, and those who challenge those categories. We feed the fear, birthed from sexual orientation, moving those who are straight to judge those who are gay. Our walls separate the thin from the obese and the beautiful from the ordinary. We separate class through possessions, income, and location of your homes. We build walls between the haves and have-nots, moving you toward self-concern when the deep struggles of others are easily within your reach. Our walls are built between generations, separating parents from their children, and within our schools, separating youth by their perceived abilities and intelligence. Wherever diversity exists within your physical world, you can be assured that through our influence, our walls are being built. We encourage the feelings of superiority within each of you, and we raise you up glorifying your own righteousness with those who live within your walls, whatever they may be. We manipulate you through the illusion of your separateness while God fights to unite you all as one. Our influence infiltrates every aspect of your lives. Not even your Holy Bible is immune from our division!"

After a moment, Rachel asked, "How could the Holy Bible build walls, or divide people? You've been telling me it was written to encourage love for all who surround us."

The demon's eyes rolled back in his head, then reappeared more demonic than they were just moments ago. He began to walk across the rooftop nervously, as if he were anxious to explain.

"Yes, in the context of its totality, your Holy Bible is the written representation of God's absolute love. But we have pushed men to dissect its words, carving them up and removing them from their intended context for the sole intention of preaching hatred."

A smile came to the demon's face as he continued. "It was approaching midnight on October 16th, 1915, when Methodist preacher William Joseph Simmons and more than a dozen other men climbed Stone Mountain in Georgia. They built a makeshift altar, then buried a large wooden cross in the ground. Circling it, they set fire to the cross. On that dark night, each of the men took an oath of allegiance to the 'invisible empire.' As they watched it burn, Simmons, a man of God, crowned himself the second Grand Wizard, thereby resurrecting the Ku Klux Klan."

With those words, Rachel's skin crawled. "The leader of the KKK was a preacher?" she asked in disbelief.

"Oh yes, he was, my dear. Beneath their makeshift altar, glowing beneath the flames of their burning cross, they laid a U.S. flag, a sword, and the Holy Bible. These were the instruments of their division. Klansmen wore white robes to signify purity, burned crosses to signify the light of Christ, and carefully extracted scripture from its original context in the Bible to preach White supremacy, racism, and hatred. By the early 1920's, the Klan had spread like a virus throughout your country."

"That's petrifying. I had no idea they used Christianity to justify their racism."

"Simmons capitalized on the wave of White supremacy that had been mounting since earlier that same year, when movie director D.W. Griffith released *The Birth of a Nation* into U.S. theaters. The film infiltrated the psyche of many Americans, portraying the Klan as righteous patriots and villainizing Black people as vicious immigrants. The director sought to tap into Americans' greatest fear: the attack and violation of American families by these ruthless Black invaders. The seeds of bigotry had been sown throughout the nation, and Simmons did all that he could to reap its bounty.

"Not all Klansmen were ready to join their cause, though. Many of them were intentionally groomed into what the preacher had hoped they'd become. William Simmons systematically converted small-town shopkeepers, housewives, businessmen, politicians, and even clergy into something much darker than they could have ever imagined. He knew how to manipulate them through the vulnerabilities in their self-perceptions as good and moral people. He moved each of them through the mechanics of their own human nature. He exploited them through his preaching, justifying the Klan's cause, no matter how morally reprehensible.

"Simmons began by endorsing like-minded individuals, helping them to advance into positions of power. He recruited preachers with similar ideals, then helped place them in churches, marketing them as loving shepherds of Christian faith. Many of these preachers were Klansmen themselves. Their goal was to instill a deep-seated fear within their congregation that the immigration of non-Whites and changing attitudes would overthrow their White Protestant social dominance.

"To many people, their sermons seemed to be honorable, preaching ideals that were shared by so many Americans—a strong and uncompromising patriotism for America and an equally unbending Christian pursuit, guided by the Lord above. They preached words of charity, kindness, and love but all the while openly supported the efforts of the Ku Klux Klan. The Klansmen promoted themselves as *good* Americans who lived selfless lives, and through their undying Christian loyalty, followed the word of God. They defined themselves as a fraternity of White Christians whose purpose was to capitalize on love and to promote goodwill and the spirit of kindness…but also to strike without mercy or compromise the pernicious foreign influences that undermine liberty and seek to dominate American institutions.

"William Joseph Simmons gained widespread support for the virtuous causes of Christianity and country, but then redefined each of them to support his own dark agenda, creating his own army that grew into the resurrected Ku Klux Klan. Most certainly, the Grand Wizard was aware of the power he held by manipulating his followers' identities as patriotic Americans, convincing them that their uncompromised support would be a righteous pursuit. He understood that by promoting the virtues of both Christianity and love of country, he could gain a widespread following. He encouraged them as vital and integral virtues of every good Christian parishioner. Then, he deceitfully incorporated the Klan's agenda as if it were God's agenda, justifying their intentions as honorable in the pursuit of making America the great country it was intended to be. So ultimately, in the mind of the parishioner, if someone was to denounce the KKK, they would be denouncing Christianity and America too. Because of the distorted views that were diabolically woven into their identities, if the Klan were denounced, the parishioners felt as if they were being denounced as well. You see, White supremacy flourished through the intentionally distorted vehicle of self-identity.

"By the time their carnage had ended, the KKK had slaughtered over four thousand African Americans who were viewed as threats to our country in the eyes of the Klan. The Klan would act as judge, jury, and executioner as their crowds would storm the unsuspecting man's home. Then, by the light of a dozen torches, they would hold court in the victim's front yard, sentencing the innocent to death in front of his wife and children. Many had been publicly tortured, then lynched as the crowds of self-proclaimed patriotic Christians cheered them on. It was not uncommon for the victims to be hanged, set on fire, then dismembered. Upon their slaughter, the murderous Klansmen would then distribute the innocent men's body parts, so each 'patriot' could depart with a memento. The victims' bones became trophies for the Klan's deeds, to later display in their homes or businesses as testaments to their true commitment to God and to the United States of America.

"Griffith and Simmons were not alone in promoting our darkness though. The leader of your country, Woodrow Wilson, legitimized their endeavors by welcoming a personal screening of *The Birth of a Nation* into the White House. After viewing the movie, President Wilson gave credence to their dark agenda with two simple sentences: 'It's like writing history with lightning. My only regret is that it is all so terribly true.' His words rang through every household in America, and although he did not overtly proclaim that he supported the KKK, his dog whistle sounded clear and loud to so many Americans, foremost to the members of the Klan. That, Rachel, is what true darkness does. It hides like a wolf in sheep's clothing, deceiving men through its cloak of righteousness, offering false cause of the pain, fear, and anger that inevitably exists in each of your vulnerable lives. It tricks the unsuspecting into promoting and feeding it, like raw meat to an insatiable wild beast. The seeds of inequality, hatred, and greed were sown into the soil of this nation at its birth, and their bitter fruit has since been bountiful in the capital.

"After the president's statement, darkness bloomed in the hearts of millions of Americans who had always looked to their leader for guidance in the pursuit of national prosperity. As a result of the president's inferred endorsement, the embrace of White supremacy surged through the hearts of many Americans. And be assured, as it did, the power within our collective influence surged with it. Even the American flag—the same flag that represented freedom, equality, and justice for all—seemed to be redefined through your leader's shadowed praise. Hatred and racism had been legitimized globally from the highest political seat in your land, and we grew stronger from it."

Rachel was shocked at how insidious and cunning the demon's darkness really was.

"I can't believe the President of the United States would openly endorse hatred."

Titus continued, "Many Americans stood shocked as well. It seemed unfathomable how the president and so many other seemingly good people could support such immoral and inequitable standards for American citizens. So, to many Americans, the flag suddenly stood for something much less than it was intended. If orchestrated properly, that is what each one of you good people are capable of. And trust me when I tell you, if we moved you to support the unthinkable before, we will move you to support the unthinkable again. You see, the tragic events throughout history will continue to reoccur until those within your world have truly learned the lessons that exist within each of them."

Rachel was filled with anguish. She sat in silence for a while before she spoke.

"My heart's broken for all those innocent people. Their families watched as they were tortured, then murdered in front of them, simply because of the color of their skin—and the president of the United States subtly endorsed the murders. But on the other hand, I can see why so many Americans were confused. And all those parishioners, trusting their spiritual leaders to decipher the word of God for them, only to have it twisted to advance hatred through their own dark agenda."

Kaw spoke up. "Regardless of denomination, or even religion for that matter, if your moral leader does not preach absolute love for all men and women, then they do not preach the truly inspired word of God. And considering the overwhelming influence we have on each of you, if they do not preach the inspired word of God, then they most definitely are preaching *our* word.

"Every leader carries with them an unthinkable responsibility. God intends that each religious leader continually engages in self-examination of their own conscience. They are intended to regularly reevaluate their true surrender to God, searching for his will. Each of them are men and women just like you, prone as you are to ego and all influences that come from it. From high on their platforms, many spiritual leaders fall into our trap of self-righteousness and judgment of others. Within your clergy's preaching, they may bestow their own will onto their congregation as if it were the will of God. This is a direct result of our influence on them, not God's. Judgement is intended to be reserved for God and God alone, no others."

Rachel asked, "Well, what about all the clergy who have moral intentions? They must find themselves judging certain members within their congregation. That would seem to be part of their role as the leader of their church, wouldn't it? How can they have differing opinions from their congregation without judging them? Wouldn't they go hand in hand?"

"When you begin by truly loving the one next to you in the way you are intended—with no judgment, only unconditional love and forgiveness—then, and only then will an illumination begin to shine within your heart, lighting the clear path you are intended to walk. When you begin by judging others, then your spiritual veil grows, dimming your inner light and darkening God's path. At that point, all guidance from above is lost as our influence of self takes over. When this occurs, judgment and self-righteousness grow stronger, so regardless of the validity of your spiritual leader's opinion, at that point it becomes misguided and quite often convoluted through the influence of ego upon them.

"You see, Rachel, you are intended to pass through God's doorway of love first…and within it, possess a truly inspired concern for whoever stands beside you. You are intended to form your opinions from a heart that is first driven by a deeper love, even if you are divided by your beliefs. You are to love them first, understanding our influence on them, the influence of ego and judgement and the perceived strength within them. Love them first, despite what they are saying and how they are saying it to you. Consider their words with an open heart. Try to understand why they feel as they do without building a wall of judgement first. With absolute intention, consider how each of us tie our own beliefs to our identity. Pause within your understanding that through your own ego and strong sense of self, you may feel attacked when another speaks from an opposing position. *Love them first,* then breathe deeply, asking for God's guidance in hopes of forming an inspired opinion before you speak.

"You are absolutely entitled to your opposing opinions, but they are intended to be formed through the guidance of your Lord. And again, all judgment should be reserved for him alone, not you. My brothers and I get credit for all motivation beyond that. We are the masons of all walls within your hearts and ultimately within your world. And regardless of your perceived intentions, they push each of you further from God's healing Spirit, separating you from his guidance when his true intention is to unify your entire world through the doorway of his will. When you love others in the way you are intended to, God's divine bridge will emerge within your hearts and will span even your greatest divides. God fights to unite all diversities through his essence…his essence which is love."

Rachel kept running the words 'love them first' through her mind. "I know it sounds simplistic, but love really is the answer to so many of the conflicts that exist in this world, isn't it?"

Kaw corrected her, "Love is the answer to them all. Most are just too blinded to understand its simplicity."

Within Rachel, Kaw's words brought an unexpected hope for this world, at a time when so much darkness seemed to dominate. As she embraced it, she stared off across the rooftop. Her heart suddenly lurched at an unexpected sight. At the opposite end of the rooftop, beyond where the piano sat, the weathered face of a rusted door caught Rachel's eye. Although the light of hope still lingered within her, Rachel's mind shifted to her potential means of escape before any more trauma fell upon her.

The battered door appeared to lead down to a stairwell, as its exterior brick walls tapered down below the asphalt roofline. It had one cracked window in it, which was covered with a weathered steel grate. As not to bring attention to her potential means of egress, Rachel quickly drew her eyes back to the old man who strolled across the rooftop in the opposite direction.

Titus Kaw slowly walked toward the three strangers again, who were still standing side by side in their trance. He casually hummed to himself as he approached. He was now a fair distance from Rachel and seemed to be focusing on the Hispanic stranger. Rachel watched as Kaw pointed his cane at the man. Then, as if in response to the demon's gesture, the man reached down to his wrist and removed an elastic band that was wrapped around it.

With both hands, he pulled his long salt-and-pepper hair back into a loose ponytail, cinching it with the hair band. He lifted his chin and stared over the rooftop again, toward the horizon. Now, with his hair pulled back, Rachel caught her first unobstructed view of the man's face. Something about his eyes looked familiar to her. Drawn by them, she began to take slow steps closer to the stranger. As she approached, she noticed something on his cheek. She squinted her eyes to focus, trying to make out what it was. Until then, it had been covered by his long hair, but now was in clear view. Time seemed to stop as she realized that it was a small faded blue teardrop tattoo just under his left eye.

It couldn't be! she thought as she continued moving closer.

His eyes looked clear, light, young, and so familiar to Rachel. Her heart sank at that moment, suddenly realizing that she was staring into the familiar eyes of the young boy from the Mexican prison. He was much older now but held the same bright brown eyes he had as a boy. Again, the world around her seemed to spin as she fought through her confusion.

"I don't understand, he was just a boy earlier today…he was sitting in the prison courtyard. He was just a child!"

The old man spoke up, feeling the power within her fear. "Yes, you're right, my dear. That is the boy from the prison. Only, what we saw earlier was a glimpse from forty years ago." He began to laugh again, basking in his power.

Rachel's heart suddenly beat faster at the realization of why the boy was put into the prison. He had shot another man in cold blood. The reality of her circumstance hit her like a brick. She was about to endure the pain from the blinding light and deafening scream emitted from the spiritual veil of a killer.

Oh, dear God…I'll be deaf! was the last thought that ran through Rachel's mind before she turned and began running toward the old steel door across the rooftop. Her heart beat faster, and tears immediately rose up as she sprinted toward it, never once looking back at the demon. *Please be unlocked. Please be unlocked!* she frantically pleaded to herself as she ran faster.

Behind her, she could hear the old man begin to laugh. His deep, raspy tone carried across the rooftop. Rachel shrieked again at yet another surreal and terrifying sight. A long wave of dark, rolling clouds rose eerily up from the rooftop, creating a dense barrier between her and the door. It hung knee-high and stretched across the entire length of the building, forming an ominous wall, churning black, directly in front of the stairwell.

"NO!" she screamed as she ran even faster toward it.

The demon's laughter grew as she drew closer to the long gauntlet of dark rolling clouds.

"Dear Lord, NO!" she repeated as she approached it.

Then with no warning, the wave of churning clouds shot up over one hundred feet high, forming a massive wall of darkness. Bright bolts of lightning began striking within the enormous wall of clouds. The barrier itself seemed to be alive, rolling and churning and cracking with sharp flashes of light within its body of darkness. Considering what she had already endured from the drug addict and the doctor, she was certain she could not brave the magnitude and intensity from an actual killer's spiritual veil. So, with no other option, Rachel raised both of her hands up in front of her face and broke into the terrifying barricade. Knowing the stairwell was only a few strides beyond the barrier, she braced herself to run into it. But three, four, five, six strides in…nothing!

"Dear God, where is it!" she cried aloud.

The door was gone and Rachel now stood in the midst of what felt like hell itself. She panted frantically as she glanced all around her. Booming crashes of thunder rang out from all directions and bright flashes of lightning struck, illuminating the rolling black clouds that now totally enveloped her.

"Oh my God!" she openly wept as total panic charged through her.

With no other choice, she raised her hands in front of her face, then blindly sprinted in the direction of the stairwell. After several blind strides, both of her hands struck something solid. When she opened her eyes, terror washed through her again at the realization that it was the strong chest of Titus Kaw that she had run into.

10

Horrified, Rachel glanced up at the dark features of the demon. He stood just outside of the towering bank of clouds in the exact spot he was standing just before she tried to escape. Rachel stood facing Titus Kaw, directly in front of the three strangers again.

"I can't force you to choose, Rachel, but I certainly can keep you here until you do."

His demonic tone cut through her as he raised his cane up high, then drove it back into the asphalt roof again. *Crack!*

Desperation and horror filled her as more inevitable torture was about to fall upon her.

"No!" Rachel screamed.

Bright flashes of lightning released itself from the tip of his cane as it had before. And then…

Nothing.

No blinding light.

No ear-shattering ping of steel on steel.

No overwhelming crash of static.

There was only a gentle hum and a soft light. It was barely strong enough to illuminate them both as they gazed upon the stranger.

Unlike the others, the static shell of this man's veil was very thin, a faint band of light that barely outlined the stranger's head. It appeared more like a soft aura radiating around him than the massive blinding spheres that veiled the others' minds. Although the outer shell of his veil was virtually non-existent, the band of black clouds that circled the crown of his head was just as thick and dense as the others'. Rachel wiped the tears from her eyes as she instantly began to softly weep, not out of fear of additional pain but from the chaos she had just experienced and the confusion within that moment.

"I don't understand…" Her voice cracked. "He killed a man!"

The old demon stood silent, stone-faced, staring up at the tattooed man. The gentle sound that radiated from his thin veil was almost soothing, like soft white noise one may listen to while trying to fall asleep. There was only the soft muted sound of static, no piercing ping or any other sound for that matter.

Rachel eventually gathered herself, then looked up at the man standing in front of her. She pulled a tissue out of her bag, wiping her face and blowing her nose.

"I don't understand. Why is the shell of his spiritual veil so thin? I'm trying to make sense of all this. How can you tell me that a drug addict and a xenophobic doctor's veil are so much larger than a killer's? He murdered a man—in cold blood! How could God's word be clearer to him?"

The old man took his time before answering.

"What causes some men to continue killing, lifting themselves up from the perceived power within it, and others to feel the burden of the pain from the life that they took?" He spoke matter-of-factly, with little expression on his face. "His name is Lejos Perez. He was only fourteen years old when he shot that man, and nearly forty years later, he is still haunted by the eyes of his victim. Oh, the days he spent in that prison courtyard, sitting alone, gazing up into the sky, seeing nothing more than those eyes, the same eyes he shut forever. They haunt this man, no different than a ghost would. It was those eyes that first got Lejos wondering, 'Are they still watching me from where I sent him to? Does he know that I'm paying for his life that I took? Can he feel the sorrow that runs through my heart?'"

The old man went on, "Oh, how time slows after you hear that iron door slam for the first time. Within those prison walls, so many hearts fall into hatred, anger, or resentment toward those who helped put them there. But not this man. He could not escape the guilt from what he had done and the question of where he had sent that boy. His mind, whenever idle, would fall back to it and inevitably, his great pain would rise up again. It did not spawn from his own misfortune, but from the regret for the life he had taken. He spoke very few words as he moved from day to day, month to month, and then ultimately from year to year. Thirty-eight years in all. But his heart never stopped feeling deep sorrow and regret for pulling the trigger on that fateful day."

The old demon took several steps toward the old piano and drove his cane back into the asphalt rooftop. As it hit the roof, a thunderous boom rang out and a bolt of lightning struck just over the piano. Rachel lurched as it cracked with a bright flash, then watched wide-eyed in nervous anticipation. A small black cloud suddenly began to form where the lightning had struck. It grew quickly, churning and swirling in a circular pattern, doubling its mass with every rotation it made. The old man stood silent, leaning on his cane, waiting emotionless as the dark cloud grew exponentially. After a short time, the cloud had grown massive, occupying nearly one quarter of the sky above the piano. Rolling slower now, it had become an ominous dark mass looming over them both.

Kaw leaned down and lifted the piano bench, then carried it with surprising ease over to where Rachel was standing. He then gently set it down in front of her, offering, "Sit, my dear…I insist. I need you to watch something before we move on. It is significant, I assure you."

With a hint of pause, Rachel sat down, then lifted her head so that she was facing the large dark cloud. As she did, a light appeared in the middle of it, then spread quickly, illuminating images within it as if projected from far away.

The old man remained standing next to her with his hands clasped behind his back, while the three strangers stood idle and unaware directly behind them. Kaw and Rachel watched as a small room appeared within the cloud. The room looked to be some sort of gathering place. Several rows of long wooden benches lined a concrete floor and faced a basic wooden pulpit that was adorned with a black iron cross, appearing to be a simple sanctuary. The walls within the room looked cold and confining, with no warmth or life that you would expect to find in an ordinary church. A large door constructed of black iron bars could be seen behind the pulpit with only barren concrete walls housing it. The edges of the black cloud outlined the scene as it continued to churn slowly, as if the cloud itself were alive. An old thin man clad in simple black attire with a short white beard and cinched white collar slowly entered the scene, directly followed by young Lejos Perez.

Titus Kaw narrated as Rachel watched the scene unfold. She sat vulnerable and silent, having no idea of what she was about to witness.

"Before the end of his first year of incarceration, he asked to speak to the prison chaplain about the sins he had committed. He felt a need to openly confess to God and ask for his forgiveness for the life he had taken."

The old demon turned and watched as the boy began to speak to the chaplain. Although Lejos and the priest solely spoke Spanish, their conservation was received by Rachel in English. Lejos' voice could be heard clearly, cracking with emotion as he spoke.

"Padre, I have taken another man's life. I live with the pain of this sin I have committed every day…and I ask you now for God's forgiveness."

The chaplain asked the boy his name, then said, "Lejos, God's forgiveness is without limit, but you must ask him truthfully to forgive you. You must ask him from a place that exists deep within your heart. He will know where your request comes from. Tell me now, my son, why did you take this man's life? Tell me. I will believe you."

The old man's words were soft and kind, carrying a strange peace and sincerity that were quite foreign to the boy.

Lejos tried explaining to the chaplain exactly how he felt forced to join the gang, and how they had pushed him to take the young man's life. He spoke openly about what led him to this destructive refuge, beginning with the death of both his parents from a terrible car accident when he was only six years old, and the nightmare of the orphanage where he spent most of his childhood. Lejos explained how the orphanage administrator was a bad woman, and how she would allow evil men to take some children overnight and do vile things to them. He described the horrific physical and sexual abuse he endured throughout his many years at the orphanage, and how the abuse ultimately became more than he could take. His eyes welled as he confessed to the chaplain how he tried to take his own life at the fragile age of ten. To the orphanage administrator, he was nothing more than an animal that could be sold to whoever had enough money and a need—any need, no matter how inhumane or perverse.

Tears rolled down the boy's face as he continued, "Padre, I ask for your forgiveness…" He paused, then knelt at the chaplain's feet and grasped his hands together tightly, as if he were begging.

"From deep within my heart I ask for forgiveness, not only for the life I have taken…" He began to weep as he fought to continue. "But for the many acts of sin that I committed with those evil men when I was a child."

Although his knees hurt from kneeling on the unforgiving concrete floor, Lejos held his position, with his head hung down in front of the chaplain as he begged for God's forgiveness.

"So many men did vile things to me…and many times I was made to do vile things to them." Baring his great guilt, Lejos cried aloud at the feet of the chaplain. "I carry great shame, Padre. I ask for our Lord's forgiveness for my many years of sin."

The chaplain placed his hand on the boy's head, then gently replied, "You were only a child, Lejos, and that was not your will. All these people who hurt you…they were lost. They were driven by the darkness that moves throughout this world. You need not ask for God's forgiveness, my son.

You need not feel shame for what you were forced to do within those wicked walls. The darkness seeks your shame, my child, but our Lord…our Lord yearns for you to release it."

Rachel's heart ached for the boy now. Hearing the unimaginable abuse he had been forced to endure at the hands of so many who were only concerned with their own perverse needs began to tear deeper into Rachel's core. Tears filled her eyes as she took in the boy's heart-wrenching shame and the incomprehensible pain from the innocence that was stripped from him at such a young age.

Rachel wiped the tears from her eyes, then turned toward Titus Kaw to ask a question she already knew the answer to.

"Is that true?"

The old man stood stone-faced as she prodded.

"Are you the darkness that the priest speaks of? Did you push those men to hurt that child? Is it your influence that pushes the boy to carry his shame?" Rachel raised her voice with heightened emotion. "Are you the cause of that undeserved shame he's carried throughout his life?"

The old man calmly responded, "You already know the answer to that, Rachel. You can imagine what that deep shame would do to that boy's veil, how much distortion and distraction exists within it." The old man stared at Rachel with no emotion. "Look into his eyes, Rachel. His shame and hatred toward those men feed his spiritual veil. It might as well be lead encasing his heart, blocking him from experiencing the healing love of your Lord."

Rachel paused for several seconds, then turned to him and said, "You are an animal. You do know that, don't you?"

With a cold, callous demeanor, the demon responded, "I'm no animal, dear. Animals have the ability to love. I made that choice a long time ago."

Rachel turned her head toward the brave man who continued to stand silent and idle within his trance directly behind her. The thin, warm light surrounding Lejos remained unchanged, as did the larger band of darkness that loomed above him. The soft, soothing white noise broke the silence of the moment.

Oh, what you must have seen, Rachel thought as she gazed upon the aged face of Lejos Perez. After a few moments she took a long, deep breath, and with pain-filled eyes turned her head, redirecting her attention back toward the images of the chaplain and the boy within the large black cloud.

"Tell me what happened to the boy. How did the static shell of his spiritual veil grow so thin?"

She felt dirty even speaking to the demon now, knowing what he was capable of. But she felt a great need to know more about this boy who had endured so much pain.

Kaw stood silent, absorbing the hatred she felt toward him, which steeped dark in her heart now.

"The priest seemed to be a kind man. Was he?" she asked.

"Yes, he was a man of God who held great compassion for the boy."

A sigh of relief came from Rachel.

As if viewing old movies from a reel-to-reel projector, the old man and Rachel watched as the two images within the cloud began to speak again.

Young Lejos professed to the priest how, at the age of fourteen, he eventually found the courage to escape the orphanage. He described all of his days after, which he spent alone, cold, and hungry living on the streets. He spoke of taking refuge under bridges or in alleys and how he barely survived by eating out of garbage cans. With a deep sincerity, he explained how he believed that joining the gang was his only option. So with great apprehension, Lejos approached some gang members, only to be taken in, but then beaten time and time again. It was part of his initiation into the gang, as was killing that young man.

Lejos shared with the chaplain all that he had concealed for so long. He told the kind priest that his victim's name was Fernando Garcia, and that he was only nineteen years old when Lejos took his life. Fernando was said to have witnessed a gang shooting and was slated to testify in a Mexican court of law against a member of the gang with which Lejos was now associated. The young man's voice cracked again as he explained that Fernando had no gang affiliations, that he was merely an innocent bystander who was in the wrong place at the wrong time.

Prior to his confession to the chaplain, Lejos had sat day after day in his cell, imagining the pain he had brought to this boy's family. He became overwhelmed with the tremendous guilt from his actions. He would spend hours envisioning Fernando's parents receiving the phone call from the Mexican authorities, informing them that their son had been murdered. He pictured the terror of that moment, and how they must have screamed aloud and cried in disbelief and held each other because they could never hold their son again. He imagined their deep pain, and through his intentional focus on their loss, Lejos was able to open his own heart and quite literally take in their grief. Over time, this had brought him to a place of truth within his own heart, a truth in his regret for what he had done, and for the pain he had cast on so many.

Unbeknownst to Lejos, he had already found the depth of heart where he could truthfully ask for God's forgiveness.

The chaplain knew that Lejos' words were sincere. He could feel his truth within them.

"Why did these terrible things happen to me, Padre?" Lejos asked.

The chaplain had no answer, but told him, "Despite the darkness of our own path, we each must find it within our hearts to love *all* who surround us."

"But I prayed through the torment of my childhood. Why did our Lord disregard my prayers?" Tears fell from the boy's eyes again as he bared his soul to the chaplain.

"I promise you, our Lord heard every prayer and wept by your side as you suffered. He has never left you alone, Lejos. It is not our place to question our Lord's timing in response to our prayers. Our eyes see only what lies in front of us, but our Lord sees through the centuries and may find great blessings in what we only see as pain today."

The boy sobbed as he continued, "How can you say this, Padre? It went on and on, year after year after year. My heart burns with deep hatred for all the evil ones who hurt me. I was only a child!"

The chaplain simply said, "You must forgive them, my son."

"Forgive them?" Lejos' voice shrieked with deep emotion. "You don't know the darkness I have seen. My childhood was stolen from me, Padre! I could never forgive them for what they took from me. Their sins upon me were too great."

The chaplain sat silent for a while, then a soft smile crept onto his face.

"As a child, my home was by the sea. My grandpa, *mi abuelo*..." With the word 'abuelo,' the kind man's smile grew larger. "Mi abuelo was a fisherman and would take me out on the sea with him. He would wake me up very early in the morning, and we would walk side by side down the stone street through our village, well before the sun had thought to rise. We walked and walked until we came to the white sands where his small wooden boat was beached. I would climb in and sit quietly until he pushed us out into the water. I still remember the sound of the sea lapping beneath our feet as we drifted away from the shore into the morning's darkness. Mi abuelo would cleat his oars, and with every stroke, the sound of the sea against our hull lapped louder." The chaplain's face lit up again as he continued. "You have never seen a sunrise so beautiful, my son, as one witnessed out on that sea. The most magnificent pinks and purples and blues would appear on the horizon. And then, as if God himself were rising, the first glorious rays of sunlight would break above the waters, instantly caressing my face, as I watched in silent wonder.

"Most days, the sea would welcome us, but on others, its waves would be filled with rage. There were many mornings when the waves were so angry that they would lift our small boat high into the morning air, then slam us back down into the sea, over and over again."

Engaged in the story, the boy spoke up. "Were you frightened by the angry waves?"

The old chaplain's gentle laughter filled the room, "Yes, I was frightened. Until my grandfather told me the truth about the sea."

"What did he tell you, Padre?"

"He told me that the great wind that gusts throughout this world deceives the waves. The wind promises each of them that if they surrender their will to the wind, they will be lifted so high that they will surely be the greatest wave upon the sea. Blinded by their vision of grandeur, one by one they bow and surrender their will. Then, just as they were promised, each wave is pushed high into the salty air. But as they tower over the sea and gaze across its waters, they realize that no matter how high they are lifted, there are many other waves that appear to be just as great as they are. This is when the seeds of anger sprout within each of them. So, abiding by the will of the wind, they crash into each other, again and again, fighting to be the greatest."

The old man's smile grew as he shook his finger at the boy, adding, "And into anything else in their path, too, Lejos." The boy's heart lightened as he envisioned the old man as a child with his grandfather, rowing among the great waves. The pain within his eyes slowly subsided, as the chaplain went on, "But just feet below the water's surface, the wise old sea lay still, smiling, as the waves fought among themselves."

"But I don't understand, Father. If the sea is wise, then why would he find joy in the battling waves?"

"My son, the wise old sea does not listen to the lies of the wind. He lays very, very still and quiet so he can hear the soft, whispered secrets from our

Lord that have always existed deep within his heart. Then as stillness finds the heart of the sea, his focus falls upon only the beautiful colors that appear when God's sunlight breaks through the mist of the battling waves."

With great anticipation, the boy asked, "Can you tell me what secrets were whispered to the sea?"

The beat of the chaplain's heart felt clearer and more purposeful as he went on. "Of course, my child," he offered compassionately. "Our Lord whispered that although the waves fight fiercely to dominate each other, they are not evil at all. They have simply forgotten who they truly are. And rest assured, soon the winds will weaken and the waves will lie back down. Then in the quiet calm of the morning, God's stillness will find the heart of each wave. That is when the same soft whisper will rise in each of their hearts and tell them that they are not waves at all. That is when each will be reminded that they are indeed the wise old sea."

The old man's warm smile grew as he softly chuckled, then gently stroked the boy's hair. Although Lejos did not fully understand the priest's tale, he liked how it made him feel, so he sat quietly musing as the old man went on.

"The angry waves did not frighten my grandfather, and it was not long before they did not frighten me either. So, despite wind, waves, or rain, my grandfather would row and row until the seas became calm and the land disappeared from sight. I knew we had arrived when he would finally draw his oars, dripping with the sea, into our boat. Then he would bait a large hook, tether the cord of his first spool to it, and drop it over the boat's wooden hull. I would watch over the edge as his bait fell into the depths below. When I finally lost sight of it, I knew the spool was running thin. He would then tie spool after spool, cord after cord, allowing his bait to drop deeper and deeper into the sea. You see, mi abuelo said the big fish, *el pezgrande*, feed deep."

Lejos respectfully listened to the chaplain, but he couldn't imagine what this story had to do with the evil people who had hurt him as a child.

The kind old priest went on, "Oftentimes, a fish would strike! And after a long fight, mi abuelo would pull the line in, hand over hand. Then, I would spool his wet cord as straight and tight as I could, and he had great joy if his fish made it into our boat. But other times after a strike, amid the fight, silence would fall upon his boat…and with the silence, I knew he had lost his fish. Sadness fell upon him when this happened. I knew then that I would need to spool much faster, as there was no fight. And as I did, no words were spoken as his heart was in pain with the loss of his fish. Then, after all of his line had been retrieved, I would sit quietly as he studied the end of his cord. By looking at its end, he could tell if it had come untethered from his hook or if his knot had failed between two spools of cord."

Frustration began to overtake the young man, pushing him to speak up.

"I thank you for your story, Padre, but forgive me…what does this have to do with the great pain that I carry? I do not understand."

The priest only offered him a compassionate smile, then continued, "Mi abuelo was a holy man. That is where I first learned how to pray from *deep* within my heart, out on the sea with him. If he found that his cord came untethered at the hook, he would have me close my eyes and listen as he gave thanks to our Lord. I still recall the sound of the seabirds speaking to us from above as we prayed, thanking God."

Perplexed, Lejos inquired, "Why would he give thanks? If his hook was left in the mouth of the big fish, he would then have to forge a new one."

"My boy, el pezgrande is strong. His mouth will heal around that hook, and although wounded, he can still live a good life...a long life...with it remaining in his mouth."

The boy still did not understand, his impatience growing as the chaplain continued.

"On the days when my grandfather found that his knot had failed between two spools of cord, his prayers would be very different. He would have me shut my eyes, and I would listen as he prayed for God's forgiveness."

"God's forgiveness?" the boy asked.

"Mi abuelo's heart filled with great pain for el pezgrande that swam away with a full spool of cord tailing from his hook. I could see the pain in his eyes when he knew his knot had failed. It was certain that in time, the long cord carried by the big fish would find a reef or some coral on the bottom of the sea, and when caught, it would pull tight on his hook, reopening that wound again, and again, and again."

The chaplain lovingly stroked the boy's head, then softly offered, "When the darkness of so many forced their will upon you over and over again, they set their hooks deep within your heart, and you, Lejos, have carried many long cords since you were a child. They float all around you throughout this life, waiting to be caught, pulling tight again, driving their barbs deep within you, reopening the wounds from your childhood again, and again, and again."

The boy slowly stood up from the floor and sat down on a pew. He rested both elbows on his knees, then hung his head down, silently taking in the words of the kind priest.

"Think, Lejos, think of all that you see or hear or touch. Think of all the times that a raised voice, or a room you enter, or even a smell, draws you back to those painful days, setting their hooks over and over again. These are the spiny reefs of your life, my son."

The kind chaplain intentionally paused, allowing the boy to consider his words.

"My sweet child, the only way to untether their cords from those hooks is to *truly* forgive them."

A clear battle was raging in the heart of the boy as he sat hunched on the pew. After sitting in silence for quite a while, his sad eyes opened wide, then his voice raised again.

"But you don't know what they did to me, Padre!" His tears fell again as he continued, "You cannot know the horror of those chambers. I want to heal. From deep within me, I seek redemption, but I do not have the place within my heart to forgive them for what they did to me."

The chaplain's voice remained kind but firm. "Every person was created in the image of our Lord...in mind, body, and spirit. Each of our hearts holds the capacity of our Lord himself and has the same capacity to forgive. Just as our Lord forgives all our sins, we must forgive *all* those who sin against us. I tell you now, Lejos, no matter how great the sin that was committed onto you, you have been blessed with the *choice* to forgive—no matter how great the sin! I tell you today, it is your choice, my son."

The chaplain wrapped his arms around the boy.

"There is much darkness within this world and great pain falls upon many innocent people, but a greater light lies waiting, which can wash away your pain and hatred for those who laid their darkness upon you. Despite your deep wounds, you must find a way to love all who surround you. You must truly surrender to our Lord's will, Lejos, and no matter how dark it was, you must seek a purpose within the path you have walked. Just as our Lord accepts our pain, you too need to accept the pain of all those who surround you. Feel it truthfully within your heart, my son, then offer it back to our Lord."

The boy asked, "From deep within my heart, I seek redemption. But what purpose could lie within my great suffering, and the boy whose life I took, and the darkness I brought to his family? How can you ask me to find purpose amongst all the pain I have witnessed?"

The chaplain paused, standing in front of the boy for several seconds before he spoke.

"Oh, Lejos, our Lord has a higher calling for you. Otherwise, you would not have sought me out in this prison sanctuary. You felt him call to you from within your heart, then you came, Lejos...you came, my child!"

The chaplain lovingly laid his hands on the boy's cheeks, which were still wet from his tears, then gently lifted his chin so he was looking into his eyes when he spoke.

"Open your heart and try to forgive all those who have hurt you. Then, from deep within your heart, ask God to forgive you for the life that you took, and ask for forgiveness from the boy's family. Then, simply love...love more deeply today than you loved yesterday. Love all who surround you. You *will* be forgiven, my son."

Still holding the boy's face, a soft smile came to the chaplain as he slowly knelt in front of Lejos, then gently used his thumbs to wipe the remaining tears from beneath the boy's eyes.

"Maybe the meaning of all the darkness you have witnessed lies here...here on your path today, your path that brought you to me, Lejos, here in this drafty sanctuary."

The kind priest softly chuckled and pulled the boy's head into his chest, then held him with the loving compassion of God himself.

A stillness hung over the rooftop as Rachel's heart steeped with deep emotion. She was filled not only with the pain this poor boy had endured, but with the deep compassion and love that the kind priest had offered him. The images of the two men in the sanctuary melted away within the cloud. Only then did Rachel notice that the ominous black color had softened to a lighter tone of grey.

The old demon paced slowly in silence, allowing Rachel to absorb all that she had witnessed. For several minutes, she sat perfectly quiet, her mind focused first on the words of the priest, and then on all the resentment that she had carried for so long. The bars that caged her throughout her own life were becoming clearer than ever to Rachel. A more vivid understanding of the effects of her unbending pride, deep resentment, and relentless drive— all at the expense of others—was emerging within her.

As she sat absorbed within her reflection, another image appeared in the cloud. It was Lejos lying on his cot in his cell. Titus Kaw began to speak again.

"After the boy left the sanctuary that day, he went back to his cell and ran all the chaplain's words through his mind, so as never to forget them. With an open heart, he truly considered everything he was told and wondered if the purpose of all of his pain may actually lie somewhere in their conversation."

The images in the cloud began to change, correlating with Kaw's narrative as he spoke. He explained that in the months that followed, Lejos did everything the chaplain had asked. Seeking forgiveness, he wrote a letter to the parents of the young man whose life he had taken. He wanted them to understand what had led him to his false refuge in the gang that targeted their son. He explained to them how he was orphaned at the tender age of six and how he had endured terrible abuse in the orphanage. His heart ached as he described his suicide attempt as a young boy, and then again as he depicted a life of isolation on the streets of Mexico after he had escaped the chambers of the hellish orphanage. He explained that he felt that joining the gang was his only option for survival. Then, from a truthful place within his heart, he asked them for their forgiveness for taking their son's life.

Months passed, then finally a letter arrived that offered the absolution he so desperately needed. Lejos opened it with great anticipation to find that, although still heartbroken from their loss, his victim's parents had found it within themselves to offer their forgiveness to the boy. At their act of grace, a great burden instantly fell from his heart.

For many years, he fought to forgive all those who had hurt him throughout his life. This would become the great mountain that would ultimately define his journey, a mountain that would take him a lifetime to climb.

When he would try to forgive the evil men who brutally abused him as a child, the pain from his deep wounds would inevitably surface, spiking his fear and anger and ultimately deterring his efforts. Amid his prayers, like ghosts, the memories of their abuse would always advance, only to have Lejos turn from them, then fight to bury them within the recesses of his mind. And although, in that moment, it felt as if it were a means of self-preservation; in fact, this entombment of his ghosts had hindered his own healing and *truthful* forgiveness. He had not yet reached the understanding that you must first unearth that which you ask to be forgiven, whether God's forgiveness is sought for sins that you have committed or sins that others have committed against you; otherwise, a part of them may remain rooted deep within you. In the end, he was only able to offer acknowledgment of the dark influence that moved each of his attackers. And although his struggles to forgive them were ultimately in vain, he would still plead for God's light to spark within the darkness of their hearts.

As the years went on, Lejos found other ways to find peace within his mind. Whenever a hint of anger or resentment began to emerge, he would stop whatever he was doing and close his eyes so he could picture the chaplain's big fish swimming through the sea. He would envision el pezgrande's burdensome cord trailing far beneath him, relentlessly weighting him down as he moved slowly through the strong ocean currents. He would pray for God's guidance in releasing his anger before it ever had a chance to set in his own heart.

Kaw explained how Lejos was eventually given a job as a cook and server in the prison mess hall. And how many times as he worked, anger would mount between different groups of men in the cafeteria; anger that quite often would lead to bloodshed. Time and time again, Lejos watched as the inmates violently rose up against each other as if they were battling to be the greatest within the prison walls. Amidst their clash, their bodies would crash together and into anything else in their path, fighting as hard as they could to dominate each other. On the days when there was no fighting, quite often the inmates would talk openly among themselves about their lives or the crimes they had committed. With virtuous intention, Lejos began to listen and pray for each of them as they passed through his line. As they conversed, he would fight to only take in the good, shielding all words of hatred, prejudice, cruelty, or judgment. And although these harsh words commonly echoed throughout the large room, he developed the ability to hold them at bay, taking all life from them before they were ever given a chance to seed within his heart. He would only take in their acknowledgment of loved ones that they missed or their regret for the crimes they had committed. Each day, after all had been served, Lejos would close the kitchen, then walk down to the prison sanctuary. The loving man would then kneel on the concrete floor and continue his prayers for all those who he had just served. He was truthful, conveying the good within each of them as he pleaded for God's light to shine through their hearts so his magnificent colors could finally be seen. Lejos carried great faith that each man may find the stillness needed to hear the Lord's whisper remind them who they truly are.

As he offered himself day after day, the air within his lungs began to feel different. It felt cleaner and purer than it ever had before. It even felt as if his lungs had grown in capacity. All the light that touched his eyes seemed to carry a new brilliance to it, as if reflecting from heaven itself. As the years passed into decades, Lejos found the stillness of mind that allowed him to love all who surrounded him from the elusive caverns in his heart. His daily sacrifice not only changed him, but so many others who had crossed his path in the prison.

God's loving guidance had emerged within Lejos' consciousness, illuminating the clear path that he was intended to walk. Quite often, his mind would go in one direction, but his heart would move him somewhere else. He began to feel deep nudges to approach certain inmates, and after he did, little thought was needed during their conversations. His words seemed to come from a different place now, a place of deep caring for everyone that he was moved to speak with. They rolled off his tongue with great ease, as if they were not being spoken at all, only felt. They did not come from his brain, but his heart. His words were his own, but each was inspired from a higher place, conveyed to him through his thinning spiritual veil. Even if he did not fully understand his inner nudges, he developed a strong faith in their origin, and ultimately their purpose would unfold as a testimony to his unbending obedience to God's will instead of his own.

By the end of his incarceration, a profound unyielding stillness had found a home within him, a rightness to a life in a prison that was considered, by many, to be a living hell on earth.

11

"There is significance in how he came to be here. In the city of Cleveland, I mean."

The old man pointed his cane back up to the image within the cloud. It was Lejos, still sitting alone in his cell, only he looked much older now.

Kaw said, "One day, over twenty years after he was first incarcerated, a letter was pushed under his cell door. He picked it up and ran his palm over the face of the envelope. In the upper left-hand corner, handwritten in black ink, was the name Maria Perez. It was the name of his grandmother, whom he had never met. There were two stamps in the upper right-hand corner of the envelope, which had brightly colored American flags printed on them. With black ink stamped in a circular pattern over the flags, it read 'Cleveland, Ohio, USA.'"

Rachel asked, "Why did she wait so long to write to him, and why did she allow him to go into the orphanage in the first place?"

The old demon continued, "You see, Maria Perez had never been told by her daughter that she even had a grandchild. Several years before his parents' death, Lejos' mother and grandmother had disassociated themselves from each other over her decision to marry Lejos' father at such a young age. His grandmother's resentment toward her daughter was reciprocated and grew into a great wall over the years, which neither was willing to breach. Their separation was spawned by resentment but grew larger through their stubbornness and pride. And beyond that, his grandmother had been living in the United States for several years before Lejos was even born, which aided in their divide.

"It was not until years later that his grandmother found out that Lejos even existed. By then, he had been a longtime ward of the orphanage and they were not willing to let him go. When Maria Perez finally communicated with the orphanage administrators, she was told that Lejos had already been placed with a family through a closed adoption and they were not able to offer her any additional information beyond that. All that his grandmother could do was pray to God that he would be safe and that someday her and her only grandson's paths may cross. Over three decades had passed when Maria Perez got word that a man who may be her last living relative was incarcerated in the Juarez prison. That is when she first wrote to him.

"With all he had been through, Lejos had nearly forgotten he even had a grandmother. He found himself conflicted as his heart ached from what could have been, and yet was joyful to learn that he still had family who cared about him and had sought to find him. From his prison cell, Lejos began to correspond with his grandmother. For years, they wrote back and forth to each other. He eventually came to realize that despite living in poverty most of her life, she was a charitable and decent woman. Maria encouraged Lejos to be a good man and to continue to pray each day and search his heart for God's Holy Spirit—and Lejos did just that. He continued going to the sanctuary, and throughout his remaining years in the prison, he and his grandmother wrote back and forth, exchanging scripture and prayers in their letters. The two developed a deep, loving relationship without ever once seeing each other face-to-face. All their communication consisted of handwritten letters, and that was enough to open both of their hearts. Then, with less than a year to be served in his thirty-eight-year sentence, he received another letter from his grandmother."

The image of Lejos reading the letter in his cell appeared within the cloud, only his appearance had dramatically changed. His face had grown much older now and carried many creases. His hair was longer, but his sparkling brown eyes remained unchanged from the moment Rachel first saw him in the prison courtyard. They were still clear, bright, and young.

The letter from his grandmother read:

My Dearest Lejos,

Snow has come to Cleveland again, and it lightens my heart as I know the celebration of our Lord's birth is near. Yesterday the Padre at the sanctuary across the street hung colorful lights above the banner that reads 'The Cleveland Mission.' They looked beautiful with the freshly fallen snow resting on them. As of recently, a gentleman of modest means has been standing on the street corner playing Christmas music on his saxophone. So many of God's children are in great need as they wait in line for lunch outside of the Mission. He stands alone in the cold with only one leg, but through his music offers humanity to all those poor souls who are in such desperate need of it. Someday I hope your eyes may fall upon this place I live. There exists so much good here, and I think you would love the city of Cleveland…it seems almost magical to me. Never forget that our Lord lives wherever we love, Lejos. Whether it is in a prison or an old mission…when you love truthfully with your heart, you will give breath to the truth of this life. You have made me so proud, my child, and despite the prison walls that surround you, I know that your heart is now free. Our Lord's love knows no walls, and he walks with you today, Lejos.

I regret that I must share some unfortunate news with you. As of recently, I have grown ill. The doctors have told me there is little they can do for me, and it appears my time in this world is growing short. I know you will be released in a year's time, but if our Lord has taken me before then, please know that my heart will still be with you. I know you are a good man, Lejos. You have touched so many lives throughout your years within those walls. Carry that same love with you as you move back into the free world. The Holy Spirit has found a home within you. Pray for God's guidance, and direction will come to your heart…follow it, my child. Our Lord speaks to us through our hearts. Open yourself to him, and you will find the path that your feet were intended to walk.

God be with you, my child. I love you so much.

Grandma Maria

As he read the words of his grandmother, Lejos became filled with emotion. He had lived nearly all of his early life with no real family or anyone who *truly* cared about him. Now, he had a grandmother who he shared a deep, profound love with. And although their eyes had never met, their hearts felt as if they were one, entwined with a very real love that seemed to transcend the thousand miles of landscape and barbed wire that separated them.

Lejos dropped to his knees and with his elbows propped upon his cot, bowed his head and opened his heart in prayer.

"My dear Father and Son, allow your Holy Spirit to fall upon my heart. Feel the love that exists within it for my grandmother whom I have never met. Dear Lord, feel what I feel. Know the love I carry in my heart for this woman…and please know the love she carries for so many in need at the Mission. This woman, whose heart I hold within my own, has grown ill. And if it's your will to take her now, then I will pray that you will hold her tight as she enters your kingdom in heaven. I surrender myself to you and will continue to love and honor you in the same way that I have within these prison walls, whatever your will may be. But please hear my prayers for your healing love to fall upon her. Please find it within your grace to grant her your breath, so my eyes may fall upon hers just once and my arms may hold her tight, so she knows that they are real, before you take her to her final place of rest. I open myself to you, my Lord, and as I kneel within this prison cell and feel your Holy Spirit breathe within me…your will will be mine. In the name of the Father, the Son, and the Holy Spirit…Amen."

Tears could be seen running down Lejos' face as he knelt praying on the floor of his cell. His image then began to fade within the churning cloud, which had now softened to a beautiful cottony white. As Lejos' image disappeared, the surreal cloud rolled over itself again and again until all signs of it had totally vanished.

Through this process, Rachel had begun to open herself to the pain of others in a more deliberate and meaningful way. Sincere emotion filled her as she witnessed the anguish of this man who simply wanted to be in the presence of his only living family member before she passed away.

With tears in her eyes, Rachel asked, "Did she live long enough to meet Lejos?"

The old man responded, "For the next year, Maria Perez became the main subject of Lejos' prayers. From the prison sanctuary, from inside of his cell, and as he moved throughout the rest of the prison, his heart was with his dying grandmother. Despite her terminal diagnosis, he began to picture her doctor relentlessly reviewing his grandmother's case, searching for something, anything that might have been missed. He imagined the doctor finally calling Maria to explain that they had indeed stumbled across something that may offer her some hope. Then, he envisioned her growing stronger each day until her doctor was finally able to reverse her terminal diagnosis. Throughout each of his days, this became Lejos' ritual. With every letter that arrived from his grandmother, before even opening it, he would fall to his knees and thank God for his loving blessings that had mercifully been offered to the one he loved so dearly. Ultimately, on the day of Lejos' release, Maria Perez *was* still alive. The doctors had no explanation for the deceleration of her terminal illness. You see, Rachel, the thinner your veil becomes, the purer your prayers are to God. And when you pray from this place of truth and depth of heart, your prayers become more powerful.

"It took Lejos over a month to make his way up to Cleveland. He walked northeast on the sweltering highways, hitchhiking over the hot pavement. And when there were no rides, which was often, he kept moving by foot and foot alone, always northeast. Every step he took brought him closer to his dying grandmother.

"When he finally arrived at the Mission in Cleveland, he paused, taking in all the details that his grandmother had described so vividly. A tear came to his eye as he knew his long journey had finally come to an end. Lejos had no idea if she was even alive. His heart beat faster as he finally approached his grandmother's door. After hearing that unexpected knock, Grandma Maria felt within her heart that it was her long-lost grandson standing just beyond it."

The old man went on, "Emotion filled them both as their eyes first met, then again as they embraced for the first time, binding them together through their deep gratitude for a living God who guided and protected them throughout her illness and his long journey."

Rachel sighed, then paused in thought. "When was that? Did he recently arrive in Cleveland?" Half-jokingly, she added, "I think I've lost track of time."

The old man replied, "It has been just over one year since Lejos arrived in this city."

Then with guarded concern, Rachel asked, "So his grandmother…is she…?"

Kaw interjected, "Is she still alive?" He scowled, then intentionally paused before answering. "Shortly after Lejos arrived, he began volunteering at the Mission. His duties included cooking, serving, caring for the homeless, and helping with maintenance throughout the neglected church. It was not long before the Father at the Mission had recognized his caring nature and offered him a position there. He was only able to pay him $20 per day from the meager donations that they received. The Father knew it was very little pay for the work he would be doing but was able to offer him two meals a day and full access to the Mission's sanctuary, understanding what a prayerful man Lejos was."

"It's wonderful that he continued to serve after he was free."

The old demon went on, "Day after day, through each of his breaks, Lejos knelt on the hardwood floor of that old sanctuary and prayed for his grandmother. Tears often fell from his eyes as he offered all that he was for her sake. It has been over one year, and to her doctor's amazement, yes, Maria Perez is still alive."

With a joyful gasp, Rachel asked, "Was it actually Lejos' prayers that kept her alive?"

Reluctantly, the old man offered, "Yes, it was. Without them, she would have died nearly two years ago."

Rachel's heart immediately flooded with gratitude and a strange newborn hope, which she had never possessed until that moment. Hearing that Lejos' dying grandmother was still alive brought shock and amazement to her.

Witnessing God's grace, a miraculous healing from prayer in the present-day world, simply astounded her.

Rachel spoke up with heightened emotion. "I understand miracles happened with Jesus two thousand years ago, but not today, not in Cleveland!"

Kaw spoke. "Every soul that's ever passed through this physical realm has held the exact same capacity. Each has possessed the necessary tools to allow miraculous prayers to transcend the laws of physics. Although this may be difficult for you to understand, heaven doesn't actually exist up in the clouds. It exists in the hidden caverns of your hearts. So, when God's beautiful light shines out and surrounds your spiritual veil, it is your own heart that he is shining from. Your true, deeper self and all who have passed on dwell there too. Don't you see, Rachel? The most relevant war within this world is not fought on the battlefields, but between mind and heart within each of you. Jesus only used the sky to describe heaven because it is endless space, totally intangible and limitless. The vast space in your hearts is the same. The only difference is as you approach your heart's center, its space becomes dense with absolute love. Try to imagine the distance between you and the stars; if you multiply it times one thousand you will still fall short of the distance between your physical heart and its center. But your access to this state is not blocked by a barrier around your heart. Its only restriction is the static shell that surrounds each of your minds. Your mind is the key that can unlock miracles through the quantum field, the same field that is the mind of God. The love that exists in the depths of your heart is not limited by time or space, or anything else for that matter. It is a limitless state of euphoric being. But your full acceptance is what's critical. You must truthfully surrender your will to the Lord first. The key to it all lies in your own mind's surrendered state of powerlessness. If you are able to unlock that elusive door, limitless possibilities lie at hand."

Rachel's mind whirled at the true, unlimited power of prayer. She was amazed at what has always been accessible to each person in the deepest caverns of their hearts. But as she mused, her mind returned to Lejos' grandmother. Although astonished by the internal mechanics within each person and their limitless possibilities, her focus was falling on the divine bridge that was growing between her heart and the heart of Maria Perez.

Rachel's love for an old woman that she had never met was now beginning to feel more natural. Immersing herself in the pain and the love of a stranger had inexplicably begun to feel right. She was shocked that in an instant her heart could feel so much fuller than it had just moments ago. Rachel clearly felt a new strength within her, not spawned by money or class or possessions, but a power that had begun to seep into her heart through her own thinning spiritual veil from the essence of God himself. For the first time in her life, she held the most peculiar balance of power and profound peace simultaneously within her. Her unconditional love for all others was continuing to grow, and with it, a stillness within her own consciousness had begun to emerge.

As Rachel brimmed with excitement, Kaw scoffed. "It's true, Rachel, that each soul in this physical realm has been given the ability to open their hearts, allowing God's miraculous doorway between heaven and earth to open. It is transcending your physicality through a *deeper* love for them. It is all about the thinning of your veil. Each of your prayers' effectiveness depends on the density of that veil, but you are not the only one who dictates its thickness—and with that, the depth of distortion around your consciousness. Believe it or not, there are many souls in heaven who continue to intercede for the living through their own prayers."

"Yes, you explained how my mother has been praying for me from heaven. I know it's true. I've felt her presence within me."

"Yes. I think it may be appropriate to take a closer look at those specific mechanics."

The old man walked across the flat roof to its far edge, at the brick parapet. He then lifted his cane waist-high, and with its brass tip, scratched a deep line across the old stone cap. Even from Rachel's distant vantage point, the noise from it pierced the air like nails on a chalkboard. He then scored the brick face of the wall vertically, from its marred cap down to the roof line below. Rachel gazed across the top of the old building with a perplexed look on her face. He then dug the tip of his cane into the asphalt roof just in front of the brick wall. As Rachel watched, he began to whistle a slow, haunting melody that felt familiar to her. The demon continued to stare into Rachel's eyes as he slowly crept closer toward her, carving the tip of his cane into the asphalt as he walked. Rachel remembered her mother whistling the same tune when she would work around their house, but she could not put her finger on it. Kaw meandered in long sweeping swaths, back and forth, as he moved in her direction. Rachel's brow furled with distrust as he took his last few steps and stopped just feet from where she stood. His long-etched path was the shape of a snake that began at the brick wall and ended at her feet. His melody came to a frightening crescendo when he raised his cane up, then slammed it back into the rooftop again. *Crack!*

As his cane crashed into the top of the building, the structure beneath their feet began to quake. Its tremor increased so quickly and violently that Rachel felt that the entire building might implode. Fear for her life overtook her as she fought to stabilize herself, but her knees buckled and sent her collapsing to the asphalt below. Rachel watched in horror as inches from where she lay, a crack appeared in the rooftop where the winding, etched path ended. Then, as if the building were above the epicenter of an earthquake, the roof itself began to tear and crumble along the demon's serpentine path. In a frenzied panic, Rachel struggled to her feet and frantically scampered toward the only thing in sight that she could hold on to, the old piano.

As she ran, the demon's laughter rose around her, compounding her panicked fear. The fissure tore through the top of the building, then blasted through the brick wall, as if it had been struck by a cannonball. Bricks and stone rained down onto the street below. Rachel wrapped her arms around the upper body of the piano and held on as tightly as she could. The massive wood structure chattered violently from the quake. The crumbling divide was growing wider now, migrating closer to where Rachel stood. Huge chunks of concrete and asphalt sheared from the roof then dropped into the growing abyss below. The demon casually leaned against an iron smokestack, calmly taking in Rachel's fear as the chaos ensued. Suddenly, the whole building felt as if it dropped several inches, slamming Rachel and the piano down with a violent crash. She watched in shock as a surreal scene unfolded in front of her. Huge boulders and rocks of all sizes were suddenly thrust upwards through the winding void, coming to rest just above the building's roof line. As the final rocks settled into place, all movement throughout the building subsided.

Traumatized, Rachel reluctantly released her grip from the piano, her hands trembling.

Eventually, her heavy breathing began to slow. As her fear began to fade, she turned and surveyed the unbelievable sight behind her. She hesitantly departed from her place of safety and cautiously stepped closer to the unusual rock formation that spanned the full length of the roof.

All was quiet now except for the soft sound of trickling water. As she moved closer, she noticed a slow-moving serpentine stream running over and around the rocks. The water was murky at the bend where she now stood. It looked to be muddled with fine black silt and deep-green algae that churned within it, as if it were just stirred up from the bottom of a stagnant pond. Its rocky bed followed the demon's winding path, which ended at the opening in the brick wall. The strange riverbed spanned twenty feet from bank to bank, and its rubble rested just above the roof's surface. The largest boulders could be seen far off in the distance, well beyond the iron smokestack that towered high above another bend in the river. The demon appeared bored as he leaned against the iron stack, staring off at the city below. In front of him, the boulders in the riverbed had transitioned into smaller ones. Those then tapered into smaller ones, which tapered down into smaller rocks and then into gravel. As the rocks progressively got smaller, the water running through them became clearer and clearer. The final span of aggregate was of fine white sand, which ran up to the brick wall's opening. The water that ran through it looked as if it had been filtered, sparkling like crystal-clear water from a spring. It glistened as it gently rolled over the brick's edge, then softly cascaded down to the street below.

Titus Kaw leaned forward, shifting his weight away from the smokestack. He spoke matter-of-factly as he began walking toward her.

"It was used centuries ago in India, and in many other countries for that matter. This riverbed is actually an ancient water filtration system, made to remove all impurities that have contaminated it—all the toxins from your physical world."

Rachel replied, "I don't understand."

Kaw went on, "When rain falls from the heavens, it is pure and can be consumed with no fear of harmful contaminants. It is not until it pools in this world that it becomes infiltrated with the pernicious impurities that can be harmful when consumed. Without a system of filtration, foreign bacteria, harmful organisms, and other contaminants are introduced into the water—and then into your bodies, if ever consumed."

Rachel walked along the winding stream, noticing the clarity of the water improving as it flowed through the various levels of rock and sand. As the water moved through the finer aggregate, it became clearer and clearer.

Rachel spoke up. "All right, I think I understand how the filtering system works, but why are you showing me this? What relevance does this have to a dying woman or the prayers from her grandson...or to me, for that matter?"

Without a response, the old man slowly made his way over to the piano, slid the bench out, and sat down. He pressed down on the keys with both of his hands. Multiple hammers struck the piano strings simultaneously while he listened to the note's tone.

"Why is this relevant? Because this is heaven, Rachel...well, I should say, this is your second heaven. This is the place you pass into when your physical life here on earth has come to an end."

Worried and confused, Rachel fought to understand.

"As I told you before, the first heaven, which is your physical world, was created as a place of redemption. The second heaven, the spiritual realm you pass into, was created as a place of purification. The murky water that courses through this riverbed represents the souls of the departed that have not yet been fully cleansed from their physical experience."

The old man raised his voice. "You need to cross that river, Rachel. You need to cross over into the second heaven. And you need to go now."

A look of fear came over her as she rebutted, "Why? I can understand its mechanics without actually crossing into it. Why can't you just explain it to me from this side of the river?"

"Having a small glimpse of your existence beyond this physical world will help deepen your understanding of your eternal life. You will be able to witness the reciprocal nature of prayer between your physical world and the spiritual realm within heaven."

A large grin came upon his face as he began playing the same tune he had whistled just moments ago. Rachel's eyes filled up when she remembered the song her mother loved so much.

The demon began to play *Moon River* on the piano and sing in a deep, slow, steady tone. As he sang, Rachel walked over to the edge of the river and gazed into it, focusing on the water as it ran through the rocks. A cool, thick mist drifted in from the north, which quickly obstructed her view from all but the riverbed at her feet. She stood, frightened and alone at its bank. The demon's music cut through the thickening haze as she searched for the courage to step into the water.

Rachel spoke up. "So this is where our souls come to be cleansed?"

The music stopped playing, and the sound of slow footsteps could soon be heard approaching her from behind. The demon's dark shadow appeared, and his raspy voice rose out of the rolling fog.

"That's absolutely right, Rachel. The process your soul undergoes is much like the filtering system in front of you. After you cross over, your soul slowly progresses through multiple stages of purity within your second heaven, and as it does, it becomes clearer, cleaner, and purer than it was in its previous state. This is where you go to eliminate the spiritual veil that separates your consciousness from the mind of God. But all progression must flow from your own free will."

Kaw continued, "Throughout your lives, each of you are inevitably exposed to feelings that arise quite naturally but are in opposition to the essence of who you truly are. They are introduced through your human nature, which is driven by your ego. It is all part of your human experience. The way you choose to live your life, the manner in which you treat others, and what you create within your own minds all determine your level of contamination—it's what makes up the static within your individual veils. These contaminants will determine what spiritual level you pass into after you die. Some souls need more filtration so they pass over into the boulders, while others need less. They pass into the gravel or even into the sand. The life you live within this physical world will determine the distance of your spiritual journey after you pass.

"My brothers and my influence are the infections that exist within God's being, and we have been festering since the beginning of time. Our influence floods your physical world and drowns all who are born into it. As you progress through your life, it is God's intention that each of you find your way through the murkiness of your physical consciousness, up to the surface. You achieve this by loving deeper and living your lives as God intends. The depth of your love and the purity of your intention act as antibodies within the consciousness of mankind, fighting back against our infection of ego—in turn, shrinking the inner core of your veils. As I have told you, selfishness, greed, prejudice, jealousy, hatred, and complacency are just a few of our toxins. When you choose to live your life moved by these tendencies, they seep like poison into your being, fortifying your spiritual veil and feeding our egoic influence upon the day-to-day thoughts of the living.

"When you die and pass into the second heaven, the dark inner core of your spiritual veil will thin, but will not totally die with you. As it dissipates, the inflow of ego into your conscience will decrease, and as it does, what you create within your mind will inevitably change. This leads to the static shell around your mind becoming very thin. In turn, God's Holy Spirit will blow into your consciousness, awakening you from the dream that was your physical life. Although you have already been forgiven for each choice that you've made, your soul must go through a filtering process dictated by your own free will before it is able to be reintroduced back into the highest level of heaven, back into your unobstructed unity with God. All space within the highest heaven—the third heaven, is occupied by love, and love alone. That space is so pure and dense with God's love, there is no room for anything else. This second heaven is where he gives each one of his children a clearer understanding of their intended purpose that might have eluded them throughout their lives. With a clearer voice, God guides each of you to rise beyond the veils that have blinded you, and as he does, a higher understanding of who you *truly* are will emanate within you.

"This next point is critical, Rachel. The overall influence of our darkness upon your world can only be diminished through the choices you make throughout your physical lives. Once you have passed into the second heaven, your ability to directly influence darkness will be lost. What you create in your mind will no longer influence the egos of the living throughout the world. God reserves that gift for his children who reside in the physical dimension, the ones who remain totally immersed in ego. You will have the ability to shed your entire spiritual veil as you progress toward the highest heaven, but any effect on the physical world will need to come through your divine inspiration within the hearts of those who are still living. They alone can diminish our darkness.

"Within the second heaven, all intervention must happen indirectly through your prayers of intercession for the living. If the prayers of those who have passed are powerful enough, they can penetrate the veils of those being prayed for and inspire them through their own intuition. Divine inspiration can appear in the physical world as one's own notions, or through physical signs that may hold relevance to them, or even through their dreams."

Rachel interrupted him. "I thought dreams were just manifestations of whatever was on our minds before we fell asleep?"

"Well, some of your dreams are exactly that, but others hold great meaning and manifest in your conscience as a result of the prayers you are receiving from heaven. When you sleep, your consciousness detaches from its physical state, and when it does, your spiritual veil often becomes thinner.

Although you may not remember exactly what transpired in your dreams, their remnants may linger, moving you after you have awakened.

"The progression of souls who have passed into the second heaven is dependent on their prayerful intercession on the living as well as their deeper understanding of the choices that they made throughout their physical lives. Inspiring your loved ones who are still living is not only critical in the journey of the living, but in the spiritual journey of those who have passed. This purification process is based on their willingness to let go of their human nature and willingly surrender to God's will, which spawns from his true nature. With each progressive level of the second heaven, your veil will thin more and more. And as it does, you will find a clarity to God's guidance, inspiring you through your own heart. But the choice to abide by his guidance will always belong to you.

"Each who passes is given open access to the unobstructed consciousness of the living, so through God's guidance, each soul is able to feel how the choices made in the physical world reverberate through the universe. Every thought of the living ripples throughout the unified consciousness of God. That knowledge is critical in understanding his truth, and, in turn, willingly moving those souls toward it, within this spiritual realm. By his own law, God cannot force your progression toward the third and final heaven. The law of free will applies in this spiritual realm too, just as it does in your physical world. All transition through the second heaven is based on the free will of the soul who is passing through it. As it is within your physical lives, the choice of complacency or progression lies in each of your hands."

Rachel said, "It is still hard for me to understand exactly what to do after we pass. How do we find God's guidance? How do we find our way to the sand?"

Kaw replied, "You will know, Rachel. It begins the moment you step into the water. It begins with the thinning of your veil. It will allow God's love and knowledge to flow into your consciousness much more vividly than it did throughout your physical life."

Rachel nervously looked down into the water and across the riverbed toward the misty bank on the other side.

From behind her, Kaw spoke. "One last thing before you go, my dear. When you return from this spiritual experience, your veil will return too, and with it, a blinding of what transpired in this realm. But if you are truly moved, remnants of this experience may linger within your heart, no differently than a vivid dream. Go ahead now, I'll be waiting for you."

Rachel nervously inquired, "Aren't you coming?"

Kaw began to laugh again. "You, and you alone, can cross this river. I made that choice a long time ago." The old man snickered, then turned and slowly walked away, disappearing into the thick mist.

Apprehension filled her as she was immediately bombarded with conflicting thoughts. *If I do cross into heaven, what's waiting for me on the other side? What if I can't find my way back? Will God be waiting to judge me for the mistakes I've made in my life?*

Understanding that she had no other choice but to cross, she took a deep breath, then carefully stepped into the shallow water. As soon as her foot entered the river, a wave of emotion filled her heart. All the love and light and peace and power and security that she could ever imagine came rushing into her all at once. It felt as if there was a literal explosion of love within her heart that instantly spread throughout her whole being. All of her senses suddenly became heightened. Her vision was clearer, her hearing became amplified, and a welcoming aroma of pungent wildflowers sent her olfactory senses into overdrive. All she took in was crisper and clearer and more real than it had ever been throughout her physical life. So, with slow deliberate steps, she began to cautiously move through the strange waters toward the opposite bank.

Although she was moving very slowly, her consciousness felt like it was about to take flight. Within seconds, Rachel felt as if she was flying past stars and planets at the speed of light. None of this made any sense to her. She felt a depth in her heart she had never known before. An intense sense of love seemed to cradle her as she moved toward a place of unity with all living things. What she felt could not possibly be put into words, but somehow, she knew it was real and it was good. And although she was walking into the unknown, she felt as if she was approaching someplace familiar, as if approaching her true home. The security she knew as a child intensified as she moved deeper through unexplainable layers of unconditional love, each one rendering her more secure than the last. With every step, her apprehension felt as if it were releasing itself from within her. All of her great fears, which had burdened her since she was a child, miraculously shed from the depths of her being.

Then, just as Rachel felt that she might explode from the love and acceptance that now filled her, the impossible happened. In the matter of a single step, she relived every moment of her physical life. It was beyond her understanding, and in terms of the laws of physics, it was not even possible, yet it happened. Every word she had ever spoken, every choice she had ever made, and every thought she had ever processed came rushing back to her within that fleeting moment. The only difference was that instead of only feeling what ran through her mind, as she did in her life, she felt the consciousness of every individual whose life had been impacted by her own. She felt it as if she were the people themselves.

Rachel gasped as unimaginable joy as well as regret filled her all at once. Heartfelt tears formed thin streams as they rolled down her cheeks then dropped into the murky water below. She felt the warmth and security that wrapped her as she grew in her mother's womb. Then, every aspect of joy that her parents felt as she witnessed her own birth through their eyes, a moment that Rachel found bittersweet, as she also felt the disconnection from God as her spiritual veil wrapped her consciousness for the first time. She felt the joy of each kid from her old neighborhood as they ran and hid and laughed through countless games of kick-the-can. She experienced the lingering security from her friendship with Peggy, as she fought to navigate her young life in a household dictated by an abusive, alcoholic father. Rachel had no idea how much her simple life had positively impacted so many different people around her.

She experienced all that radiated from her choices through the consciousness of each person who had crossed her path, even through the eyes of her pets. The deep joy of her childhood dog, Tinker, coursed through her heart as they ran together through the grape vineyards behind her house. Although her father was a man of few words, Rachel suddenly understood the depth of his love for his only daughter, undiminished from her birth until the day he died. She felt the pride that radiated like light from within her parents as they witnessed all of her accomplishments throughout her life. As a young mother, she was able to feel the warmth and love that her babies experienced when she cared for them. There was so much more good that came from her life than she ever knew, and as she experienced it again, she felt her love ripple through the universe.

Some of the smallest deeds, which she had disregarded or viewed as inconsequential, had significantly moved the universe in the direction that God had intended.

One such event happened when she was just fifteen years old. Rachel and her cheerleading squad had spent the morning washing cars at a school-sponsored fundraiser. They were just wrapping up for the day and a few of her friends were eagerly waiting for her in their parents' car so they could depart. Rachel filled a bucket of clean water as they coaxed her to 'hurry up' from across the parking lot. As Rachel relived that moment, she felt the frustration of her friends as they sat waiting, and she also felt the insecurity of a teenage girl who frantically rushed so she would not disappoint them. As the girls prodded her from the car, she struggled to haul the large bucket of water toward a line of pear trees that encompassed the parking lot where they worked. It was a beautiful late spring day, and all the trees were flushed with the rich new growth of light green leaves and pink buds that pushed out in abundance from their limbs—all of them, but one.

Throughout that day, Rachel had breathed in the crisp spring air. She had always loved the spring and the inner renewal it seemed to carry with it. But as she laughed with her friends, washing cars and soaking in the beautiful day, her eyes kept returning to one tree that appeared to be dying. All of its leaves were brown or had fallen off. It was smaller than the rest of the trees and leaned a bit to one side, as if it hadn't established the proper root system to support it. As Rachel witnessed this seemingly insignificant moment in her life, she felt her concern for the small tree and her true intention as she hurried to give it a healthy drink of water before she departed. As her friends raised their voices, she quickly nourished the withering tree. She had nothing to gain from this act of kindness, only the sacrifice of potentially being ostracized by her friends at an already-vulnerable period in her young life.

A sudden burst of light and love overflowed within her with an intensity she had never experienced before. Upon this selfless act, she felt the jubilation of every angel and occupant within heaven rise up together. Miraculously, Rachel felt the tree reflect the love she was giving. An exuberant, joyful praise rang through her heart like the most powerful and beautiful embrace one could ever imagine. Time and time again, she witnessed countless acts of kindness that she had considered inconsequential throughout all stages of her life. The only difference was that now she could feel their effects on all the living that she touched, as well as their impact on the shared consciousness of the world. Rachel finally realized how critical the depth of her love really was. Each loving act and selfless thought rippled through the universe, diminishing darkness as it spread.

As Rachel continued moving through the strange waters, she experienced pain and regret as well. She relived moments of resentment, jealousy, greed, and disregard for many who surrounded her—all normal feelings that most have experienced. She witnessed all repercussions from the choices she had made throughout her entire life, the good and the bad. But, the regret she felt for the pain she imposed on others fell softer upon her heart than she had expected. It was miraculously tempered by the unconditional love of a God whose truthful forgiveness surged through her being as she relived those moments. She could not feel her regret without first feeling the understanding from the one who loved her more than anyone else, God. She gained a profound understanding of the influence of self, which moves each person every day of their lives. His unconditional love for her seemed to become clearer as her life's review progressed.

It is God's intention that when we review the pain from the choices we have made in our lives, it will be softened by the love that swaddles each of us from the moment we cross over. He does not seek our punishment, only our understanding. As our veils thin, so does our ego, which is the source of so much of our pain. God does not seek our shame or toil to inflict his guilt upon us. On the contrary, he wants each of us to *truly* understand our impact on all those who surround us throughout our lives, then release it, as if it never happened at all. The guilt and shame that linger will only add to our veil, pushing us further from his guidance and the security within his love. He wants each of us to accept his full forgiveness with open arms, and that entails each of us truthfully and fully forgiving ourselves too.

Rachel moved forward through the murky water, taking in the pain from injuring others as a young girl through thoughtless words or hurtful actions. She felt their hearts ache, but leaned on God's radiating love and forgiveness as she bore witness to her own choices. She experienced the loss of her first child, who she had miscarried halfway through her third trimester. She was so close to delivering that they had even chosen a name for her. She experienced the pain that flows through each person as they fight to navigate through their uncharted lives. All that was idle in the dark closets of her mind was suddenly released as she finally felt the full impact of her choices on the universe around her. She realized that the dark secrets she had kept were not secrets at all, but understood intimately by God and all within heaven, and in that moment, each became painfully clear to her.

She reviewed much of her life that she was not proud of—choices made at work, or at home, or in her relationships—choices that unknowingly created darkness that reverberated through the unified consciousness that the universe springs from.

As she neared her crossing, she felt an unexpected cleansing from within her soul. There was a clear release of something unknown to her, something that felt natural in the physical world, but now felt totally foreign to her. It fled simply through her understanding of the truth—the truth about what her physical life really was, and how every aspect of it impacted all that is—the truth about love, and how critical it is to the universe around us.

Just as Rachel was about to cross over onto the riverbank, the fog beyond its rocky shore began to break, giving way to a stunning and miraculous scene.

12

Deep green tufts of long grass covered the river's rocky edge. Unusual tropical flowers with the most vibrant colors Rachel had ever seen lined the winding river, fading into the distant fog. Each appeared to bow at the foot of the trickling stream, releasing crystal-clear droplets of dew into the babbling water, left like gifts from the retreating blanket of mist.

Rachel stepped out of the stream into an expansive field of tall, soft grass peppered with countless varieties of colorful wildflowers. Both of her feet were inexplicably dry the moment she pulled them from the water. The heavy mist still covered most of the landscape, but progressively more and more flowers were breaking through as the haze slowly began to dissipate. Rich green pastures rolled higher and higher in every direction. Large mountains outlined the horizon and were blanketed with beautiful patches of trees with vivid lime-green leaves that swayed together in the warm cross-breeze. The mountains towered over low drifting clouds that brushed across the blooming pastures far below. The vibrant colors of the foliage amidst the drifting haze seemed to bestow a whimsical aura upon all that was in her range of sight.

Multiple flocks of large and small birds soared across an early summer sky in every direction. Bees buzzed and butterflies danced from flower to flower in an almost choreographed rhythmic manner. Cicadas chattered from the distant woods, and all seemed to be alive and joyful and strangely moving as one in this place of unimaginable beauty. A thick sense of peace and harmony hung over this strange land, as present as the fog itself.

Rachel intimately connected with all that she gazed upon. When she watched the flock of geese flying overhead, she could feel the grandeur of their flight within her heart. She could not explain how, but she felt the concern of some birds for others flying behind them as they continually repositioned themselves to minimize their air resistance. She felt their joy as well when they surveyed the beautiful landscape below them. There was a profound unity that she now shared with all living things. Even the trees and the flowers seemed to speak to her with a quiet tranquility through her own heart.

Rachel's being felt lighter than it ever had before. Again and again, she took in large breaths of clean mountain air, deliberately focusing on its qualities as it filled her lungs. The air felt different now, as if its oxygen had been increased tenfold. There was a simple harmony to her state of mind and an intense sense of love, security, and unity with all that surrounded her.

The joyous sound of children laughing and the playful bark of a dog broke through a low cloud bank hanging over a distant pasture. As more fog lifted, she saw several groups of people moving together through the fields. All cultures seemed to be represented—black, brown, tan, and white men and women happily intermingled with each other. Their bodies looked normal but appeared almost translucent and seemed to radiate a captivating aura that moved around and through each of them. They carried a youthful excitement about them, laughing and conversing as they joyfully moved together through the tall fields of wildflowers. But when they spoke, it was not with audible words; it all transpired through their hearts. They communicated through a shared telepathy from within their consciousness, which seemed to bind their alluring unification even more closely. And although no words were spoken, somehow they were translated with more elation and vividness than words or laughter could ever convey.

Rachel made her way along the river, then up a gentle slope passing through a small outcrop of tall evergreens. The large trees offered a fresh, pungent aroma of pine that felt as if it were cleansing her soul with every deep breath that she took. Beyond their thick trunks, from this higher vantage point, the pastures of tall grass and wildflowers looked as if they stretched for miles. From all directions, huge swaths of warm breeze continued to brush over the fields, coaxing large patches of flowers and tall wispy grass toward the ground and releasing them again. When Rachel turned toward the long winding river, she saw what appeared to be the most beautiful sunrise she had ever seen. Magnificent pinks and oranges and yellows and many other colors she had never seen before broke over the river's bank and gently caressed her face with indescribable light. This strange light did not only touch her skin but permeated her soul, lovingly blowing through her, then holding her from within. When she squinted her eyes toward the sunrise to witness its grandeur, she saw that it was not the sun from which the light shone, but from hundreds of people gathered together upon the riverbank. As Rachel focused on the diverse people, the strongest, most secure love that she had ever felt surged through her, raising all within her up to an elevated state of selfless euphoria. It erupted out from each of their hearts with a power and purity and unity of spirit which she had never witnessed before.

As her eyes swept across the crowd, she saw that each was clad in simple white clothing with off-white accents. Some wore dresses and others wore freshly pressed button-down shirts with suspenders. Some of them covered their hair in veils or turbans, while others wore nothing at all on their heads. Some were draped in robes, while others wore bulky slacks with white T-shirts. The entire world looked as if it were represented in this beautiful, serene place. Everyone appeared to be so happy and at peace with one another as they joyfully went about their individual business. And although each was busy with their own task at hand, they moved in synchronicity with each other, as if they all shared the same goal.

Some of them knelt along the river with their heads bowed in prayer. Others sat with their legs crossed in a meditative position, while others knelt on their hands and knees with their eyes closed. Each who prayed was joined by another individual with their hand resting on their backs as if they were somehow aiding them in their efforts. Those from seemingly different cultures intermingled, indiscriminately aiding one another in their prayer despite their apparent cultural differences. Strangely, it felt as if there was no religion at all in this magnificent place, only one grand, unifying love conveyed equally for all of humanity. All genders, color, and cultures felt insignificant here. The traits and ideologies that each identified with throughout their physical lives suddenly felt like binding shackles in the light of this beautiful, inclusive love. Shackles that had once divided, but now, could no longer oppress. All that had once separated them somehow felt as if it had miraculously melted away.

None spoke, but when Rachel focused on them, she could feel their prayers as faint voices within her own consciousness. They held such sincerity and concern for each other, as well as for the recipients of their prayers. When Rachel focused and blocked out all other distractions, she could feel them taking in the pain of the people they prayed for, those who were still living.

Others sat together in groups, listening while people who looked to be teachers spoke from the front of their gathering. All that was taught carried a sincere love and lightness with it. A sense of equality and oneness flowed around and through each of them, and although Rachel was aware that different spiritual levels did exist, she could not detect any social hierarchy at all. Everyone seemed to be equal here. Every person or living thing that moved in this realm felt as if they were infinitely bound together by an abiding love that surged through each of them—the same universal love that tethers all the world's people and religions together. Although much of their conversations were faintly received within Rachel's consciousness, their unity of heart and unbounded love clearly tied them together. Rachel slowly made her way down the soft, grassy slope to a lush opening where wildflowers sprung from the green pasture.

What's happening to me? she thought.

Then, a soft familiar voice rose within her own consciousness.

"Nothing out of the ordinary, my love."

A kind, warm laughter followed, rising within her. Even before she could turn her head, she felt another tear form in her eye.

"Mom?" she replied.

When she turned, she couldn't believe her eyes. Both her mother and her father stood next to each other, smiling back at her with the same loving glint in their eyes that they had carried throughout her life. Rachel was overwhelmed, not only because her deceased parents were standing in front of her, but because they looked so much younger now, even younger than Rachel was herself.

They wrapped their arms around her and pulled her in tightly to their bodies. A gush of love rose in all three of them simultaneously, and each could feel the truth that moved through the next. They held each other, suspended in a moment of heightened emotion and peace of heart.

Her father said, "What are you doing here, Rachel? It's not your time."

The joyful couple reluctantly released their daughter, then stood in amazement, smiling and admiring her.

Rachel excitedly spoke up. "Oh my God! You guys look amazing. I don't understand. Mom, you are so beautiful! And, Dad, you look like you did when I was born. And how are we doing this? How are we able to speak to each other without actually saying anything?"

Both of her parents began to laugh together, and their happiness radiated in Rachel's heart and throughout her entire being.

Rachel spoke before they had a chance to answer. "I can feel whatever you're thinking, but it's not easy for me. It comes across very faint, from within my heart, I think?"

Her parents beamed with love, and again, Rachel felt it.

Her mother then replied, "That's normal after you cross. Your spiritual veil is very thin in terms of your physical world, but it is still very thick, in terms of heaven. You, and you alone, have the choice to remove it—and if you do, all communication in this second heaven will become much clearer to you. Your purpose doesn't end when you cross into heaven. There's still a great journey left that each of us is intended to take. The more you learn, understand, and progress, the thinner your veil will become and the deeper your unity with all will grow. That's how you draw yourself closer to God and the third heaven, Rachel.'

Rachel replied, "Like the river?"

Her mother beamed again, then responded, "Yes, dear. Your second heaven is just like the river. Your mission requires lots of work, not only through your physical life but after you pass. It is required for your upward progression through the spiritual levels of the second heaven."

Then she added, "But it's not like any work you've ever done in your physical world. You reap the benefits as you work. It feels more like a gift than anything else! We learn about all the intricacies of love and how intimately it is bound to our true identity. We then intercede for the living through prayer. That is how we sow the seed of inspiration in your hearts. There are teachers to guide you through your progression. Then as you advance, you are flushed with higher levels of knowledge through the loving spirit of God. That is how we shed our armor, Rachel. That is how we purify our souls from the impurities that felt so natural to all of us throughout our physical lives."

Rachel replied, "You said that my mission entails a lot of work. What do you mean by that? What mission?"

Rachel's mom responded, "Each of us has a mission or an intended purpose to our life, that we all agree to before our birth into the physical world. I know this must be difficult for you to understand, but before you were even born, you asked God for it. Unbelievably, you requested many of the struggles that you have faced throughout your life. Because of the law of free will, you cannot know what form they will take, but these adversities are a particularly important facet of your individual mission."

Rachel answered, "I don't understand. Why would I ever ask God for any struggles throughout my life? I'm sorry, it just doesn't make sense to me, Mom."

"Because, dear, before you were ever born, your soul held a clear understanding that when you face adversity throughout your physical life, your struggles can move you closer to an awakened state of being. When you suffer and are still able to love others in the way we are intended, you diminish much more darkness than a life lived with little or no adversity. The amount of darkness that you diminish throughout your lifetime will help determine what level of heaven you will ultimately pass into. So, a starving mother in Africa who still finds it in her heart to love, forgive, and live charitably will pass into a higher spiritual plane than one who lives an entitled life with little or no adversity, all other factors being equal. This does not mean God's love is diminished for those with less adversity. It merely means the underprivileged mother underwent greater struggles and God recognizes that. When you face challenges throughout your physical life and are still able to love others truthfully, your soul will evolve. Your evolution from your physical experiences will determine what paths still lie ahead. That is our mission, Rachel. That is where the meaning of life lies."

Rachel paused for a moment, taking in her mother's words. Then she nodded before responding, "I think I understand the process each of our souls undergoes throughout our physical lives and even after we pass into this second heaven. But the meaning of life, the actual reason for all of it, I still don't understand. Why would God put himself and all of us through so much pain? What is the actual purpose of the full process?"

Her mom said, 'The answer to your question lies in the word 'perspective,' Rachel. From an egoic perspective, you perceive your soul and your physical body that stems from it as your own. But from God's perspective, each soul that has ever crossed into the physical realm has crossed over as a direct expression of God himself. Every life has been a functional organ within his being. So, to truly understand the meaning of life, you must first understand that the billions of souls that have been drowned in the ego of this world were not individual souls at all. From the beginning of time, each of you has been a unique mechanism for God to drown himself in ego."

"Why would God want to drown himself in the one thing that brings him and us so much suffering? I thought he wanted to free us from the pain of ego, not submerge us in it."

Her mother replied, "God wants nothing more than to extinguish all ego throughout creation, but his nature prevents him from eliminating darkness simply by imposing his will upon it. All progression must manifest through the free will of the souls who were created in separation from God but are still unified as one within his spiritual consciousness, the same consciousness that each of us are intentionally veiled from. Darkness deceives, enslaves, and imposes its will upon each of us. God longs to free us from that enslavement through his truth, and waits patiently for it to slowly arise through our own choices and free will. He has allowed each soul their own path to forge through the darkness of your physical world. God has sacrificed his own peace and impenetrable security within the highest heaven and has chosen to cut nearly every tether to his home and submerge countless expressions of himself into the murky darkness of this world—all for the sake of our salvation. Through living more sacrificial, loving lives, each of us are able to diminish some of that darkness that still festers within God's being. God's will exists in the hidden caverns deep in each of our hearts, but each of us must fight through the distortion of our spiritual veils to find it."

Rachel said, "But it sounds like he is sacrificing us, not himself. We are the ones experiencing the pain in life."

Her mother explained, "Rachel, all that exists, exists as one with God. He feels every bit of heartache that you and everyone else in your world feels—and feels all your joy too! It is your lingering veil that moves you to still perceive yourself as a separate being from his being. Once you begin to progress through the second heaven, the illusion of division between God, yourself, and everyone else will slowly dissipate. This is the realm where God has left larger breadcrumbs for every soul, to ensure each will have a pathway home. Don't you see, Rachel? From the beginning of time, God has slowly been diminishing the damaging effects from the original fall within his own consciousness. Our first and second heavens are his mechanisms to eliminate that distortion in his own being, without it infecting the blissful serenity within the highest heaven. That is each soul's purpose within our lives. That, my dear, is the meaning of life itself."

A glint of understanding sparked in Rachel's eyes. "That is how his love remains perfect…through those of us who learn to love deeper. Isn't it, Mom?"

Rachel's mother beamed at her daughter's understanding, and as she did, they both felt her joy radiate through them.

"That's right, my love. He has created each soul in a temporary state of separation, but our unification within his spiritual consciousness remains. Your world was created as a stage for each of us to diminish darkness, but we must do it with a physical mind whose every thought has first been influenced by the darkness itself. The first and second heavens are the mechanisms for God's perfect love to remain perfect."

Deep emotion rose in Rachel, then instantly washed through her mother's being, drawing them closer than they had ever been before. Rachel said, "It's hard to comprehend the full depth of God's sacrifices—all to ensure the eternal purity of his essence...of his love. I have never known a love that was anything like that."

Compassionately, her mother answered, "Well, that love knows you! That same love exists at your core and of everyone else who has ever lived."

For the first time in her life Rachel understood who she really was and what a critical role she was playing in God's ultimate plan.

"Thanks, Mom. I think I finally understand how important my life's journey really is. And thanks for your patience...there's just so much more to my life than I ever knew."

A sense of peace moved through her as Rachel redirected her questioning to the third heaven. "Okay, so can you tell me a little more about our highest heaven, Mom? How long does it take most people to make it to the end of the river?"

They both looked past the bend in the river where the crystal-clear water trickled over a small tranquil waterfall, the same spot where the roof's brick parapet once stood. In its place, a patch of wild lilies grew from both sides of the small, picturesque waterfall.

"Time is different here, Rachel," her mother said. "It is not linear, like it is in your physical world. That is how you were able to relive your entire physical life in only a few seconds. Then through your access to the unified consciousness of all, you were able to intimately understand how your choices impacted each of their lives. That is also how God can witness each of our lives as if we were his only child. He experiences our every thought, understanding each of us much more intimately than we could ever understand ourselves. He can't wait to feel each of his children explore the depths of their own hearts, and when they overcome the great struggles throughout their lives and are still able to love others truthfully, he rejoices in it. God shares all of your pain throughout your challenges but shines when you continue to love despite them."

Rachel asked, "What happens when you make it to the threshold of the third heaven? What happens when you transition beyond the waterfall?"

Rachel's mother paused before she answered, as if she wasn't sure if she should answer at all. "It will be difficult for you to understand with the veil you still carry, but it is the most beautiful moment you could ever imagine. When you are ready and your veil has fully dissipated, your reflection of God's mind and the love that is his essence will surge through you with unobstructed clarity. Then and only then, you will be given the choice to shed your physical identity and step into full unity within the mind of God. That is where you exist as one within the purest form of love—that is the third heaven, the paradise we are all working toward. That is our true home, Rachel."

A shimmer of fear ran through Rachel. "Can you explain what you mean when you say that we shed our identity?"

Rachel's mother smiled again. She gently wrapped her hands around the back of her daughter's head, then lovingly pulled her into her chest and said softly, "Oh, my dear girl." With deepfelt tenderness, she kissed Rachel on her head, then distanced herself a bit so she could look into her daughter's eyes.

"I think we are getting a little bit ahead of ourselves here." She took a deep breath, then hesitantly continued. "That is why a progressive understanding of love—and in contrast, through your intercession into the consciousness of the living, a deeper understanding of self—is so important. By the time you reach the sand, you will understand that you, the real you, the deeper you, is perfect without the ego that separates you from others through your identity. You are the purest form of love, Rachel. You are the binding element that orchestrates life itself, always moving it in the direction it is intended to go. You yourself are the essence of God, as am I and everyone and everything that has ever lived. As you stand at the waterfall, you are given the greatest gift of all, the same gift that Christ was given at the cross: the choice to sacrifice yourself for the sake of all others."

Rachel's fear spiked again. "Is it painful, Mom?"

Her mom answered, "Oh no, my dear…there is no pain in that beautiful sacrifice, only bliss. It frees you from all pain in the form that you have known it. This is the place where pain does not exist and all live as one within the consciousness of God. Although we willingly step into the unity of a God who lovingly accepts the pain of each of his children, that pain is instantly devoured by the grandeur and purity of his love. It is the most serene place that exists. It is our true home, Rachel."

Rachel paused, taking in all that her mother was explaining. "But how could any place be more beautiful than this? I've never felt as alive and at home as I do right now!' Tears welled up in her eyes. 'This second heaven feels like my true home, and you and Dad are here with me. I can't imagine a place more beautiful than this. Mom…I don't want to go back to my physical life. I want to stay here with you and Dad."

Her mother spoke up. "Rachel, your father and I are with you every minute of every day. We feel all of you, every moment of your life, no differently than if we were still alive holding you in our arms. You need to understand that when you hurt, your father and I hurt with you, and when you love more deeply and sacrifice yourself for others, we shine with you. You are never, ever alone, Rachel. And don't forget, we pray for you more than you could ever know. We pray with all that we are so inspiration may spark within your heart.

"You must go back, dear. You still have too much work to do in your life, in your mission. So many people's lives are hanging in the balance of the choices that you have not yet made. Make sure you walk through the doorway of love first, Rachel—that is the key to living a true and purposeful life. Remember, we will be with you throughout all of your life experiences, and we will be waiting for you when your time comes to cross back over into this realm."

"But what about—" Rachel began to speak, but her mother interrupted.

"But what about the third heaven?"

Both of Rachel's parents began to laugh together, lightening her concerned heart.

Rachel teased, "You knew what I was going to say. That's not fair, Mom!"

Her mother reaffirmed, "We will be with you in the third heaven too, dear. Each of us will have the full knowledge of our individual lives in paradise—every moment and memory of them. And we will be together just as we are here, only without the obstructions from our egos that still burden us to some extent, even here in the second heaven. We will never be apart, living, moving, and loving as one within the highest heaven. I don't expect you to fully understand, but have faith that with every spiritual level you progress through, your understanding will grow, and with that, your fear will dissipate. By the time you arrive at the falls, I can assure you, nothing in this universe will strike fear into you."

Bustling activity continued all around them as groups of joyous people moved through the pastures beyond where they stood. The delightful sound of an excited dog's bark cut through the chatter. The expression on her parents' faces immediately lit up, and as they did, Rachel felt a burst of joy rise within her own heart. Suddenly, a playful black dog clumsily barreled through the tall grass at their feet. The young dog looked up at Rachel and began to merrily bark.

She crouched down and scratched his ears. "Hey, boy, what's your name?"

A clear joy radiated from the pooch as he joyfully wagged his tail. He reared up on his hind legs, then rested his paws on her bent knees and began licking Rachel's face uncontrollably. A wave of the dog's loving and somehow familiar presence moved through her. She gently pushed him back to get a better look at him, rubbing his ears and gazing into his eyes.

"Oh my God... *Tinker?* Tinker, is that you boy?" she shrieked.

The happy dog excitedly pushed off of Rachel, then began to run wide patterns through the pasture at full speed, as if he had just been toweled off after an unpleasant bath. Again, a burst of love and unbridled elation rose as he sprinted through the tall grass, and as it did, the joy of their resurrected love simultaneously surged through Rachel's and Tinker's beings.

Behind Rachel, the pleasant ring of a child's laughter could be heard. It felt almost healing as it approached. Suddenly, a lovely little girl came charging through the wildflowers, giggling as she made her grand entrance. Wearing a neatly kept white and tan dress with the most unique floral patterns, she looked to be around six years old. She wore a beautiful hand-woven flower crown that was made of interlaced long-stemmed wildflowers. The band of flowers capped her head and lazily draped throughout her long sun-kissed hair. The little girl stopped and stared up at Rachel with wide eyes, as if she had seen a ghost. Rachel's mother cleared her throat. On cue, the young girl shifted her attention to the excited dog, as if reminded not to be rude, and began vigorously scratching his belly.

"You're a good boy, Tinker! You are a crazy dog, but you are a good boy."

She laughed as she rubbed the happy dog's belly, and her joy instantly spread throughout all in heaven.

Rachel spoke up, intending for the child to hear. "So, who is this beautiful young lady?" With curiosity in her eyes, she looked up toward her parents for a response.

They both looked back at Rachel with sincere, yet solemn smiles.

Her mother paused, staring into her daughter's eyes, then gently said, "Try to focus, Rachel." She smiled supportively and nodded her head, lovingly coaxing her daughter to try.

Rachel looked over at the little girl, who was still joyfully occupied with rubbing Tinker's belly. When Rachel focused, the child's lighthearted laughter reminded Rachel of her own daughters when they were her age.

A sudden wave of understanding moved through her, and with it, a tidal wave of emotion quickly followed. Rachel crouched down and laid her hand on the shoulder of the busy little girl. The young girl turned and locked eyes with Rachel. Then, with her inner voice cracking, Rachel asked, "Abigail...is that really you?"

With her trembling hand still grasping the little girl's shoulder, Rachel knew that she was touching her daughter for the first time, the daughter she had lost during her miscarriage over a decade ago.

Tears immediately fell from Rachel's eyes. "Oh my God, how could it be? I don't believe it's you! You are so beautiful."

The ecstatic little girl excitedly interjected, "Of course, it's me, Mommy. Grandma told me not to just run up and hug you when I saw you, even though I wanted to! She said you may need a minute first."

They both began to laugh, and for the first time wrapped their arms around each other in a heartfelt embrace that seemed to heal the pain of her deep loss in an instant. Rachel pulled away from the little girl so she could look into her eyes and study the lines of her face.

The beautiful child shared Terra's defined jawline but had Meghan's eyes. "Look at you, Abigail. You are so beautiful! I never thought...' Rachel wanted to make up for lost time, raising her daughter up, explaining to her how special she was, but her emotions were too overwhelming. Her inner voice became stifled.

Abigail spoke up. "It's okay, Mommy, you don't have to fight to get it out. I can feel how happy you are right now. It's okay, I love you too, very much...and I think you're beautiful too!"

They embraced again as Rachel wept the most beautiful tears she could ever imagine. With a loving smile, the little girl gently pulled away and happily went back to scratching Tinker's belly. As she did, she shouted with great excitement, "Tell Terra and Meghan I can't wait to meet them both. We can have a tea party at sunrise up on the high pasture!"

Rachel wiped the tears from her eyes, then said, "I'll tell them, Abi!"

Rachel's mom and dad beamed with joy at the sincere connection they felt between Abigail and her mother.

Rachel's father spoke up. "Why don't you track down some of your buddies, then head over to the pond and find a frog. I'm sure Tinker would love a new friend to play with."

The beautiful girl's unrestrained laughter rang out at her grandpa's suggestion. Then, with a new mission at hand, she popped up with enthusiasm to head back across the flower-laced pasture with Tinker.

With tears still in her eyes, Rachel quickly called out, "Abigail! Remember how much your mommy loves you."

With a grand smile and wide eyes, her daughter responded, "I will, Mommy…I love you too. And promise you won't forget to tell Terra and Meghan about our tea party up on the high pasture!"

Rachel brimmed with emotion. "I will try my hardest to remember, Abi. I promise, I will."

Abigail coaxed the playful dog. "You wanna go for a walk, Tinker? You wanna go find a frog? Come on, boy, let's go!"

As Rachel's daughter was about to depart, Rachel interrupted, "Abi! Wait a moment…"

She then took a deep breath, then walked over to where her daughter stood. With the care of a loving mother, she gently straightened the draping band of flowers that rested on her head.

Cleansing tears streamed from her eyes, and her inner voice cracked as she spoke. "Now, Abi, you take care of grandma and grandpa and Tinker until I come home, alright?"

Abi beamed as she answered her mother, "I will, Mommy! I promise."

The jubilant little girl joyfully squealed as she scratched Tinker's ears. Her innocent glory sent great waves of love rippling through all of existence. Euphoric and beaming with joy, she glanced back at her mother one last time, then ran off through the wind-swept flowers with Tinker nipping at her heels.

Rachel shed healing tears of love and loss as the sound of their footsteps and the joyful barking of her childhood dog faded off into the pasture.

Both of her parents lovingly explained to their daughter how much they loved her, and of course, how happy they were that she was finally able to hold Abi for the first time. Together, they turned and embraced her one last time.

As Rachel's mother released her daughter, she spoke up. "Rachel, it's nearly time for you to go, dear. But before you do, there's one very special person who would love to meet you. Would that be okay?"

Still emotional but curious, Rachel responded. "Who would that be, Mom?"

A slight grin came across her mother's face as she responded, "It's Jesus, dear. Jesus would love to meet you."

Rachel's stomach immediately dropped. "Mom, are you serious?"

Her mother answered, "Yes, Rachel, he's waiting for you right now…if you're willing."

As she considered her mother's unimaginable proposition, Rachel began to focus on all the choices that she had made throughout her life. She envisioned the deep resentment she carried from her divorce, and the judgment she had imposed on so many others, and the unkind words she had spoken, and the harmful choices she had made that served herself alone, regardless of their impact on so many others. She shook her head at her mother, then simply said, "No, I can't, Mom."

Rachel's mother replied, "I shouldn't have to remind you that he loves you more deeply than anyone, and that Jesus forgave you for all of your choices, even before you made them."

Her eyes welling up again, Rachel responded, "I know he has. I felt the truth and depth of his forgiveness fully. This is not about Jesus…this is about me, Mom. I have to fully forgive myself first, and I'm just not there yet…I hope he'll understand."

Her mother simply responded, "I think he might." She began to chuckle a bit. "Promise me you'll continue to work on that, Rachel—forgiving yourself. There are some unfortunate souls that become stalled by their own guilt, even within the second heaven. Although God's unconditional forgiveness rings clear within their hearts, their shame from the choices made in their physical life can drown it out. When you fall victim to such guilt, you risk stalling your forward progression—and that, my dear, is a tragedy. All progression through your eternal existence is based on your own free will. All you need to do is call out with a truthful heart, and Christ will be waiting to guide you, but you alone must allow him to."

Rachel kissed both of her parents one last time and promised them she would work on truthfully forgiving herself, then turned toward the river to depart. As she did, she noticed that the waters of the river also branched upstream in the opposite direction of the large bend and looked to be filled with massive boulders far off in the distance. A curious orange glow flickered from within the largest crop of boulders, which caught Rachel's eye. As she studied it from a distance, a foul smell of sulfur drifted in over the water.

"Mom, Dad…is that what I think it is? That eerie glow coming from the middle of those boulders…is that hell?" Rachel asked, but part of her didn't really want to know. Something inside of her told her it was not a good place, and although it was part of the second heaven, it appeared to be isolated from the peace that moved within it.

Rachel's father explained. "It is not the place you understand it to be, Rachel, but yes, God did cast the fallen angels down to this spiritual realm where they will exist eternally within those distant boulders. But the boulders are not the place of eternal damnation for our lost souls, as many people believe. God loves each of us far too much to eternally condemn us. It is the hearts of those who have passed that dictate where they go. Even after their initial enlightenment through their own life's review, some poor souls harbor such hatred and disdain for mankind that they must pass through their waters, beginning the process of dissipating their heavy veils. But God's love never falters. He continues to reach for them, waiting for each of them to call out, searching for the love in their own hearts that is necessary to progress. The only souls who are condemned eternally are those who first have the full knowledge of good within them but still choose evil, as the fallen angels did."

He walked over to where she stood and hugged his daughter again, then left her with a departing kiss on her head. He slowly walked away, then turned and added, "Simply walk through the doorway of love first, Rachel, and you'll be fine. I'll see you soon, dear." Then with a snicker, he added, "Well, not too soon!" Her father began to laugh at his own joke, and as he did, the heavy mist rolled back in from the faraway mountains. His laughter began to fade within her heart as his silhouette slowly disappeared into the cool blanket of mist.

The dense fog that had approached soon obstructed all but the riverbed, so Rachel turned and stepped back into the water and cautiously made her way to the opposite bank.

By the time she had arrived, she had fully forgotten all that had transpired within the second heaven. But somehow, her heart felt different. The bars of ego that had housed it throughout her life had somehow become clearer to her. Her dense spiritual veil felt as if it were dissipating. Even without the memories of her miraculous experience, she was now bathed in the beauty that existed beyond the physical world and felt as if she were ready to move in the direction that she was intended to. The deep unconditional love from a benevolent God was now filling her. Until that moment, God's love touched her as an outside light radiating upon her, but it felt as if it now beamed outward from the core of her own heart. Only now, she held the understanding that access to this loving God and all in heaven had always been within her reach. For the first time ever, she had unknowingly cracked her heart's window open, which allowed God's Holy Spirit to move through it, radiating from within.

Rachel stepped out of the river, back onto the asphalt rooftop. The moment she crossed back into the physical world, the deep love she now carried within her surged through the demon. And with it, much of his power was instantly diminished.

The drifting haze still obstructed her view as she tentatively stepped away from the water. The eerie sound of a single key strike from the old piano cut through the fog, then another.

Rachel blindly moved through the dense fog bank toward the eerie notes. She listened carefully, following them through the vast, drifting mist. Their tone became louder as she progressed. Then, the faint outline of the old demon seated at the piano broke through the thick cloud. He sat in front of the large instrument with his shoulders slouched over its keys. As she moved in next to Titus Kaw, Rachel noticed that his complexion had changed. A pale tint washed over his face now. He gasped several times before speaking, appearing frail and much feebler than just moments ago.

The old man slowly asked, "How was your visit, Rachel?"

She stood in silence, fighting to remember what had transpired, but her spiritual veil had returned and now clouded all of her memories from heaven. Her only recollection was walking over to the edge of the river; all else had tragically been lost. Rachel inquired about the last conversation she could recall.

"I'm not sure what just happened. I remember walking over to the bank of the river, but then everything beyond that gets foggy. The last thing I recall is you telling me that Lejos' prayers aided in his grandmother's recovery. Everything else is...I don't know, it's just gone."

"That's right. As I told you, when you cross back through the second heaven, all of your memories from the other side will fade away. And as for Grandma Marie, although impeded, her illness has continued to progress. As of recently, she is struggling to walk, and although continually encouraged by her grandson, she has lost the desire to eat or even drink anything." He gasped several times, as if fighting to find his own breath. "Although Lejos' prayers are clearly powerful," he paused for another short breath before continuing with weak defiance, "it seems they may be falling a bit short. I'm quite confident that her days are numbered."

Despite his words, Rachel remained filled with hope for the old woman. "Are you all right?" she asked.

"Oh, I'll be fine. My brothers and I tend to feel a bit...off whenever one of God's souls opens themselves to his Holy Spirit, as you just did."

Rachel struggled to understand exactly what he was talking about. And although she could not remember what had happened, she did feel a powerful new lightness that brought a newfound security and rightness to the moment.

Kaw spoke up. "Congratulations, Rachel. It appears you have just hit your summit, but unfortunately for you, my dear..." The old man paused again to take several more short breaths. "This means your climb has come to an end."

The old demon fought to lift his cane up high. Then, with all the depleted strength he could muster, he drew it back down onto the asphalt roof. *Crack!*

The building violently dropped again, sending Rachel crashing back down onto the rooftop. As she lay motionless, the heavy mist that had housed the two of them began to dissipate, retreating to wherever it had originated. It wasn't until Rachel opened her eyes that she realized it was not the brick wall that the haze was escaping over, but the worn edge of the old oak stage that stood unaltered in the gym at Eastwood Elementary School.

With her forehead still resting on the stage, she began to make small sweeps over the slats of oak with the palm of one hand, as if to convince herself that they were real and that she was actually back home again.

13

Fully aware that the demon was to put her to a moral test at the end of their long journey, Rachel's heart began to beat faster. Wasting no time, Titus Kaw began to speak with a weakened voice from the other side of the stage.

"It was March 18, 2007, one and a half years after your first day at Jackson Pharmaceutical. You were at the Ambassador Hotel in Washington, D.C., and were celebrating your recent victory after your final meeting with the medical officer of the Food and Drug Administration."

The old demon continued to fight for the breath he needed to speak.

"You had just found out your company had secured the officer's approval in his recommendation to the FDA of Hybalarium as a licensed drug for moderate to severe pain."

Rachel sat upright, shaken from her transition back to the old stage. Unsteadily, she made her way to her feet. Her lighthearted glint, which she carried just moments ago, seemed to extinguish with the demon's account.

"I believe it was Martin Schmidt, your company's president; James Orbash, Jackson's top attorney; Dr. Randall Fitzgerald, their chief medical director; and, of course, the young, beautiful face of Hybalarium, Rachel Dawson."

His voice seemed to grow stronger as her concern grew.

"You were the chosen one, Rachel. You had spent your first eighteen months with Jackson learning everything there was to know about their proposed 'miracle drug.' You were finally ready to taste the fruits of your first major endeavor with Jackson, and Hy-Bal was like your child, your firstborn, whom you nurtured and cared for throughout its infancy. And on that fateful day, it was finally time for it to walk on its own! You took such pride in what it would someday do for the company in which it was spawned, and what it would do for you too. Oh, Hy-Bal was your baby. And when you began selling it, you made sure that it thrived, no matter what the costs!"

Rachel gathered herself, reached into her bag for another tissue, and blew her nose again. Her demeanor had changed from enlightened to a nervous, guarded state. She looked concerned and withdrawn. Initially, she said nothing as the demon recounted her early activities at Jackson, as if he had a fact sheet on both her and her company in front of him.

Kaw quickly regained his composure as Rachel's insecurity spiraled.

"Your company misled doctors, patients, and regulators about your drug's risks of addiction and overwhelming potential to be abused. I believe 'misbranded' would be an appropriate description."

Rachel stood stifled, like a deer in headlights about to be struck by a speeding truck. Kaw glared at her with accusing eyes as he slowly circled her.

"For over a decade, you boasted false claims to thousands of medical professionals about your new drug. You actually paid physicians, the good doctor being one of them, millions of dollars to overprescribe Hy-Bal. And your wealth grew as a result of it. You and the rest of Jackson's sales force documented those doctors' payoffs as services rendered for speaking engagements."

The demon motioned with air quotes as he went on, "Jackson Pharmaceutical's 'Enlightenment Program' was geared toward educating other physicians on the benefits of Hybalarium. But we both know what it *really* was—a kickback for pushing your narcotics!"

The demon's voice spiked as he grew stronger.

"The more prescriptions written and the higher the dosage of milligrams prescribed, the more money funneled back into their pockets through Jackson's Enlightenment Program, a program that turned patients into addicts. Through your false pretenses, your sales of Hy-Bal soared, and as a result of this program, the drug was over-prescribed to hundreds of thousands of patients. You convinced the doctors that your miracle drug posed a lower threat of abuse and addiction to its patients than the shorter-acting painkillers of the time. *That* false claim was used by Jackson as the focal point of the largest, most aggressive marketing campaign ever launched by a narcotic manufacturer."

Meekly, she rebutted, "The FDA approved it, and it was Jackson that marketed it. I was only doing my job. I was an inexperienced kid fresh out of college. I was only doing what I was told to do."

"You, Rachel, *you*, out of all people knew beyond a shadow of a doubt that your company's claims were false. You even created phony charts validating their claims of lower addiction rates. Throughout its trial run, in its infancy, you whole-heartedly supported the Enlightenment Program, knowing fully what the results may be. You beamed victoriously when Jackson adopted it as an accepted selling tool. Your hands are just as dirty as Jackson's. I felt every one of your lies. You knew exactly what you were doing, my dear!

"Together, you and Jackson paved the road for armies of opioid addicts. And as a result of you and your company's greed, over a million are dead—one million! Your 'miracle drug' is responsible for nearly as many bodies as the Khmer Rouge. And like their slaughter in the Killing Fields of Cambodia, your victims are innocent and chosen just as indiscriminately. But don't fool yourself into believing that Jackson's death sentence is any more humane. The only difference is that instead of killing them with machetes, you draw your victims' deaths out, torturing them and their families slowly with your own profit-yielding blades. Yours just come in an orange vial and cut your victims from the inside out."

Rachel stared at the floor as Titus went on.

"Within a few years of its licensing, Jackson Pharmaceutical's sales of Hybalarium exceeded the one-billion-dollar mark. The highest sales ever, in the shortest period of time, for any Schedule II narcotic. Hy-Bal flooded this country, and it was not long before an unprecedented spike in rates of addiction and crime-related incidents began to rise as a direct result of that flood. Soon after, the Mexican drug cartels recognized the incredible opportunity that you so graciously presented to them. They immediately slashed heroin prices in half, creating a less expensive alternative for the tens of thousands of new opioid addicts. One after another, their bodies began to drop, and neither you nor Jackson ever looked back, did you? Your profits had become so astronomical that they dictated your response, which ultimately was no response at all. Despite the obvious carnage, which you knew you and your company were responsible for, you just kept selling while glorifying yourselves through your enormous profits."

All of Titus Kaw's accusations were true, and Rachel knew it. From her very beginning at Jackson, she had invested all of her time and effort into this one drug. She would dazzle doctors with her facts about its patented formula and its unique chemical makeup that allowed it to effectively relieve pain without a high rate of addiction, like their competitor's pain inhibitors, only it was a lie. Hybalarium was her pet project, and she would have walked through fire to ensure its success in the marketplace.

So many of her sales practices just seemed to be subjective at that time, a gray sea of half-truths in which she had become comfortable wading. The power and money derived from 'the sale' became her drive, while providing for her family remained her justification for any questionable tactics that she chose to use.

Rachel knew the demon had lurked within every dark corner of her past, and that knowledge soon began to root within her, turning her stomach yet again. She felt as if she were drowning in a tidal wave of sobering truths from her long-forgotten past. Any consideration that her practices at Jackson were immoral or illegal had long been calloused over under layers of self-justification and time.

As Kaw continued to exhume these dark secrets, Rachel seemed to depart from herself, and was left to gaze through unveiled eyes upon a shell of what she had always considered herself to be. Rachel felt a certain hollowness to her being now. Her heart felt like a freshly skinned knee, sensitive to each verbal strike, thin and vulnerable to the emerging truths behind her life. Her mind raced with her inevitable demise. Her salesmanship would not save her this time. She was guilty, and both she and Titus Kaw knew it. The fact that the top brass at Jackson shared her responsibility would be to no avail in the eyes of the demon, or as she now understood, in the eyes of God.

"It's time to come clean, Rachel." There was a false overtone of concern to Kaw's words. "This is your time to step up, dear. Just one phone call to the FDA, and you can put a stop to all the pain and suffering you and Jackson Pharmaceutical are causing." His laughter had never sounded so evil as it echoed across the gym. "Our boy Lejos seemed to navigate prison quite well…I'm sure you and your management at Jackson will do the same!"

As she stood helpless on the stage, her nausea overtook her, nearly pushing her to expel the contents of her stomach. She started to feel lightheaded, so she began taking slow, deep breaths.

"After you are incarcerated, at least your kids won't have very far to walk to get to their new home."

For the first time ever, the clear consequences of her greed and total disregard for the welfare of the masses rapidly emerged in Rachel's mind. And with them came vivid images of Rachel in a federal prison, and her children being raised by her ex-husband and his new wife in the house next door.

As she envisioned these painful images, Rachel's panic intensified. Her worried mind spun as she felt the walls of the gymnasium closing in around her.

For a fleeting moment, she felt a push from deep within to do the right thing, and she now knew where that push was coming from. She envisioned herself making that call to the FDA and confessing what she and Jackson had been doing for so many years. She knew that one phone call could end her company's immoral practices that were responsible for so many avoidable deaths. She also knew that by confessing, she would implicate herself and would be subject to the same judicial repercussions as her company. After all, Jackson Pharmaceutical was still producing Hybalarium to the tune of hundreds of millions of dollars each year, and it was still being sold like gumballs through many of the same unethical tactics that Rachel and her colleagues continued to use.

She felt torn and kept flitting from scenario to scenario, her mind whirling as she listened to the demon's accusations. Unfortunately, every potential outcome would end in self-tragedy. She either called the FDA, pulling the plug on Jackson's unethical operation while totally implicating herself, or continued business as usual with nobody else being the wiser, bearing the burden of her greed, whose weight, as she now knew, was shared with God and the universe around her.

She silently considered, *If I were to call the FDA, I would be prosecuted by the federal government for fraud and probably homicide, and I would open myself up to unimaginable civil lawsuits by hundreds of thousands of the victims' families. In the best-case scenario I would lose everything, including my kids, and end up in prison for God knows how many years. After I was released, I would be without a job and blackballed from any other pharmaceutical company in the country.*

Another wave of nausea rolled through her. With that thought, the black stones on her scale of justice came crashing down to one side.

Her mind flitted again. *If I don't make the call…*

A long deep breath followed. *If I don't make the call…*

Her lip quivered as she stalled again. She didn't want to go any further than that. She wanted to stop right there without ever letting another single thought enter her mind ever again. She drew one final breath in. *If I don't make the call and I walk out of here and I go home, nobody but me will ever know any of this ever happened.*

Tears immediately crested her eyes and quickly ran down her face. With one last painful breath, her choice was made. Rachel reached down and picked up her bag. Then, with no acknowledgement of Titus Kaw whatsoever, she began walking toward the steps that led to the lower level of the gym. She now carried a new understanding of the path she was intended to walk, and for her own sake, had chosen to close her eyes and her heart to it.

With her inaction, a burst of power surged through the demon, thickening the spiritual veils of all within the world. Silently tailing her to the lower level of the gym, Titus Kaw's mouth quivered, aroused by her choice to protect herself despite the obvious carnage her miracle drug was causing. Then with an intentionally subdued tone, prodded her, "I'll be seeing you, Rachel. I must drop you a postcard when I arrive at my new spiritual home."

Rachel was already fighting to forget what felt like some surreal turbulent whirlpool that she had unexpectedly been caught up in, spinning her in dark, uncontrollable waters, dragging her down deeper and deeper, ultimately feeling as if she had been drowned in the end. She moved toward the doors of the gym that led to the school's exit as if pursued by a predator. She was the same woman who had entered the gym earlier that day, and yet she was not. The perspective of the life she had always known had been torn wide open. She now felt as if the blood of one million victims was dripping from her, leaving a long pool trailing far behind her across the gym floor. And with that came the now-present realization that this trail of blood had followed her every step for more than twelve years. The excruciating pain of a blinded life and the sudden clarity of what she truly was now cut her deeply. Her heart felt as if it was made of lead, and all within her buzzed with the dull muted tone of self-inflicted emptiness.

Her mind bounced in every direction. Vivid images of her fellow salespeople and herself boasting about their enormous sales, raising themselves up, feeling the power within their achievements. Then in dark contrast, the faceless masses with needles left at their side, lying dead or dying, their bodies forgotten in some back room or all alone in a dark alley as a cold soft rain fell on them in their final moments within this life.

For the first time, she envisioned their families and the battles that must have raged within them. The love for a son, or daughter, or a parent fighting against the very darkness of that drug—the darkness of this world. Her new reality became clear, listening to the demon; but at the same time, her mind was far, far away.

As she approached the doors, she heard some indecipherable mumbling coming from behind her; coming from Titus Kaw, as if he were conversing with someone else. Then, just as she was about to exit into the corridor, a sound rang out that instantly cut deep into her core, opening an intentionally locked door to one specific day from her long-forgotten childhood. It was the hollow, tinny *clank* coming from the old cowbell that hung from the rafters at the top of the climbing rope.

Rachel stopped, then turned back toward the stage to find the old man casually leaning on his cane with the long hanging rope grasped in his other hand. He was swinging it in a wide sweeping circular pattern. *Clank!* Again, that dull tinny noise pierced her heart as the top of the rope swept against the cowbell again.

"Funny how a simple sound can bring you back, isn't it, Rachel? One last request before you depart, my dear. Per my brothers' suggestion, I'd like to give you one particular update before we diverge paths for our last time."

Rachel listened, but her heart and mind were somewhere else now.

Titus Kaw glared into her eyes with a lifeless expression.

"My brothers thought that before you depart, you may like to hear about an old friend of yours. I'm sure you'd remember her…" Then with a softened tone, he cut her again with his words. "You remember that dirty little piggy, don't you, Rachel?"

With the demon's words, Rachel's very soul felt as if it melted away into nothing. She suddenly looked as if she were a victim devastated by a tragic accident, witnessing horrific sights that she should never have seen. Tears welled up in her eyes again as she began to walk slowly in shocked silence back toward the demon.

The old man went on, "You remember her dirty clothes…and of course, let's not forget about that dirty little bow she always wore. It was the one thing she owned that ever made her feel pretty. Did you know that, Rachel?"

Tears streamed down Rachel's face now as she slowly approached the demon.

"You remember all the specifics of that day, don't you, dear?" Kaw asked.

She didn't respond at all as she stopped just feet from the old man, her eyes fixed upon the climbing rope as Kaw finally released it. Rachel's tears continued to emerge as she stood transfixed by the rope. Rachel's rebuttals had ended. She only listened now, willingly opening herself to the demon's words, as well as all the deep cutting pain that they brought.

Her memories stirred black as he went on.

"It was recess on the last day of your fifth-grade year. You had just spent a very special summer with your new friend, Peggy Bender. Oh, but how things changed after the school year began. It was that little bastard Timmy Watson that did it! That's when he said it to you. That's when he called your father a drunk, nothing more than a field hand."

Rachel stood broken and vulnerable as Titus Kaw exhumed her suppressed memories. She appeared to be gutted, only a fragile shell of who she was earlier that morning, frail and silent and vulnerable to his every word.

"You remember how Timmy's words burned, don't you? How *could* you stay friends with her? You had no choice! She was poor and her clothes were always so dirty, and her father was a drunk and a seasonal field hand. No wonder her nickname was *Piggy*. She deserved it, Rachel. There was no way your friendship could continue. You were better than that. You were better than her!"

"No!" Rachel screamed at the old man. "She didn't do anything wrong. She was just a little girl. She didn't deserve that." With a burst of emotion and tears, Rachel expended all that was left in her. She didn't think she had any tears left to cry, but she was wrong.

"She never knew why you dismissed her. She never asked for a reason, and you never offered one. Those first couple of days she really had no idea. Something felt a bit off, of course, but maybe you were just busy? But then that moment came when you glanced up at her, making that unexpected eye contact with her in the hallway, right before you snubbed her as you turned and walked off with those girls from that new development down the street. Oh, that's when she felt it, Rachel. That's when she felt your wall, fresh and new and strong! Little did you know it would become such a significant part of who you are today—and who she is."

"Initially, it was quite hard for her. There were lots of tears and questions to her mother, of course. 'Why? Why is she ignoring me? I didn't do anything to her. Why doesn't she like me anymore?' Oh yes, she was sad, and, what's the word...*lost!* Yes, yes, she had become quite lost after that. But as the months passed, she moved on just fine, no real friends though. But kids are resilient, aren't they?"

Rachel's voice cracked, "Why...why are you doing this to me? Haven't you tortured me enough?"

Kaw pushed on. "Then the last day of school arrived. It was recess, and all of you were playing and laughing together in the schoolyard—well, most of you anyway. At the ring of the bell, you were all headed to the gym for your final physical evaluations of the year. That was a very big day in the life of a fifth grader. Do you remember how you felt that day, Rachel? How badly you wanted to be the first girl to the top of that rope? I remember, Rachel. You wanted it so bad, you could taste it."

He sneered at her, then popped the rope with an unexpected snap. *Clank!*

Tears fell as Rachel looked up at the cowbell swaying above her, remembering. Remembering how she felt...remembering what she did.

Kaw continued, "There was only one problem. One other girl in your class could climb that rope just as well as you, and unfortunately for you, her last name started with the letter 'B'. It wasn't fair. Piggy was always one of the first in line, wasn't she, dear? You couldn't have that, you needed it too much. And maybe more importantly, it was your chance to separate yourself from her in the eyes of your classmates."

Now, taking in the little girl's pain, Rachel shouted, "Stop calling her that!"

Relentlessly, the old man persisted, "You had no choice, you had to do something. Then it came to you, watching her, sitting all alone on the playground, leaning against the brick wall of the school, reading her library book.

"Her heart actually lurched when you approached her. Did you know that? And again when you asked if you could see her pink and white bow, convincing her how pretty it was and that you wanted to try it on. She actually thought you wanted to be friends again. Oh, but we knew better than that, didn't we, Rachel? Those days were over. You could never let that happen again, could you? Your need was too great and your wall was too strong.

"You took her bow into the bathroom to 'see how it looked in your hair.' Then right before the bell rang, you returned. And with that little manufactured smile, you clipped it back into her hair, ingeniously thanking her for letting you try it on. Oh, the power you felt at that moment. Lightning crashed, Rachel. High above, lightning crashed!

"It didn't take long before all of your classmates noticed her bow too. Well, all of your classmates except for Peggy, of course. At first, they giggled softly, pointing at her behind her back. But soon after, laughter erupted as the crowd gathered behind her in the hallway. She turned to see what all of her classmates were laughing at, and then like a nightmare she had just stepped into, she realized that they were all laughing at her.

"Then it happened, that cutting name rang out from one boy. '*Piggy!*' Then again from another. 'Hey, Piggy!' Then again and again. Their laughter filled the hallways! Everyone around her was laughing and pointing and calling her Piggy. Wherever she turned, they were pointing and laughing at her. Within the chaos of that moment, it felt as if all the lockers lining that hallway became unhinged and violently rattled around her, a thunderous moment of horror and deep cutting pain for the innocent girl."

Rachel regretfully pleaded, "I was only a child! It was a cruel mistake."

"Eventually your teacher heard the commotion. It wasn't until she emerged from your classroom that the laughter finally subsided. As she broke through the crowd, she found little Peggy weeping at the center of it. Do you remember the pain in your teacher's voice, Rachel?"

"'Oh, Peggy,' she offered sympathetically as she unclipped her cherished bow, then handed it to her, revealing your masterpiece. 'Who did this? Who did this to your bow, Peggy?'"

Titus Kaw looked intently into Rachel's eyes, then said, "That's when Peggy realized what you had done. Those five simple letters that you had written in red magic marker. Oh it was magic all right—it changed her forever!"

The old demon scoffed, "That was the last time you ever saw her, wasn't it? Watching her slowly walk away toward the school's infirmary with your teacher's arm wrapped around her because she suddenly felt sick and was afraid she might throw up.

"Your plan worked perfectly—so impressive! Orchestrated by a fifth grader, nonetheless. You controlled the playing field now, and that rope was yours to conquer. And conquer, you did! Remember how powerful you felt, being the only fifth grade girl to the top of the rope? That was the moment you knew exactly what you were capable of. That was the moment you knew what you had become."

Rachel looked as if she had seen a ghost. She stood envisioning Peggy's sad eyes, tears welling up within them, looking so lonely and in need. She remembered how she appeared broken as she walked away with her teacher to the infirmary. As Rachel remembered what she had done, her own pain within her chest felt unbearable, as if someone had actually pierced her heart. The pain radiated throughout her very being, engulfing her so she could think of nothing else. Rachel was hollow now, changed forever, impaled with the pain-laden dagger of the long-forgotten ghost that had finally come back to haunt her.

The old demon went on. "After she got home, with tearful eyes, she told her mother what you had done to her. Peggy's mom tried washing the red marker out of her bow, but it was ultimately in vain. Feeling helpless in her daughter's pain, she scrubbed and scrubbed for over an hour as Peggy watched, weeping. You could only imagine the faded streaked letters left by that permanent red marker. She scrubbed it until the fabric was thin and frayed, but the word Piggy was still visible, only faded to a softer pink. It was no use. The one thing Peggy owned that made her feel really pretty, like a normal little girl, was now lost forever—and it was at your hands, my dear."

Her broken heart continued to take in all the demon's words. As it did, the pain they brought seeped deep within her. Her heart, which used to conceal so many secrets, was now a cracked vessel that could withhold no more.

"Oh, and let's not forget about the incident later that same night."

Rachel's voice cracked as she inquired, "Incident? What are you talking about? That was the last time I ever saw Peggy."

A joyous grin came to the demon's face. "The repercussions from your plot did not end in the school's hallway, Rachel. After Peggy's father made his way home later that night and found no dinner had been prepared…how can I accurately convey this?" He paused for a moment. "Well, let's just say a violent darkness was unleashed!"

With heightened emotion, Rachel raised her voice. "What did he do? Tell me what happened!"

"Your father and the field hands had ended their workday early due to an unexpected afternoon rain, but Peggy's father never left the vineyards. Unbeknownst to anyone, he sat alone sheltered in the barn behind the grape wagons. He gazed across the fields in silence, watching the summer rainfall, fighting to find some elusive stillness within it. But as usual, when he opened himself, searching for some remnant of peace, he was haunted by the sounds of war—the memories from his days as a soldier.

"As they always did, the relentless rockets came again and again. Their high-pitched shrieks grew louder as they moved closer toward him and his platoon. And like always, their approaching whistles morphed into the high-pitched screams of his brothers. The sound of pain, with the vivid memories of their dismembered bodies and their anguished pleas, draped his heart like a veil of chains. There was no stillness found in that rain or any other, so Peggy's father muted it the only way he knew how. He submerged a large glass jug into the swill barrel in the bottling barn, then watched as the tainted wine slowly drew itself into the vessel. He then sat by himself on a wooden crate, trying to escape the pain of his life. By the time his jug was empty, the sky began to darken, and like a shadow, he moved through the fields toward his home."

Rachel's nausea deepened, knowing that Peggy's father was a violent alcoholic.

"When he found there was no dinner on the table—his wife having chosen to wash their daughter's bow instead of preparing his meal—oh, how he raged. And he wasted no time either, tearing into Peggy's mother like he was one of us. Through all of it, Peggy never once let go of her mother's leg. She held on tight throughout the whole beating, through the screaming and the punching and the crying, and through his wild swing with that heavy glass jug, and throughout the rest of the night too. Peggy held her mother's hand as their neighbor drove them to the emergency room. She never left her side once. Typically, the doctor would have had the young girl take a seat while he worked on his patient, but the trauma in the daughter's eyes was so clear. So, she sat on the hospital floor with both arms wrapped around her mom's leg as the doctors worked on her broken body, hour after hour. Her mother was stoic through the whole ugly event, despite all the blood and the broken bones. The little girl looked up at her battered face as she sat beside her, holding her freshly casted hand. At that moment she felt just as broken as her mother did. As she sat cross-legged on the hospital floor, Peggy said nothing, but her heart cried out to the universe, 'Why is this happening to us?'"

The demon softly added, "Little girl lost...twenty-three stitches in all—fifteen over her left cheek and eight more across her right eyebrow—three broken ribs and two broken bones in her left arm. He may have killed her if she hadn't shielded her head from that heavy wine jug."

Rachel had no idea that any of this had happened. The dagger in her heart felt as if it were being twisted again and again, shooting spikes of sharp pain throughout her being. She now carried a brokenness to her as she envisioned the horrific scene. And as she did, tears kept rising from the emptiness within.

"Her mother's injuries had been cleaned, stitched, and casted. Then just before she was about to be discharged—" Titus paused, intentionally looking into Rachel's eyes. "A nurse walked into their room who ultimately changed Peggy's life forever."

Rachel looked up at the old demon with a dim glimmer of hope in her eyes.

"She brought her mother's discharge papers, then handed her a small orange vial filled with little white pills. The nurse spoke to her mother, but her words set deep into the mind of your little friend, giving her the answer that she so desperately needed. 'These pills will help take your pain away.'"

Rachel screamed out, "You're a liar! I don't believe you!"

The demon rebutted, "I told you from the beginning. I can't lie to you, Rachel, even if I wanted to. All I have told you is the truth."

Rachel's mind spun. *It couldn't be. She turned to narcotics to escape the pain I put her in? Dear God, no!*

Rachel demanded, "Tell me if she's an addict. Tell me if she's still alive, you bastard."

In the deep emotion of the moment, all of Rachel's self-concern had unknowingly fallen away from her. All that was within her had suddenly become occupied by the pain of an innocent girl and her wellbeing.

Rachel's voice raised in octaves. "Tell me what happened to Peggy, you son of a bitch!"

The old demon smiled with a confidence that had been shaped through witnessing mankind's self-concern throughout the centuries.

"Unfortunately, my dear, as we both know, people in this world are built to protect themselves first. It's what comes naturally to each of you. It is human nature, and both of us know, Rachel, *that* is exactly what you are going to do."

With those words, a profound, foreign light suddenly filled her chest. Something unexpected shifted within her, and with that, something shifted in the universe in a way that it seldom does. The realization hit that despite all the choices she had made up until then, she still had her free will to choose selflessness at that present moment.

Rachel's mind and heart suddenly raced faster. Within seconds, her soul had been torn wide open. The deep pain for her long-forgotten friend had miraculously sparked hope within her.

With a new strength and unwavering resolve, Rachel pushed. "Tell me where she is!"

Kaw gritted his teeth. "Think about the ramifications of what you are considering. The prison walls I've shown you are very real, and mark my words, they will be waiting for you. Think about your children. Where will they go once you're gone? Think carefully. If you move forward with this, you will live to regret it!"

A surprising calm came over her as she stared with confidence into the demon's eyes. "You said that you have to tell me the truth. So, I'll ask you again. Where is Peggy?"

As his brothers witnessed, Titus Kaw knew he had no other choice. So hesitantly, he acquiesced.

"I'm sure you won't find her. Amongst the great crowds, I mean..." Defeat washed through the demon as he went on, "But I suppose, if you insist...you could try looking at that old mission in Cleveland. She's been homeless and hopeless for quite some time now, thanks to you!"

Rachel turned from the demon one last time, then without hesitation, ran toward the main exit of the school. For the first time in her life, she began moving down the path that God had always intended her to walk. And, as she did, her soul began to soar.

Pushing through the school's large exit doors, she could hear the weakening words from the demon fading behind her.

"You'll never go through with it, Rachel. You have too much to lose!"

And as if accentuating the finality to his darkness within her life, she allowed the large doors of the school to slam shut behind her as she ran toward her SUV.

There was suddenly a new directness to her decisions. God's inner light had begun to shine brighter, offering clarity and awareness. There was an absolute rightness to her actions, and she felt it deep within her, despite any of her own inevitable consequences.

As she headed south on Lear Road toward I-90 to Cleveland, she searched for the main phone number of the Food and Drug Administration in Washington, DC. After three transfers, she spoke to a DEA agent who took down her statement on Jackson Pharmaceutical, including her self-implication in the unethical practices of their sales force. There was an unexpected peace within that moment, an unexpected freeing of her soul. It was as if some unseen cumbersome burden had suddenly been cast from her shoulders. She felt clean and fresh and renewed in a way she had never felt before.

She thought, *How could there be such joy in confessing something so horrific?*

She described every detail of Jackson's fraudulent operations. Rachel told the agent everything, with total disregard for any personal ramifications that her confession would certainly bring. Finally, Rachel was willingly sacrificing herself for the sake of so many others—and in doing so, had become a significant part of God's redemptive act.

There was one moment as the DEA officer pressed her where she felt an old tendency creep back within her, pushing her to sway from the truth, protecting herself as she had throughout her life. Only now, it set differently. It felt as if it actually carried a weight to it, like rusting iron in her heart.

So with no thought, only feeling, she redirected herself, guided by this inner compass that navigated her from a higher place now. And as she did, she felt cleansed again. It was as if some crystal-clear waters had washed her soul in that instant of redirection.

Again, it was as if she had just stepped back into the serene light of God. She could actually feel the veil surrounding her consciousness dissipate through her own selfless choices. All of her thick, dark, binding baggage released itself from the place where it had long resided.

As Rachel drove through the city, she concluded her statement with the authorities. The DEA officer took her number, then told her that another agent would be contacting her in the next few days to begin their official investigation. Rachel finished her call, took a deep breath, then shifted all thoughts to the welfare of her old friend.

Rachels's selfless act of redemption released a brilliant light throughout the universe, diminishing darkness as it surged. Back at the school, Titus Kaw's strength faltered as he feebly made his way back to the bench of the old piano. He sat down gasping with labored breath and wide eyes of disbelief, searching for any and all justification for his defeat.

14

Behind the Mission, two provocatively dressed women and one man stood around a large, rusted oil drum, watching the flames rise up from a crackling fire within it. Their faces were illuminated from its changing light.

"You're up, Peg," the man instructed.

A thin woman with distinctive platinum-colored hair, known to all as Platinum Peg, rolled up the sleeve of her black leather jacket. Then with the help of her friend, she wrapped her bicep with an elastic surgical band. The veins in her pale bruised arm quickly rose up into a deep, bulging blue trail. The man carefully heated some brown powder, which was heaped in a soup spoon. As the heated powder crystallized, it transformed into a brown bubbling liquid. Another woman submerged the tip of a hypodermic needle into it, then drew the plunger back, preparing the fix that Peg so desperately needed.

As Peg's friend injected the heroin into her vein, her great need subsided and the pain within her slipped away. Peg's eyes rolled back into her head as she swayed toward the old stone building. She took two labored steps backward, then awkwardly eased herself down onto the remnants of an old mattress that lay on the ground behind the brown stone wall of the Mission.

Watching her friend, trepidation filled the eyes of the other woman but the man simply said, "Peggy just needs a little rest. She's fine!" He laughed confidently out loud as he pointed to the woman who anxiously awaited her fix.

"You all right, Peg?" the woman asked with concern. "Peggy, you all right?"

Peg lay on the mattress, unresponsive. Her breathing began to slow as a grayish tint washed over her face. Deep concern filled her friend when subdued, phlegmy gasps rattled with each breath Peggy struggled to take.

Her friend knelt at her side, then gently shook her. "Peggy! Wake up, kid. Peggy?" Now with grave concern in her eyes, she turned to the man. "She's fading, Pauly!"

The man then crouched down next to Peg, firmly lifted the back of her head, then slapped her across her face. Peg looked like a lifeless rag doll. Her body hung limp, with no response from his stinging strike. Seeing her slip away, he immediately zipped up the needle, spoon, and bag of powder into his case, then shouted as he hurried toward the empty lot next door.

"The front of the Mission is swarming with doctors…get one, get her some Narcan, quick!" He disappeared behind an abandoned building just east of the Mission.

As Peg's friend ran to find a doctor, her pulse grew faint. A brownish drool bubbled from the corner of her mouth as her heartbeat faded, then stopped beating all together. Her lifeless body lay perfectly still, strewn out on the old mattress.

Christ's broken body hung down from the large cross just inside the back stone wall of the Mission. As in her life, Christ was at her side, but remained veiled from her sight.

15

Large crowds of people moved chaotically outside of the Mission while others waited in long winding lines. Temporary stanchions interlaced with long draping ropes had been set up to divide and organize the masses who all sought medical care. Multiple large white vans with The Cleveland Hospital's logo on their doors were parked, lining the curb directly in front of the old church. People in white lab coats hurried to the vans for medical supplies as they treated the overwhelming deluge of patients. Toward the west side of the crowd, a doctor gave his written statement to two police officers while paramedics wheeled another faceless victim of the opioid crisis past them on a gurney.

Dr. Sam Pierson pulled past the crowd, then parked next to the curb just beyond the Mission. He sat inside his SUV, staring at the different faces in the frenzy contemplating why he had come. He reached his hand over to the passenger seat and laid it on his overnight bag, which he had packed the night before. Sam cracked his car window, allowing some fresh air to gently blow in. It was the end of summer, and the cool dusk air brought the promise of fall. He fought, taking emotional inventory, but could not pinpoint what had moved him to drive to the Mission that afternoon. He had every intention of flying to Miami for the weekend, but as he approached Burke Lakefront Airport where his plane was fueled and waiting, a strong unexpected inkling tugged at his heart. So, uncharacteristically and without question, he continued driving west along the Shoreway. Strangely, he felt compelled toward the old mission to see if he could lend a hand at The Cleveland Hospital's free clinic.

Sam did not understand why he had decided to do something so spontaneous and out of character. He simply did not know. Maybe he needed something more in his life, something hidden from his view until then. Maybe it was the smugness of the other doctors the evening before when they said Sam would never give up a weekend for a 'bunch of illegal aliens and prostitutes.' Or, maybe it was the strange way the light seemed to caress the old mission's sanctuary as Sam gazed down on it from the window of the hospital's lounge. Whatever it was, he could not quantify it, but he was there nonetheless; compelled by the unknown, surrendering to it, and at that moment, feeling a peculiar rightness in his surrender. An unexpected newness hung in the air, and with each breath, it almost felt as if he was absorbing it.

The doctor got out of his SUV, then walked through the busy crowd toward a nurse. She was holding a clipboard, writing a prescription in front of a long line of underprivileged people.

Sam caught her eye as he approached.

"Good afternoon, Doctor. We didn't expect you here today. Are you here to work?"

"Why not?" he replied with confidence.

The nurse approached Sam so she could brief him while out of earshot of the waiting patients.

"These will not be typical examinations. We need to get them in and out as quickly as we can. We have a lot of patients to look at and not a lot of time or volunteers. Many of these people are homeless. They are malnourished and some haven't been seen by a physician in decades. Our pharmaceuticals are limited, but I'll stick with you and fill them as we move through our line. The hospital has set up a soup and sandwich station under that tent if they're hungry. Any questions?"

"Nope, let's do this."

With a nod of her head, the nurse turned, then both she and Dr. Pierson walked together toward the front of the long line.

The nurse then instructed, "Here's your first patient, Doctor."

Dr. Pierson glanced down the meandering row of bodies, then turned to survey his first patient. She was an elderly woman who looked frail and in clear need of medical attention as she struggled to hold herself up. Her breathing was labored. It appeared as if simply standing was too much for her to endure.

Sam noticed the pain in her eyes, so he walked over to a nearby staging area, picked up a folding chair, and brought it back to where she stood.

He set it down next to her, then said, "Please sit down. Why don't you tell me what brought you here today?"

The old woman had to take several short strenuous breaths before she was able to respond.

"I am having a problem with cancer, Doctor. The other physicians have told me there is nothing left that they can do for me." She paused to take two more short breaths, then explained, "They call it glioblastoma…it is in my—"

The doctor gently interrupted with a compassionate smile. "In your brain?"

Surprised, she responded, "Yes, yes, that's right. It's in my brain. Unfortunately, they told me it's terminal. They told me it is only a matter of time before…" The elderly lady became overwhelmed with emotion. She eventually gathered herself, then continued to explain to the doctor that she was not expected to live much longer.

Dr. Pierson spent the next twenty minutes taking her vitals and asking her a wide array of questions. As she spoke, he seemed to listen to her not only as a medical diagnostician, but as a man who had come to help her in whatever way he could.

He looked into her eyes, which carried a gentleness despite the obvious pain she was in. He noticed her expression awakened with a lightness of youth when he asked about where she was born. Then again, he noticed how her lips came together and her expression became withdrawn when she spoke of her terminal diagnosis. Strangely, he was looking beyond her cancer now, looking deeper into who his patient truly was. The dusk air felt cool and crisp and new and welcoming. As the doctor intently listened to his patient, all around him and in him seemed to slow, then strangely join as one. He did not know what was happening as he took in the words of this stranger, but something unusual and new was transpiring; something beyond his cognitive understanding, but poignant and very real nonetheless.

When he had completed his exam, the doctor instructed the nurse to order a full screening of her blood, along with other tests that would need to be performed in his office the following week.

The nurse responded, "Excuse me, Doctor, could I have a minute?" She motioned the doctor away from his elderly patient.

As they walked away Dr. Pierson inquired, "Is there a problem?"

"It's just that these free clinics are not set up to treat cancer patients, especially cancer patients that have been given a terminal diagnosis. There are specific guidelines set by The Cleveland Hospital on what we are and are not allowed to treat. I've been instructed—"

The doctor abruptly interrupted the nurse. "I am instructing you to run a full panel on my patient's blood work. And if anyone has a problem with it, well, they can take it up with me directly." The doctor scribbled his orders onto the clipboard, then signed it. "Am I understood?" he asserted.

The nurse complied, "Yes, sir. I'll order the panel right away."

He then walked back to his patient, who spoke up as he was approaching.

"I hope I haven't taken too much of your time." Her voice cracked as she continued,

"I think I just wanted another opinion, another doctor to tell me if there...well, if there was any hope for me or not."

Dr. Pierson gazed into the eyes of his patient, then replied, "I promise you that I will do everything in my power to give you the answers that you need, Mrs....?"

Some beautiful tears of long-forgotten hope welled up in the old woman's eyes as she softly responded, "Perez. My name is Maria Perez."

In an instant, the massive walls within the doctor's heart had cracked, and the large stones that stood strong for most of his life began to shear and fall from it. Walls that veiled his heart from so many of his patients—great walls of prejudice that were set firmly by his father—unexpectedly had begun to crumble. A strange, brilliant light now shined through, bringing with it an unfamiliar security well beyond that which his oppressive walls had ever offered. In an instant, Dr. Pierson felt more renewed and whole than he ever had before.

At the end of Maria Perez's examination, the doctor smiled from a sincere place within him and told her that he looked forward to seeing her in his office. As Maria slowly walked away, he paused, suspended in a heightened state of awareness and unfamiliar peace, all from the simple act of serving a stranger.

16

Just beyond the parked vans, Rachel slowly pulled past the crowd in her SUV. She stared at the passing faces as she crept by, wondering if she would even recognize Peggy after their twenty years of separation. She eventually parked her car next to the curb, then sat inside searching for the courage to open the door. Her heightened nerves brought butterflies to her stomach. She folded her visor down, then looked at her own reflection in the mirror. Dried paths of mascara trailed down her face. Shocked by her appearance, she reached into her glove compartment for a wipe to clean herself up. Suddenly, she was startled by an unexpected *tap, tap, tap*. Three taps rang out from her tinted passenger side window, as if struck by a fistful of rings. Rachel looked up and saw the torso of a woman standing by the curb just outside of her car. When she rolled the window down, to her amazement, she found the sex worker from the rooftop leaning down and looking into the open window.

"My God, Honey Love?" Rachel impulsively blurted out.

Surprised, the woman responded, "Do I know you?"

Rachel fumbled with her response. "No. I...ah...no, I'm sorry, I don't believe you do."

It crossed Honey Love's mind that this strange woman could be the wife of a past client, so instead of interrogating her, she simply said, "I'm sorry, I was just expecting somebody else." She then turned away and began walking back toward the Mission.

"Excuse me!" Rachel raised her voice. "Excuse me, do you happen to know any of the people who are staying here at the Mission? I'm looking for somebody. She's an old friend of mine?"

The woman stopped, then turned. "I know some. Who ya looking for?"

"Peggy is her name."

After a short pause, Honey responded, "Platinum Peg? Yeah, I know her. Everybody knows Peg. She's a working girl like me. I just saw her taking a break by the fire behind the Mission. Do ya want me to get her?"

Rachel's heart lurched, but also stung with the bite of her words. *A working girl like me.* Deep pain instantly surged through her chest, but she swallowed it back down to where it came from.

"Yes, would you tell her an old friend is here to see her?"

Honey agreed, then began to walk toward the back of the Mission.

On the other side of the large crowd, two paramedics lifted the gurney that held Peggy's lifeless body, then slid it into the back of their ambulance. Peg's friend, who had tried to help, wept as they slammed the doors, but still could not escape the relentless need for the fix that she had just been denied.

Unaware of what had happened to Peg, Honey continued walking toward the back of the Mission in search of her friend.

When she was nearly out of earshot, Rachel hopped out of her car and shouted over the hood. "Bender, Peggy Bender is her name! I just wanted to make sure it's the right Peggy."

Honey immediately stopped in her tracks. She stood perfectly still for several seconds, with her back to Rachel, then cautiously turned to face her.

"Who the hell are you?" Honey Love demanded from a distance with a strong defensive tone.

Confused, Rachel repeated herself, "I'm an old friend of hers. Peggy and I went to grade school together in Avon Lake."

With obvious trepidation, Honey slowly walked back toward Rachel. Then, carrying the fear of a frightened child, she said, "Nobody has called me by that name for almost twenty years now…who are you and why are you here?"

Rachel's eyes opened wider. Tears of both regret and joy immediately surfaced. It felt as if every emotion she had ever felt washed through her at that moment. With a pain-filled exhale, she hurried toward the confused woman who stood guarded on the sidewalk.

Rachel stared into her old friend's tired eyes as she approached.

"My God, Peggy. I don't believe it…that was you all along! It was you!"

Rachel threw her arms around her long-forgotten friend and drew her in with a heartfelt embrace. She was so grateful that she had found Peggy but could not find the words to adequately convey her regret for what she had done to her as a child.

After a few seconds, Peggy pulled back and studied the stranger's face. With their arms still entwined, she was struck with a memory of her and this stranger as children, eating grapes together on a lawn blanketed in fall leaves.

"Rachel…Rachel Dawson? Is that really you? Oh my God, I don't believe it!" Peggy had never had any communication with anyone from her old neighborhood before. After so many years of separation from her family, most of her childhood memories felt like someone else's life altogether. She only had distant disconnected memories now, which faded with each passing year.

The joy within Peggy's eyes soon faded as the stabbing memories of their last encounter suddenly rushed back to her. All the details of what Rachel had done to her in front of their classmates quickly returned with painful clarity. Without a single word spoken, Rachel knew what Peggy was thinking.

"I am so sorry, Peggy! I am so, so sorry for what I did to you that day. You didn't deserve any of it. My heart breaks knowing what I did to you."

Peggy's eyes departed to some far-away place as the gnashing memories of that moment replayed themselves over and over again inside of her mind.

Anger quickly grew in Peggy as she stared into Rachel's sorrowful eyes.

"You have no idea how badly you hurt me, Rachel. How could you do that? I was just a little girl...I thought you were my friend!" Peggy's voice cracked with heart-wrenching emotion. Unable to speak, she held her tongue while she fought back her tears.

Rachel could feel the pain and anger that coursed through her and knew that both were justified.

"I was weak, Peggy. I was just a stupid, insecure child, and I am so sorry for hurting you like that. I know you have no reason to forgive me for what I did, but I'm asking you to try. Even though I don't deserve it, I'm asking you to try to forgive me. You were a good friend of mine and you didn't deserve any of it."

Peggy stared at the ground, flushed with the pain of a victimized child. The vivid memories from the hallway of their school cut into her heart like a plunging dagger. After that horrible attack, Peggy had sat up in her bed night after night rehearsing the hate-filled words that she would someday inflict on Rachel, wounding her just as deeply as she had been wounded herself. For so long, with painful detail, she envisioned Rachel suffering just as she had. She hated her and dreamed of the day they would cross paths again so her redemption could finally be served. Now, finally, after so many years of resentment, it felt as if the universe had finally delivered her assailant so her long-sought atonement could finally be realized.

Although Peggy had prayed for this moment for so long, the truth was, she had simply grown weary of hating and resenting so many people. The majority of Peggy's hard life consisted of deep painful moments; and although Rachel had hurt her significantly, she was tired. So tired of being angry at the world. She was tired of so many things in her life, and at that moment it felt as if she stood at a crossroad where her instinct was to strike. But from some unexplored realm within her heart, she suddenly felt moved to surrender instead.

So, with both hands, she wiped the tears from her weary eyes; in the midst of her deep resurrected pain, she found the strength to somehow release it. Peggy drew her tired eyes up to Rachel's, then with a painful sigh, softly said, "We were just kids, Rachel." Then with a weary voice, she uttered three simple words, "I forgive you."

Immediately, the burden Peggy had carried for so many years was released into the universe. Tears fell from both friends as they held each other, separated merely by their flesh. Their hearts beat as one, unified in that unexpected moment just as God had intended.

Rachel pulled herself away, then said, "Grab your things, I'm taking you out of here. I'm taking you home."

Peggy didn't know what to say. It had been so long since anyone had shown any real compassion for her. She was stunned.

"Please, Peggy, let me take you home. I have two beautiful daughters and it would mean so much to me if you could meet them." Then, as if it would solve all the issues in both of their troubled lives, Rachel added, "I'll make you a nice cup of hot tea."

With those simple words, the 'child' reappeared in both of their eyes, and with it, they both began to laugh.

With her own act of grace, Peggy's apprehension had fallen away. So, without another word spoken, she put her arm around her long-lost childhood friend and began walking back toward the car.

"All right, let's go have a cup of hot tea."

The two women got into the car, then departed for Rachel's home. Both of their hearts beat nervously, open to the possibility of reconciliation.

The western sky burned orange as the sun descended toward the lake's distant horizon. From her passenger seat, Peggy watched in awe as the heavens' beautiful colors beckoned and the day's dimming light slowly slipped away.

Why don't I ever watch the sunset…it's so beautiful? she thought. *I live so close to the lake but have never taken the time.*

As Rachel drove west on Lake Road, Peggy's mind retreated to a foreign place where she viewed her own life from outside of herself. Stepping away from her pain-filled world, even for a moment, had given her reason to look inward at a clearer image of what she had become.

As she gazed out at the changing colors over the water, she unintentionally uttered softly, "Why...?"

Rachel spoke up. "What's that, Peggy?"

Forcing a smile, she replied, "It's nothing."

When Rachel turned down her long, winding driveway off Lake Road, her old friend remarked, "I should have guessed...you live in a mansion."

"It's not so great," Rachel responded, solemnly.

Both Terra and Meghan were next door doing their outside chores with Shannon's two kids. Dave and his new wife were pulling weeds from their flower beds as Rachel parked her car in her driveway next door.

Rachel sat in silence, thinking, before she spoke, "Would you mind waiting here for a moment?"

She opened her car door and made her way across the driveway in the direction of her ex-husband and his new wife.

"Can we talk?" Rachel asked as she approached them.

The tone in her voice captured both Dave and Shannon's attention. Ever since their bitter split, all communication from Rachel had been hostile, at best. But something in her voice sounded different now.

Dave responded, "Of course, what's up?"

They both stopped working, then walked over to where she stood in their front lawn. The children curiously watched from a distance but continued their yard work.

"I know this is your weekend to have the girls, but I have an old friend of mine I'd like them to meet. Would it be okay if they came over for a couple of hours and...well, I don't know how long she is going to be here, but it would mean a lot to me if they were able to meet her."

This was the first time Rachel spoke to them with any hint of civility, and it was clear to them both that something had transpired within her. Dave looked over at Shannon, then raised his eyebrows in search of her approval.

His new wife spoke up with an upbeat tone. "Yes, of course. They should meet her!" Shannon looked over at Terra and Meghan, then shouted, "Girls, come quick. Your mom has an old friend she'd like you to meet."

The two girls happily dropped their rakes, then ran over to where the three of them stood. Rachel looked into the eyes of her daughters. For the first time, she saw a pain in Terra's eyes she hadn't noticed until then.

Meghan spotted the concern in her mother's eyes. "Are you okay, Mom?"

"I'm sorry...yes, I'm fine." Rachel put her arms around both of her daughters and squeezed them tight. "I hope you both know how much I love you."

Confused, Terra's eyebrows furled as their mother released them.

Terra spoke up. "I love you too. What's going on? Are you sure you're okay? You're acting weird."

Rachel spoke up. "I have an old friend of mine in the car. She is...well, she's not feeling well right now, but she needs our help. I need you both to take her into the house and make her some hot tea. Meghan, get her a blanket and get our first aid kit out of the pantry. I saw that her toe is cut and needs some attention. It's very important, girls. Go on now. Her name is Peggy. We went to Eastwood together."

As the girls started moving toward her car, under her voice, Rachel said, "Spoil her, girls. Make sure she feels loved."

Meghan excitedly responded, "We will, Mom!"

The two girls hurriedly opened the car door, introduced themselves, then escorted Peggy into their home.

As the three of them entered the house, Dave inquired, "Who is she, Rachel? Is she all right?"

"She is a friend of mine from my old neighborhood, and well, I don't honestly know if she'll be okay. I hope so." Rachel took a deep breath, then said, "Shannon, I loved you. You were a close friend of mine, and what you did...was not alright. You hurt me more than you could ever understand."

Pain rose within Shannon as she heard the anguish in her old friend's voice. She nodded her head, accepting the responsibility, as Rachel went on.

"I'm just so tired of being angry. I'm tired of hating you both for what you did to me."

Dave interrupted, "We didn't mean for this to happen. You know that you and I had been disconnected for a long time, and we just..." He looked into his ex-wife's eyes, then simply said, "I am sorry, Rachel. I understand I hurt you and I am sorry for that."

Rachel paused with another deep exhale before she spoke. "I am releasing you both from the resentment that I've carried for so long. I'm done punishing you for what you did. I want to move on from this...from *all* of this." She took a deep breath, then closed her eyes and fought to open herself, asking for God's strength in this impossible task. She exhaled with tears in her eyes, then professed, "I forgive you. I forgive you both."

With those words, the painful weight of her deep burden fell from her shoulders. Miraculously, in that instant, she felt lighter, newer than just moments ago. These were more than just words she shared with them. She felt the truth of her words deep within her. So, within that unexpected moment, they were all freed.

With a deep sigh of extraordinary air, Rachel departed and hurried to check on her old friend. Lost for words, Dave and Shannon turned and gazed into each other's eyes in disbelief.

When Rachel entered the house, she found Peggy sitting in the back room that faced Lake Erie while her two daughters waited on her. She was wrapped in a blanket, happily sipping hot tea in a comfy overstuffed recliner when Rachel walked in. Meghan had Peggy's feet submerged in an electric foot massager that was filled with warm water and vibrated gently as they soaked.

Rachel let out a lighthearted laugh. "Where did you find that thing, Meghan?"

It had been a gift that Dave and the two girls had bought for their mother four Christmases ago, but was still boxed in its original packaging, buried deep in the back of their coat closet.

Peggy exclaimed, "Oh my God, I may never leave. Your girls are treating me like a queen!"

Rachel walked over to Terra at their kitchen sink. She held a washcloth and was filling a bowl with warm sudsy water for Peggy's wound. Rachel pushed the hair away from her daughter's face, then gently kissed her forehead.

"Thank you, Terra. Thank you for taking such good care of her."

Terra responded with concern, "Is she gonna be okay? She doesn't look well."

Rachel took the bowl of water and the washcloth from her hands, then said, "I don't know, dear."

She saw the genuine concern in her daughter's eyes, and gently smiled at her as she turned to head out of the kitchen toward her childhood friend.

Peggy was grinning as Rachel approached. She returned her smile, then slowly knelt down at her feet. Beautiful emotion filled Rachel as she humbly submerged the washcloth into the bowl of warm, soapy water. With a compassionate tone, Rachel said, "Close your eyes. Just relax."

Peggy set her hot tea down on the end table, then leaned back into the soft feather pillow that Terra had placed behind her head. With a comforted smile, she closed both of her eyes, resting her mind as well as her body.

Rachel turned the electric foot massager off, then gently lifted one of Peggy's feet out of the water and began to slowly wash it with the sudsy cloth. As she tenderly ran the warm wet cloth over her foot, the dried blood around Peggy's toes became liquid and fell in diluted pink droplets into the vessel below. Now, the only sound that could be heard was the warm water dripping from her foot into the still water below.

While Rachel cared for her old friend, Terra wrung out another washcloth over the sink. She then slowly approached Peggy, knelt at her side, and caringly ran the soothing cloth up and down the outside of her arm that lay on the armrest of the recliner. When she was done, she gently rolled her arm over, exposing the underside of her thin forearm. A long, clear trail of needle marks quickly came into view, following the winding, blue vein like a seam with no thread. Defensively, Peggy turned her head, directing her startled gaze upon Terra. Her initial instinct was to yank her arm inward, concealing one of the many sources of her great shame; shame that she had carried for most of her life. But something felt different now. Something significant was changing within her. In the heart of this family's foreign, unconditional love, miraculously her shame felt as if it had somehow softened. So, with fearful eyes and apprehension, Peggy vulnerably exposed her truth to the loving girl. Terra nodded her head with compassion and began to gently cleanse the same wounds that Peggy had concealed for so long.

As Rachel lovingly cleansed the wounds with her daughter, her mind fell into a sincere place of prayer for her old friend. She closed her eyes, searching for God, while continuing to run the washcloth up and down Peggy's foot, caressing it as she prayed.

Dear Lord, I know I never talk to you, but I'd like to change that. I want to start to walk down the path I was intended to walk, and to search for my mission in this life, which, although out of my sight, I know now exists. I feel as if I may finally be heading closer to it. I ask that you forgive me for all the lives that my drug has taken, and give me the strength I will need to try to make this right. And, dear Lord, I ask that you please stay with Peggy and help her find the strength to overcome this binding addiction. I know it has enslaved her for most of her life, and although the chance for her recovery may be slim, I have seen what you can do and I have faith in your grace. Feel what I feel in my heart and know that I am asking from a deep place within it. Help her, dear Lord, to find the strength she so desperately needs to finally break its chains.

Rachel prayed and fought to open herself truthfully to her friend's debilitating struggle. As she did, deep pain rose within her and the most beautiful tear rolled down her cheek, then fell into the basin below. A lightness soon emerged within her heart and the air in her lungs began to feel different. Washing her friend's tired feet, she felt as if Christ's hands were somehow upon hers, nurturing her and caring for her as she deserved.

Rachel continued to care for her friend as she fell deeper into prayer.

As I kneel before you, Dear Lord, I vow that I will stay by her side. I will support her, comfort her, and provide her with all that she needs to start a new life…a good life. I vow to you, with all that I am, that I will make atonement for my great mistakes and finally care for my friend and all who surround me in the way that I was intended to. In your name I pray. Amen.

Over the cliff, the sun's crescent melted into the horizon and then disappeared altogether, leaving magnificent pinks and purples and soft oranges washing throughout the dusk sky.

17

As Rachel tended to her childhood friend, a man well-known to all at the Mission walked slowly and purposefully into its abandoned sanctuary. Approaching the front of the old church, his echoing steps slowed when his eyes fell upon an old man who lay sprawled across the front pew of the sanctuary. Lejos quietly sat down next to the man, who stirred a bit as the pew creaked from the weight.

"Lejos, is that you?" the old man said without lifting his head.

With a gentle smile and soft words, Lejos replied, "Sleep, my friend. Now is your time to rest in the arms of the one who loves you like no other." His smile grew as he began to lovingly caress the matted hair on the old man's head.

The weary man returned his smile, then closed his eyes again and muttered, "You're a good boy. May God bless you."

"God has already blessed me, my friend. Just last night God blessed me like he has never before."

As Lejos continued to stroke his head, a warm comfort blanketed the old man. He then faded back to sleep. Clear, soft breaths passed over the pew as he fell back to the place of his recurring dreams. While he dreamed, the hint of a smile grew on the old man's face as he found himself running through tall grasses toward a hill just beyond the woods of his childhood home. He dreamt he was a child again, and as he did, the most beautiful peace flowed through him. He laughed and ran and played and breathed with the lungs and the heart of a child.

Softly smiling, Lejos drew his eyes from the man down to the dusty sanctuary floor. He stared at the worn, oak slats where he had knelt and prayed to his Lord so many times before. His mind drifted as he considered the vast wonder that existed within God and this place where he resides. His thoughts fell into a deep and sincere gratitude for God's love for all of his children. As his friend slept, Lejos' mind and heart whirled like a growing wind. He reflected upon all the beautiful details that ran through him in the midst of the miraculous prayer that occurred just one night ago.

He drew his eyes up toward the beautiful wooden crucifix that hung just below the broken stained-glass window and fought to recall all that had transpired within his unique moment of prayer. It was the moment darkness was cut down to its knees; it was the moment of the miracle.

He recalled how all was quiet as the bodies of the unwanted lay sleeping, strewn throughout the old church. As the late summer sun descended toward the west, its gentle light broke through the high stained-glass window, summoning his attention. Multiple cylinders of beautiful colors radiated high above the prayerful man, each brilliantly defined by the thick particles of dust that seemed to dance and roll weightless in the air.

He recalled kneeling on the sanctuary floor, praying for his dying grandmother and searching for God's will. Each day had become a battle for her own survival as she slowly grew weaker and weaker. From a place of great sincerity, he thanked God for the deceleration of her cancer. He then fought to find her heart, picturing her struggling with her walker as she delivered food from the Mission to her neighbors who were in need. He envisioned her beautiful smile cutting through the biting pain that he knew she carried. He pictured her eyes, once bright and full of life, which now appeared sunken and tired as she fought to keep them open throughout her days. His heart ached as he transcended the separation between their physical bodies, fighting to unite them as one within his own heart. He willingly tried to take in all that she felt as he truthfully asked God for his healing love to fall upon her.

As Lejos fell deeper into prayer, his spiritual veil began to grow very thin. And as it did, his heart began to feel light and full, and the clarity of God's Holy Spirit grew within him with more guidance and purity than it ever had before. It felt as if the purpose of his life's journey now lay at hand during that beautiful moment of prayer. He did not understand what his purpose was, but had great faith in God's path, which now came to him through clear inklings from his own inspired heart.

Tears rose in his eyes and sweat formed on his brow as he took in the pain of his terminally ill grandmother. Consistent droplets of dense salty water began to roll off his chin and fall onto the sanctuary floor. As the minutes ticked into hours, he felt a strong notion from within to open himself to yet another who was in great need of God's grace.

Marking his conviction, the faithful man disregarded the deep ache in his knees and spiking pain from his back, which now felt pinched like knotted sisal rope. Despite his discomfort, he delved deeper into his consciousness, truthfully searching for God's will. He trusted all that emerged from his heart now and intimately understood that it was the vessel in which God's intention was being delivered. The light within him grew, then fell upon one of the sex workers who worked in front of the Mission. God's will was clearly moving him toward the heart of Honey Love.

Over the years, Lejos had gotten to know her well. On occasion, he would help her and her friends when they were hungry or in need of a shower or shelter within the Mission. He did not know exactly why his heart had fallen upon hers. He knew now not to ask, but only to fully open himself to her suffering. As he searched, he pushed all resistance and distraction away from his physical consciousness. He had surrendered to God's will, and his truthfulness within his surrender had opened a new door, allowing a beautiful light to shine in. The light brought clarity to him, illuminating an untrodden path that led deeper into his own consciousness, deeper than he had ever traveled before.

As Lejos began to pray for Honey Love, he recalled a conversation he once had with her about the start of her destructive addiction as a young girl and how it had torn her family apart. She had explained to Lejos that her drug abuse had transformed their household into a virtual hell, and how her mother couldn't take it anymore. She openly spoke of how painful it was when her parents, who were already struggling with her father's alcoholism, hit their breaking point and kicked her out of their home. She was frightened, homeless, and alone, totally controlled by her addiction. Although it broke her mother's heart, she couldn't watch her daughter destroy herself while she idly stood by. So, she asked her to leave and never return unless she was totally clean. That was the last time Honey had seen her mother.

Running the images of Honey Love through his mind, Lejos searched his heart for the overwhelming isolation, hopelessness, and fear that living on the streets must have brought. He pictured her searching through alleys or behind old buildings for any place of refuge out of others' sight so she could rest for just a few hours, or the night if she was lucky. He took in the loneliness and fear she must have felt as she sought rest but was forced to keep watch for lurking strangers who may hurt her if she was ever found.

Lejos opened himself to all of her suffering, pleading to his Lord for the truthful path to her heart so he could fully understand it. God's offering quickly came as a distant memory of one specific evening when he and Honey sat in the sanctuary alone, talking. He had asked her about the first time she had been forced to offer her body to another to satisfy her unyielding addiction.

"How difficult that must have been for you," Lejos offered sympathetically.

"It was in room 1009," she painfully recalled. Her emotion spilled out as she explained how a stranger, devoid of empathy, unleashed his twisted need upon her, a need that could only be satisfied through the pain of an innocent girl. Honey told Lejos that she was only fifteen years old at that time but was alone and living on the streets. She was hungry and in desperate need for a fix; so despite her great shame, she was forced to sell the only thing she had left, her young body. After the motel door had closed, she broke down crying and could not bring herself to do it. So, she apologized to the stranger and handed him his money back. But when she tried to leave, he moved in front of the door, making it clear that she had no say in what happened to her that night.

With tear filled eyes, she professed to Lejos that she blamed herself for the attack, describing the great shame she had carried since that horrific, pivotal night.

He willingly opened his heart in search of her great, unjustified shame. Tears fell from his eyes as he envisioned her innocence being stripped from her and the torturous aftermath, her very being diminished at the brutal hands of another. As he freely accepted the debilitating shame from Honey Love's attack, something miraculous happened.

Like long forgotten ghosts, the painful memories of his own attacks and the deep, archaic shame that followed came drifting back into his consciousness. And although it felt as these ancient ghosts had returned with slashing daggers, his great pain arose as a divine bridge that intimately connected his heart with hers.

Falling deeper into prayer, an unexpected structure appeared that was veiled in a cool, dark, drifting haze. Lejos could not see it with his eyes, only within his mind, and as he moved deeper into this realm, the heavy mist about the structure began to rise.

A large cold stone formed within his chest as the veiled structure became clearer. Then, amid his prayer, his deepest fear suddenly cut into his heart. He paused, hesitating, not daring to move another inch, holding his breath in a state of panicked disbelief as the reality of the dark place became fully illuminated. Lejos began to shake as the rising mist revealed the enormous iron-clad doors of the orphanage where his childhood torment took place. He now knew that his greatest fears hid behind those long-forgotten doors, lurking in the chambers where the nightmares of his youth lived.

The resurfacing memories were so vivid that it felt as if he had actually returned to this painful place. Lejos dropped his chin, drawing his eyes from the ominous entrance, down to the worn stone threshold beneath it. He closed them as tightly as he could, then pushed his forehead against the large doors. With a cracking voice, he softly pleaded aloud, "Dear Lord, why…why do you bring me here, when my heart searches to find the pain of another?"

More tears crested his clenched eyes and rolled down his face. The security he felt in his connection to God was instantly pierced by the unimaginable darkness that hid waiting for him inside.

All light within him had now fled. The cold dark stone in his chest was full of tremendous weight, and seemed to hang down in some dark, hollow place. Lejos began to weep openly, understanding fully that he stood on his intended path, the path that his Lord had offered him. Engulfed in fear, he paused, focusing merely on the sound of his own breath as it rose from the deep hollow place within him.

His fear echoed as he pleaded aloud, "Dear Lord, I have not the strength to move into this place of my darkness. I beg of you, my fear is too great. Please find the grace to forgive me for my weakness. Take me back to the place of peace and security within your arms."

As he wept, the image of his Lord came to him. He saw Jesus standing alone in the Garden of Gethsemane the night before his crucifixion. As Lejos prayed, he sought strength from Christ's weakness. He recalled Jesus' words as he asked God to allow him to forgo his imminent suffering on the cross.

Lejos spoke the soft words of his Lord aloud. "My Father, if it is possible, may this cup be taken from me. Dear Lord, let this cup pass…"

Fear cut through him as he drew in another deep breath. More tears fell from his chin, as he knew he stood in the place where God intended him to stand. With hesitation, he pleaded for strength as he continued, "My Father, if it is not possible for this cup to be taken unless I drink from it…" He exhaled, softly weeping with his forehead pushing harder against the orphanage doors. "May your will be done, not as my will but as your will."

With trembling hands, Lejos turned the cold, tarnished brass knobs and pulled the tall steel-clad doors open, making himself vulnerable to his long-entombed memories. Their rusted hinges cried out, surely awakening all that lay sleeping within. A heavy mist hung thick over the damp stone floor and followed the doors like ghostly waves as they opened. With fearful eyes, he gazed into the dark chambers for the first time since he was a child. He searched for any sign of life throughout their long, still hallways. At first glance, one would think it looked more like a medieval torture chamber than an orphanage for children. All was stone—damp, cold, lifeless stone. The structure was hundreds of years old and had witnessed great pain over the centuries. The corridor's main hallway stretched as far as his eyes could see and was blanketed in a thick luminescent fog that slowly drifted, nearly motionless over its stone floor. Giant stone arches stood on massive pillars that spired up from the floor, lining the walls of the hallway. Lejos recalled that as a child, the towering columns reminded him of an army of endless soldiers standing at attention within their formation, waiting for their order to advance.

His mind raced knowing what loomed in the darkness, but his conviction to his Lord's offering was now too great. With a quivering voice he whispered, "Dear Lord, take me to the heart of the wounded child that lives within me. Guide me to the shame that I have carried for so long." Filled with apprehension, he forced three quick strides through the heavy mist. As his legs swept through it, they created movement in this evil place, where until then there was none. Lejos jolted as the two massive doors suddenly slammed shut behind him. The air was cold and wet, and he trembled, awaiting the impending monsters of his youth to arise.

He stood gazing through the darkness, hearing only the sound of his own breath, when he noticed some movement next to one of the stone columns. His heart beat faster and tears formed in his eyes as he realized it was an old, decrepit hand that crept around the pillar.

With a cracking voice, Lejos pleaded aloud, "Dear Lord, stay with me!"

The ghostly hand looked disfigured as it tightened its arthritic grip around the large, concealing stone. Then, as if pulling itself out from the depths of hell, the orphanage administrator who trafficked Lejos for so many years stepped out from her place of hiding.

At the sight of the woman, Lejos felt as if he had instantly regressed into a petrified six-year-old boy, the same age he was when his abuse first began. In his mind's eye, he wore the same tattered secondhand clothes that he wore at the orphanage. Tears crested his eyes, then quickly streamed down the young boy's face. He immediately drew his shaken eyes down to the safety of the floor. The child within him wanted to turn and run toward the closed doors, but his feet could not move. He was frozen in a state of shock and fear. Panicked and quivering, he had no choice but to gaze upon the ghost of the woman who had changed him forever, the one who first stole his innocence, carving his soul, reshaping him into less than he was intended to be.

The cruel administrator began to laugh at the child's reaction to his most fearful repressed memories, which for the first time were being unleashed into his consciousness.

"I can feel it in my bones...you do remember what we did to you. I hope you did not forget that you are ours, boy. No different than any other possession. Ours to keep, or ours to discard altogether if we choose!" The evil woman's laughter echoed throughout the dark chambers.

The ghost of the perpetrator moved through the mist but maintained her distance from the petrified child. She wore the same meticulous business suit cut too tight for her over-indulged body as she did when Lejos was under her oppression. Her skin was a ghostly white now, and her eyes seemed to bulge outward as if the dense hatred within her had grown, forcing them out from their sockets. They were lifeless and black like the eyes of a doll. She glared through the mist with loathing disgust and twisted desire at the sight of the boy. The outline of her body appeared defined at times but then, without warning, seemed to shift and blur as if she had suddenly become an extension of the eerie mist that drifted beneath her. The frightened boy's skin crawled, feeling the stranger's presence not only in front of him but within the mist. It felt as if the woman herself drifted over the floor, brushing against the boy's bare legs.

Lejos stood alone in fearful anticipation of what was about to happen to him. The monster drew her finger up to the child, and with a familiar tone ordered, "Come to us, boy...come to us, as you did before." She motioned to the child, commanding him with her finger.

Her voice echoed fear through the boy's core. *Us? Come to us?* the child repeated. He silently prayed from within, *Tell me the others are not with her, my Lord. Tell me they do not move within this dreadful place.*

As if the cruel woman knew the fear that ran through the child, she began to laugh, resonating her dominance throughout the orphanage. Fighting to escape further torment, Lejos turned and ran toward the front doors of the chamber. Tears rolled down his face as his quivering hands reached up for the large tarnished knobs. When he turned them, loud creaks cried out as if the doors themselves were in agony. Before he could muster the strength to push them open, a realization fell upon him that brought him to his knees. In the terror of his suffering, he had forgotten that he was standing on the path that his Lord had offered him.

Although he was now drowned in the pain of his ancient repressed memories, the embers of his promise that he made to his Lord still smoldered within him, the promise of his full surrender to God's will. Conflicted and weakened from his trauma, the brave child collapsed onto the damp stone floor of the orphanage. As he lay frightened and alone, he knew that he had not yet completed what God had intended.

The eerie haze slowly moved closer to the boy and enveloped him completely. It wrapped the child like a chilled blanket that had been left out on a cold, damp night. He shivered silently, watching his warm breath meet the biting air. He lay vulnerable, searching for the will of his Lord, basking in his own deepest fears. Then, amid his weakness, he closed his eyes and prayed for the strength to continue down this path that only he could walk. He now understood that in fully surrendering, he had been offered the chance to heal his deeply wounded heart.

Understanding where the source of his own great shame lay, he bravely began to search for his buried memories of his childhood assailants, whose attacks remained entombed deep within his subconscious. And although he knew what terror awaited him, lurking in the shadows, he continued his plea.

"Take me to their chambers, my Lord, no matter how dark my path.'"

The faithful boy slowly stood up from the mist, then ever so cautiously began to move toward the perilous vaults that held the ghosts from his past.

As Lejos forged deeper into the hidden caverns of his mind, he transcended his own greatest fears through the strength of his Lord. Still kneeling in the sanctuary, the brave man pleaded aloud, "Dear Lord, I ask you now, take me to the place of my undeserved shame."

As the brave child deep within him searched for the courage to advance, the ghosts from his long-buried past began to emerge from the eerie drifting haze. The boy watched in debilitating fear as the misty chamber soon swarmed with an aggressive army of his resurrected ghosts. Each perpetrator stared at the child with a needful lust in their eye. Lejos wept as he pleaded to God to stay with him, and with the heart of a divine warrior, nervously moved into the den of his long-repressed demons.

One by one, the tormentors from his youth aggressively moved toward the boy, reaching for the child as they approached him. As their hands lunged toward him, painful memoires of their abuse came flooding back into his mind. And although his repressed memories brought great pain, the child soon realized that the dreaded ghosts from his past could no longer oppress him. They were no longer able to grasp or restrain the child. As they lunged at the boy over and over again, their hands harmlessly brushed over his arms as he entered into the heart of their lair. Tears streamed down from his eyes, but despite his deep-cutting pain, the child pushed through the crowd with fortitude and resolve. He continued to steel himself to their advances as he purposefully moved toward the core of his ancient pain. The daunting ghosts gnashed and fought each other like wild dogs for their chance to tarnish the child with their memory as he passed. From the heart of the crowd, Lejos searched the mind of his inner child for the deep, archaic pain that arose amid their attack. Then, just as he felt he could not withstand another second with his unyielding ghosts, his Lord guided him to a place of refuge within the words of the kind chaplain.

"*Darkness moves throughout this world, my child. It longs for you to carry great guilt and shame, but our Lord yearns for you to release it. You need not feel shame for what you were forced to do within those wicked walls. Each of us was created in the image of our Lord, and each are blessed with the same depth to forgive as he does. Just as our Lord forgives us for all our sins, we must find it within ourselves to forgive all who sin against us. No matter how great their sins, you have been blessed with the choice to forgive.*"

In the midst of his attack, the brave child's rare and beautiful heart miraculously began to shine. Then, with its brilliance radiating from within, he opened his arms to the heavens and gazed up at the high stone ceiling of the orphanage as he pleaded aloud, "Forgive them, my Lord, as they know not what they do. They are blinded by the darkness that moves throughout this world. Hold them tighter than the rest, because their need for your healing love is so great. Forgive them for what they have taken from me and allow your Holy Spirit to fall upon each of them so light may live within their darkened hearts. As I pray here today, I beg for their deliverance, and pray with truthful heart for the sake of Honey Love, my grandmother, and all who are afflicted within the Mission. In your redeeming name I pray, my Lord, amen."

Spawned from Lejos' heartfelt prayers and courageous sacrifice, amid the calm, a magnificent bolt of lightning suddenly crashed far out over Lake

Erie.

At the point of its strike, the most beautiful white cloud began to take shape. Its outer edges began to roll into itself again and again as it tumbled. Quickly growing, the cloud's core opened, forming an enormous turbulent ring of pillowy cumulous clouds in the sky. The miraculous ring of cottony clouds then pushed outward, one hundred times faster and more powerful than the darkness, dominating the entire sky within seconds. As its pure white band raced toward every horizon, the sky within its core was left painted with the most alluring hues and remnants of soft, clean pillowy clouds left gently drifting in the dusk sky.

As the heavenly ring breached every horizon, the great pain within the prayerful man's heart suddenly began to recede. Through the guidance of a loving God and his own truthful surrender to his will, Lejos transcended his severing pain into a higher realm of consciousness. Like heavenly armor, a strange security emerged within him as he finally found the depth of heart to ask for the forgiveness of those who had broken him as a child.

Within heaven, all the armies of angels sang out in unison, rejoicing at the beautiful sacrifice Lejos had made. The full Trinity shined as one, triumphantly casting beautiful beams throughout the heavens. As pure love coursed through Lejos' heart, the frightened child within him vanished, and through his selfless act, all the cancerous fear and shame and guilt that had burdened him throughout most of his life was instantly cut down by God's great sword of forgiveness. In that moment, the ghosts of his youth dissipated within the mist, and with them, their carving blades vanished, as well. By the grace of his own forgiveness, and through relinquishing his own will to his Lord, Lejos had set the wheels of the universe in motion to free them all.

As he knelt alone on the floor of the Mission's sanctuary, all within him stirred with the presence of God. The thick spiritual veil that had once cloaked his consciousness was now thinner than ever before. His beautiful selfless prayer had opened a window that allowed God's Holy Spirit to blow into the old sanctuary.

As Lejos continued to pray, the breath of God himself blew through the open doors of the faithful man's heart, then into the old church. It rolled over its pews with the power of one thousand locomotives, yet with the subtlety of a soft summer breeze. It spread through all who lay within the forgotten place. As the broken old man slept wheezing on the front pew and dreamed of running through the fields as a young boy, he began to feel as if it was not a dream at all. He squinted his eyes as the warm sun caressed his face and breathed in the pure summer air as he laughed, then sprinted faster down the grassy hill behind his childhood home. As he slept, the deep phlegmy rattle within his chest began to loosen and the age-old cancer rooted deep within his lungs miraculously dissipated with a single breath. The lost and abandoned and unloved that were scattered throughout the sanctuary were suddenly flushed with a long-forgotten lightness of heart. A deep and profound peace and the foreign light of hope strangely radiated within each of them. Their broken bodies and weary minds brimmed with God's Holy Spirit and were healed in that miraculous moment of grace.

God's Holy Spirit charged up the high walls of the sanctuary, filling every corner and all creatures within it. The mice that scurried through its walls and the pigeons that nested high in its corners suddenly paused in a curious moment of stillness. A strange serenity fell upon them as they unknowingly witnessed Lejos' rare miraculous supplication. And although undetected by the human eye, even the sprawling oak outside of the Mission was altered in that moment of grace. Its massive limbs stretching out in all directions, fighting to take in as much sunlight as they could, were inexplicably altered forever. Years later it could be seen that its lower limbs had slowly opened in the most unique manner, allowing sunlight to fall upon the new growth beneath it, which until then, had been forced to fight for it from its shadowed home below. All that lives within this world has an intelligent spirit behind it, and at that moment, all that moved within and around the Mission, moved as one with God.

Lejos' whiskey-brown eyes glimmered golden now, like sparkling sunlight reflecting off still waters. The brave man's cleansing tears shimmered within that beautiful moment of sacrifice. The air in his lungs felt fresh, and his heart beat clear and carried within it the most incredible balance of power and peace as he finally *truly* rested in the arms of his Lord.

As God's breath moved throughout the sanctuary, just west of Cleveland, Rachel Dawson leaned against the back fence of her property and with three quick swallows, emptied the last of the red wine from her glass. She was scheduled to speak the following morning at Eastwood Elementary's Career Day, but at that moment her troubled mind was solely occupied with simply surviving. Despair filled her heart as she unlatched her back gate and moved through the windswept grass toward the cliff's edge.

Tears of hopelessness rolled down her face as she prepared to take her own life.

Right then, all the love and light and sacrifice, and the truthful intention within Lejos' beautiful prayer reverberated throughout the universe. Then in the most unique moment, the purest, whitest cloud Rachel had ever seen appeared over the lake, then began to roll over itself, drifting toward the cliff where she stood. It was left in the wake of Lejos' miraculous prayer. Whimsical purples and pinks and brilliant heavenly hues—all cast from the setting sun—brushed over the beautiful cloud as it moved swiftly in her direction.

With desperation in her heart, Rachel looked down into the crashing waves, then closed her eyes and began to pray again. When she eventually opened them, she saw that the unique cloud had moved inland and was resting directly above her. It appeared to circle ever so slowly, as if it had somehow found its home. As it rolled above her, she watched as it began to slowly dissipate. And although it could not be seen with human eyes, a gentle rain had begun to fall upon her heart, a rain that came from Lejos' prayer for Honey Love.

Back in Cleveland, a few blocks east of the Mission, Dr. Pearson casually conversed in the hospital's lounge about flying to Miami for the weekend. He slowly sipped his coffee and contemplatively focused on the Mission's old sanctuary, its steeple gently bathing in the alluring hues from the soft light of the setting sun. Just as he was about to step away from the window, a beautiful white cloud caught his eye. As he watched with curiosity, it drifted toward him, then continued moving over the hospital where he stood. It circled above, then slowly began to dissipate in an unusual manner. Unaware, the doctor watched as Lejos' powerful prayers for his dying grandmother rained down upon his hardened heart, instilling in him a divine intuition that would inevitably emerge.

Oh, our prayers most certainly change this world, but our Lord does work in mysterious ways; even the most powerful prayers manifest in his time, not in ours. Our eyes see only what lies in front of us, but our Lord's gaze through the centuries, and may find great blessings in what we only see as pain today.

Although many of our prayers fall upon the hearts of those who we pray for, there are moments, through God's divine wisdom, when our prayers fall upon the hearts of others. And although they may not even be cognizant of it, when God's inspiration ultimately surfaces as their own intuition, it could free us all.

Love moves the universe just as darkness does. All the kindness and joy and forgiveness and laughter and love and prayer that each of us offers from deep within our hearts moves this place in the direction that God intends. The fruitful lives we choose to live shift all that is and all that we are closer to our selfless origin—closer to our true home. And when we truthfully pray or sacrifice for another, from the hidden caverns deep within our hearts, transcending all physicality and unifying ourselves as one, we do on earth as it is done in heaven.

As Lejos mused over his beautiful moment of prayer from one night ago, his heart soared. Lovingly stroking the head of the slumbering old man, a deep profound peace radiated from his core. God's miraculous gift of healing still lingered deep within his heart. So, he closed his eyes, then once again gazed into the deep abyss of his own consciousness.

Thank you, dear Lord. Thank you for staying with me. Thank you for blessing me with your loving guidance. Thank you for freeing my heart.

Light suddenly sheared into the inky black expanse of his consciousness, then, with a flash, ignited into a magnificent Caribbean blue. The beautiful color filled all space within Lejos' mind, flooding every corner of it. Golden sunlight flowed through it, illuminating its cavernous confines. Multiple schools of beautifully colored fish suddenly appeared, quickly cutting through the luminescent waters of his mind. Welcoming God's will, Lejos opened himself to all that was flooding into it.

A large shadow appeared in the distance, its features becoming clearer as it labored closer. Lejos could feel the great weight from its heart even before he knew what it was. Through the powerful currents of the Caribbean, the kind chaplain's Big Fish slowly swam into his view. Its long cumbersome cord hung down into the depths of the endless ocean beneath him. He swam slowly with great effort, carrying his painful burden. Its weight had grown tenfold over the long, difficult years of his life. The large hook, still barbed through the old fish's mouth, was heavily corroded and disfigured from its many years of mounting rust. The hole in its lip had been healed, then reopened time and time again, leaving a grotesque fleshy wound, calloused thick around the rusted hook. Heavy barnacles crusted the long cord along its entire length. The oppressive line spiraled endlessly down into the sea, its surface sheathed with long trails of heavy seaweed fluttering through the strong ocean currents.

Opening his heart to the weight of the Big Fish, Lejos saw the shadows of his own pain, which he had borne for so many years. Only now, their weight was gone, released forever through his own act of grace and forgiveness.

As Lejos gazed into the tired eyes of the Big Fish, the shank of the rusted hook suddenly fractured, and the age-old cumbersome cord released itself from his mouth and slowly spiraled down into the unseen depths of the sea below.

With two strong thrusts of its great tail, the Big Fish quickly cut through the Caribbean water; then, with a long-forgotten lightness of heart, swam off into the warm southern sea, never to be seen again.

ACKNOWLEDGEMENTS

To my editor Brie Horvath, who is more daughter than niece to me. This book would not have been possible without your guidance and perseverance.

To Kyle Paul for front and back book cover artwork and design.

To Yvonne Craigo for artwork in the body of the book.

To Philip Keller ("Trapper Jack") for his inspiring podcasts *Touched by Heaven: Everyday Encounters with God* and *Blind Faith Live: Real People, Real Miracles*.

To Dr Issam Nemeh of Path to Faith for his prayerful, loving heart that aided me in feeling God's light for the first time.

If you would like to contact the author, please email ghostsoftherighteous@gmail.com

Made in the USA
Columbia, SC
22 February 2025